Barnard's Hill
Settlers In T' Dale

Anthony Gilroyd

Order this book online at www.trafford.com/07-1892
or email orders@trafford.com

Most Trafford titles are also available at major online book retailers.

Note for Librarians: A cataloguing record for this book is available from Library
and Archives Canada at www.collectionscanada.ca/amicus/index-e.html

Printed in Victoria, BC, Canada.

ISBN: 978-1-4251-4480-7

*We at Trafford believe that it is the responsibility of us all, as both individuals
and corporations, to make choices that are environmentally and socially sound.
You, in turn, are supporting this responsible conduct each time you purchase a
Trafford book, or make use of our publishing services. To find out how you are
helping, please visit www.trafford.com/responsiblepublishing.html*

*Our mission is to efficiently provide the world's finest, most comprehensive
book publishing service, enabling every author to experience success.
To find out how to publish your book, your way, and have it available
worldwide, visit us online at www.trafford.com/10510*

 www.trafford.com

North America & international
toll-free: 1 888 232 4444 (USA & Canada)
phone: 250 383 6864 ♦ fax: 250 383 6804 ♦ email: info@trafford.com

The United Kingdom & Europe
phone: +44 (0)1865 722 113 ♦ local rate: 0845 230 9601
facsimile: +44 (0)1865 722 868 ♦ email: info.uk@trafford.com

10 9 8 7 6 5 4 3 2

Acknowledgments

To Derek and Lorraine Mace. A published author and writer, Lorraine took time to help me beyond measure when she was herself under pressure to meet a deadline.

Saying 'Thank you' isn't enough.

To Irene Pizzie, my editor. Without your patience and professionalism, the lads and lasses of Widdersdale would have been sitting in the .Black Bull' forever.

They want to say, 'By gum Irene, tha't' a grand lass,'

To Sue Beechey. You gave me the cover idea.

To friends in America. Thanks. I owe you a warm beer.

To my family, for allowing me many days in the computer room.

'But, perhaps they liked it that way?'

To Bob, our old collie dog. Just because I love you.

To my publishers.

Cover artwork, an acrylic sketch by the author

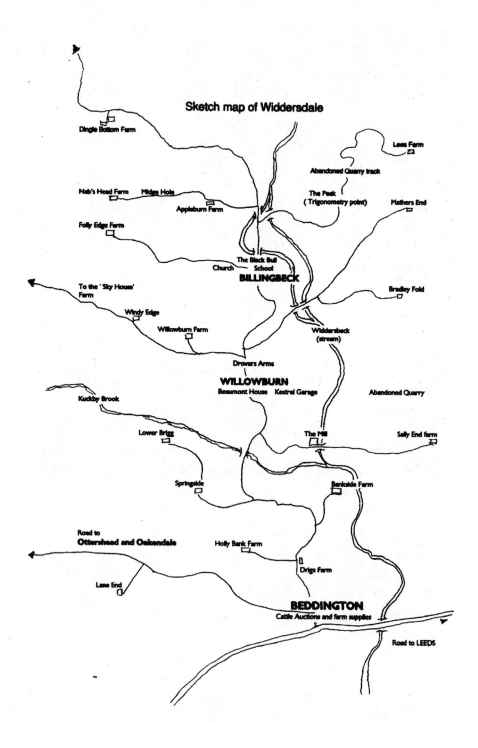

Sketch map of Widdersdale

One

A gentle warm breeze carried the sharp crackling sound of a distant tractor across the high moor to where a young man was leaning against an old weather beaten gate that was bleached white and gnarled by countless years of exposure to the harsh northern winters.

Peter was enjoying his moment of relaxation. He loved the magic of the Dales.

He lived with his family just outside Leeds in what's known as the West Riding of Yorkshire.

He smiled to himself as he thought of his wife Susan, and their son Jim. He would be waiting for his 'Daddy'. He would hold out his arms, to be picked up, as he always did.

Jim was almost five, a lively, fun loving child with his mother's bright intelligent eyes and an eagerness to explore life. He too loved the Dales in his own way. Like most children, he was always full of questions. After all, there was a whole big new world waiting to be explored.

Susan and Peter first met during their teenage years.

They had been walking in Widdersdale. Susan was with a group of college friends, and Peter walking alone, along the ridge of the Dale.

He had decided that it would be a good idea to call in at the Black Bull at the end of the day. It so happened that Susan's group had chosen the same time for a spot of refreshment.

Peter was immediately attracted to the tall young girl sitting chatting with her friends. She had a ready smile and a cute way of wrinkling her nose when she was amused. She had sun bleached hair and gentle blue eyes, shining with the sheer joy of life.

Peter had been totally captivated. But he was very conscious of his rough boots and old corduroy trousers. He knew that his hair was not as it should be, blown about by the wind and falling over his sun tanned face.

He was suddenly aware of feeling distinctly grubby.

Susan had smiled to herself. Peter's interest was rather obvious.

The next time that they met was in Guiseley.

Peter was dashing out of the library, late as always for his dinner.

He quite literally bumped into Susan, causing her to drop several books, which scattered across the pavement. Peter apologized for being so clumsy.

It was at that moment that they made eye contact, they recognised each other immediately.

'I remember you. The Black Bull, Billingbeck' Susan had said.

They both laughed, the ice was broken. That was how it all began.

Soon, they were wandering the Dales, enjoying each other's company.

Peter smiled to himself. Such were his thoughts as he spent a few more moments gazing down across the patchwork of fields that dropped steeply towards Billingbeck.

The tiny village nestled, partly hidden among a luxurious cluster of trees, halfway down the sweeping valley of Widdersdale, deep in the heart of the Yorkshire Dales.

Higher up, where Peter was, sparse grass struggled to grow among the vast expanse of windswept heather. Below, the patchwork of fields, enclosed by white limestone walls was so typical of the Dales.

A narrow stream gurgled noisily as it hurried down towards the sparkling waters of the beck far below. Here and there, sheep were grazing, the distant sound of their bleating adding yet another dimension to the wildness of the moor.

High in the cloudless sky, a solitary hawk hovered, held aloft by the warm air rising off the hillside. It hung, almost motionless, just a flick of a wingtip, as it searched for the slightest movement below.

Up here, in this remote spot, time meant very little. The inevitable cold sleep of the long dark winters was followed by the eager joyful rush of springtime as life flooded once more into the valleys, life that had been sleeping, waiting, deep in the frozen earth.

Then came the summers. Oh, the beautiful, lazy summers.

Peter had fond memories of warm sweet smelling days without a care. Summers that lasted almost forever and finally drifted into the wonderful months of autumn. Mystical and sleepy, a time that belonged to the past, reminding Peter that all things must one day step aside and make way for new life. When nature slowly took back what was hers and allowed her cloak of wonderful golden browns and reds to settle across the land. Deep purple mists and lengthening shadows, a gentle time in which to prepare for the inevitable blasting greyness of winter.

So it had been for thousands of years.

But, Peter could see how some things had changed over the years as he looked across the broad landscape of this beautiful Dale. He could see the inevitable hand of man.

Here and there, small farms and barns dotted the hillsides, themselves grey and timeless. Everything was so perfectly in keeping with the Dale.

There were hundreds of miles of dry stone walls, and the ever changing colours of the land as farmers used the fields differently according to the time of the year. The gentle folk of the Dales had however, learned to respect nature.

They knew that, overnight, or even in a moment, spring could change back to winter. This year nature had been kind.

With some reluctance, Peter got back into his van.

He worked for a television rental company that was opening shops all over the north of England. Renting television sets was big business now. The 1960s had brought so many changes.

Peter had done his growing up in the 1950s when the effects of the war were still obvious. Now, of course, everything was so different. Aged twenty-five, he was finding life very exciting.

Driving down the narrow road that wound its way towards the bottom of the Dale, Peter turned his thoughts towards home. He drove through the tiny village of Billingbeck and saw the Black Bull Hotel nestling cosily among the gently swaying trees. He smiled to himself.

How well he remembered the Black Bull. He had been so fascinated by the tall young girl with the captivating smile.

Soon, he was pulling up outside the little flat that they called home.

It was part of a red brick Victorian building in the small township of Guiseley, not far from Leeds. He entered the lounge and was greeted by the usual thing. Young Jim dropped his toys and ran to his dad.

Peter picked up the little chap and twirled him round.

'And what have you been doing all day young man?'

'I've been helping mummy to do the shopping,' Jim said.

'Put him down,' laughed Susan.

'Come here,' Peter said.

He grabbed her and gave her a kiss.

'Do you want me to go back to work?' Peter pretended to look hurt.

Suddenly, there was a knock at the door.

Susan went to see who their visitors were with Jim, as always, following close behind.

Peter, who had flopped into a chair, recognised the voices.

It was Bill and June, Susan's parents. He jumped up from his comfortable chair and went to the door to greet them.

Peter got along very well with Susan's parents. They were down to earth people and good company. Bill was an agricultural engineer. He was a lanky chap with a very quick mind and a ready smile. He had many things in common with Peter.

They shared a lot of similar interests and were often accused by the ladies of forgetting about the world around them, as they bit deeply into some complicated conversation concerning agricultural machinery or some such totally boring subject.

June, on the other hand, was so like her daughter that they were often mistaken for sisters. She had the same quick amused expression and the same sparkling intelligent eyes; she had her daughter's fair hair and they had a talent for being able to communicate without speaking. They so often knew what the other was thinking.

June owned a little florists shop in Leeds.

'Great to see you,' Peter held out his hand.

'I think I know why' Bill said, 'would it be anything to do with the fact that it's Thursday?'

Bill was smiling.

'You two deserve a night out occasionally,'

Thursday was 'folk night' at the Black Bull. It was always a good night's entertainment, Peter and Susan really enjoyed being able to go over to Widdersdale, not only for the music, but also to for the pleasure of the company of quite a few of their friends who usually turned up. Friends that they had got to know over the years.

Susan chatted away with her mother as they played with Jim on the rug by the fire. Young Jim didn't have much to say, but he knew that he could take liberties with his grandparents that were otherwise not allowed. He was always spoiled when Bill and June came, and, like most children, he was very good at exploiting the situation to his maximum advantage.

But unfortunately, it was bedtime.

Susan carried the warm and contented boy up the stairs and laid him gently in his bed. There was a smile on his face. She bent down and planted a gentle kiss on the top of his golden head.

A warm soapy aroma enveloped her. She looked down.

There were two small heads side by side. One, a sleepy little boy and the other, a rather battered old teddy bear that had, at one time, been cuddled by Susan!

She closed her eyes and allowed the love that can only be between a mother and child to drift over her.

'Sleep tight, my little baby,' she whispered.

It was a private moment that would be remembered forever.

⇌

They had no way of knowing, but this evening was to change the direction of their lives forever. A chain of events were about to fall into place that would lead them into an adventure that was far beyond their wildest dreams

⇌

The narrow road into Widdersdale could be easily missed.

Just by the cattle auctions at Beddington, the narrow turning was hidden among low trees. The late spring sun was low in the sky. It lit up the awakening countryside to perfection. At the bottom of the Dale, the limestone walls were tinted pink in the light of the gradually sinking sun.

Many of the remote farms and barns were enveloped in deep shade, almost hidden among the foliage of the ancient trees. Soft grey walls and stone roofs looked as though they had been always been a part of the landscape

Little streams rushed down from the high places and made tiny silver waterfalls among the mossy rocks.

'Oh, isn't it all so very beautiful,'

Susan put her head on Peter's shoulder, 'Each time I come to Widdersdale, I think that I appreciate it more,'

Peter laughed,

'It's very special to me too. After all, it's where I met thee,'

'Yes, there's always something that spoils it all,' Susan was quick with her answer.

There were a lot of sturdy looking black and white cows grazing in the lush grass of the lower fields. Higher up, there were groups of spring lambs jumping and cavorting about, under the ever watchful eyes of their mothers.

The road to Billingbeck wound its way closely round the contours of the Dale, following the obvious route round large outcrops of limestone rocks and steeply sloping woodland.

Approaching Willowburn, there was a level place just beside the road where a small farm nestled under the steeply rising hillside. Its name was 'Bankside'.

As they drew closer, they saw a man working on one of the walls.

His cap was pushed well back, revealing snowy white hair, his face was burned the colour of old mahogany from a lifetime of exposure to the weather. Peter stopped the van and wound down the window.

'I see you're working late again Dick,'

'Aye.' Dick slowly straightened his back. 'Mending t' gap in t' wall,'

Susan looked beyond Dick and smiled to herself.

His scruffy black and white dog was sitting patiently in the back of a battered, muddy Land Rover watching his every move with eager anticipation, hoping, no doubt, that she would be allowed to do some work up on the fell side.

'That'll be Peggy,' Susan pointed to the dog. 'She wants to be off up the hill,'

'Tha'll be off to t' Black Bull, I recon?' Dick said

Peter nodded.

Dick gave a final wave and resumed his work on the wall.

Peter and Susan continued on towards Billingbeck.

Susan laughed.

'We have lots of time. There is no doubt that Old Ned will hang on to a couple of seats for us,'

'Popular place on Thursdays. Good old Ned,'

Most of Billingbecks villagers visited the 'Black Bull'.

As well as being a pub, the Black Bull had the Dales only petrol pumps in its back yard; it also had an ironmongers shop attached. All of this was the empire of Bert Eckersley. Bert was a red faced chap who had the look of a rather prosperous farmer rather than a pub landlord.

His pub food was legendary and his cellar was known to be the home of a drop of 'Webster's Ale'. Considered by many to be among Yorkshires finest.

There were usually a few ramblers and families taking motoring holidays to be found in the Black Bull.

The villagers had favourite corners. Quite a few of the farmers on the other hand, preferred to congregate in a group round the bar.

The young couple parked the van in a corner of the pub car park and gazed for a moment into the dark pool that ran alongside the pub. Peter held onto Susan's hand.

'Remember the scruffy young chap who spent his evening gazing at the beautiful girl with the blond hair and the amazing eyes?'

Susan laughed.

'Oh, I've seen scruffier individuals. You weren't all that scruffy. A bit windswept perhaps. But, there was no mistaking the look on your face. You were a bit obvious,'

Peter smiled,

'Just think. If I hadn't been there at that time, I wouldn't be here with my wonderful wife now,' he winked and slipped his arm round Susan's waist. He whispered in her ear.

'I love you,'

Susan snuggled closer, a smile of contentment on her face.

A few people were sitting outside on the benches enjoying the evening sun. Bert glanced up as Peter and Susan walked into the cool interior of the pub.

'Good evening,' he said. 'It's nice to see you two again. How's my friend, young Jim?'

'Oh, he's tucked up in bed. June and Bill are looking after him,' Susan said.

Bert knew exactly what Peter and Susan would be wanting. He nodded towards the back room.

'Ned's in there. Better make it another pint?'

Susan grinned and turned to Peter.

'No doubt, Ned'll have some good village gossip for us,'

They collected their drinks and made their way towards the back room.

It was the largest room in the Black Bull. It had the grandiose title of 'Music room'. On Thursdays.

Over in the corner sat a chap who grinned broadly at Peter and Susan. He was obviously a local chap. He was wearing a collarless shirt and a Harris Tweed coat.

He was of indeterminate age, though Peter always guessed that he was about sixty. It was of course, Old Ned.

Peter lifted a hand in greeting to his friend.

Ned indicated towards two seats beside where he was sitting at a corner table.

'Sithee. I saved thee a couple of seats,'

That was typical of Ned. He had saved seats in an otherwise almost empty room.

'Hello Ned. Good to see you again. I got you a pint,'

Peter placed the overflowing pint glass on the table. Ned didn't answer.

He picked up his pint and took a long swig. Finally, he placed the half empty glass on the table, wiped his mouth on his sleeve and muttered,

'Nice to see thee too young man. And thy young lady,'

Ned had his finger on most things that were going on in the Dale.

Peter and Susan could always be sure to hear a good tale and enjoy a bit of dry old Yorkshire humour.

Ned lived in Billingbeck, He had only been away from the Dale once in his life. It was when he was called upon to fight for his country in the trenches of Flanders during the Great War. He had been a young lad then. Little was known about wife. She was not a local girl. She had arrived in Billingbeck as Ned's young bride when he came back from the war.

She was a gentle lady with a quiet way of speaking.

Gradually, the room began to fill up. Most people knew each other and nodded to friends sitting at other tables.

One by one, the band arrived. All six of them were red- faced lads, loaded up with guitars, a set of drums and various other assorted instruments.

They spent some time plugging into the pub's complicated electrical system and testing various instruments to the accompaniment of loud squeaks and howls from the loudspeakers. Finally, satisfied, they settled down.

The lead guitarist was a young lad with very trendy long hair and a gleaming white smile. He tapped his foot several times, and the band struck up.

They began with a Beatles song that was very popular at the time, 'I wanna hold your hand'. It was a noisy, but vaguely romantic song, and the lads made a fair job of imitating the Beatles.

Like most of their generation, both Peter and Susan were fans of the Beatles. They smiled at each other and intertwined fingers under the table.

The Farmers and their families forgot their Yorkshire roots and brass bands, as they tapped their feet with gusto.

Not so Old Ned.

'You can't call yon music. Its damned awful,' muttered Ned.

Susan smiled at him

'Perhaps you will have to get used to it Ned. I don't think it's going to go away,'

Ned screwed his face up.

'Thee and t' young 'uns. Yon Glen Miller in t' war time. Now, he was a good un. Even though he were one of them Yanks,'

'Don't you like Americans Ned?' Susan said.

'No. They used to come flashin' round here in yon Jeep things, showin' off and buyin' all t' beer, but Glen Miller, now he were a good 'un,'

The band didn't play too loudly. They were well aware that the villagers and surrounding hill folk would be chatting to each other.

The Black Bull was where a lot of deals were done among the Dales farmers in the area. Or so they would tell you.

As far as the men were concerned, it was the wives that brought it all together. What seemed like local gossip was, in fact, the life blood of the community. There was genuine sympathy for anyone who was having problems and, often, there was an offer of help. The good times were shared. Joy and pleasure brought smiles to the faces of the listeners.

The younger girls were eager to learn from the more experienced and wiser women. Most wives were involved in the day to day running of the farms and knew just as much as the men folk about what was going on around the holdings.

Peter and Susan listened with amusement to a farmer who was telling a tale about a pony that had been sold for a high price to a Lancashire farmer.

Anything that poked fun at neighbouring Lancashire was always appreciated. It happened that there was a Lancashire farmer standing among the local lads He listened to the tale with an amused smile. A voice could be heard above the chatter.

"T best thing about Lancashire is t' road out,'

The Lancashire farmer just broadened his grin and pushed his cap onto the back of his head,

'Aye lad,' he said. 'We send thee all our unwanted cattle,'

Everyone laughed. The joke may have been well worn, but still appreciated.

Old Ned had often heard Peter and Susan discussing their love of the Dale. They had talked, not too seriously, about settling down in Widdersdale one day. He seemed to be deep in thought as the band took a break. Suddenly, he spoke.

'Nabsyead's for sale,'

The young couple looked at him. What had brought that on?

'What's Nabsyead?' Peter asked.

"Nab's Head, thy'd call it. It's a farm on t' moor,'   They hadn't been discussing the merits of becoming Widdersdalians.

Peter had been telling Susan about a contractor that he was having trouble with in Bolton.

"What do you mean, Nabsyead's for sale?

"Didn't mean nowt," Ned replied.", He grinned and hid behind his pint glass. Then he continued, dropping his usual Dales accent.

'Nab's Head, Old Turner's son's decided to sell it. Thirty acres of good land with meadows and good water. Going for the right price,'

Peter and Susan had, at one time, discussed moving to Widdersdale. But now they had responsibilities. There was young Jim to consider… And so many other things. Peters job, the flat, friends, family. So many things.

Little did they realise at that moment, how their entire lives were about to change. Perhaps, if they had known, the next few years would have been very different?

Ned's casual comment was about to throw the Barnard family into an adventure beyond their wildest dreams.

All good things must come to an end. So it was with the 'folk evening' at the Black Bull.

All too soon, it was time to say goodbye to Ned and the other people that they knew, who were sitting round them. Ned drained his glass and wiped his mouth with his sleeve,

'Nowt like a drop o' good ale,' he muttered. 'Time to be off home to t' wife. Don't forget what I were telling thee about Nabsyead,'

Bert had put the towels on the pumps and the band were unplugging their instruments and carrying stuff out to their van.

Peter and Susan went out into the cool night air.

There was much slamming of car and Land Rover doors.

The Barnard's said a final goodnight to Ned.

'It's been a pleasure meeting you again Ned,' Peter said.

'Yes. Well, I'll say goodnight to thee. Don't forget what I told thee. Nab's Yead. It's going for t' right sort 'o brass,'

He didn't seem too steady on his feet. He just wandered off into the darkness and towards his home. There were voices out on the car park.

'G' night Alf,'

'G' night Bert See thee at t' auctions in t' morning,'

'Aye. Art thou bringin' yon heifers?'

The voices continued to discuss the following day's auctions, but Peter and Susan had climbed into the van. It was time to head back to Guiseley. The road ahead was very dark. The headlamps of the van picked up the green, winding tunnel formed by the overhanging trees. Occasionally they saw the reflected eyes of some startled sheep in one of the fields.

Peter and Susan were unusually quiet.

I wonder where it is.?' Susan said in a quiet voice.

'Where what is?' Peter looked at her. But, he knew very well what she was talking about.

There was silence for a moment.

'Nab's Head. It seems such a shame,'

'Let's find out,' Peter said. 'We have nothing to lose,'

He grinned to himself. It would be fun to take a look.

He guessed that Susan was overcome with curiosity. So was he.

What did it look like? How badly had it suffered from being abandoned for a few years?

'Gosh. I can't wait to see it,' Susan said.

'Don't raise your hopes too much. It'll probably be a total ruin,'
Peter was being practical as always.

'Oh Peter. Don't be a killjoy. I'll bet there's nothing much wrong
with it,'

Peter looked at her eager face. He didn't want to spoil her dream.

'If its any good, it's bound to be going for a lot of money,' he looked
thoughtful.

'Are there no farmers up there who want to expand their land?' They
discussed the abandoned farm as they drove home to their cosy little
flat where they were surrounded by all the comforts of life.

On the way home, they decided to call in on Peter's family.

Arthur and Ada lived in a small terraced house on the outskirts of
Guiseley. Nothing much had changed in the house over the years.

It was almost exactly as Peter remembered it in his childhood.

Old fashioned rooms, with tasselled lace curtains and rather heavy
Victorian furniture.

Peter's dad Arthur worked in a local woollen mill.

He had left school at the age of fourteen and had needed to help
supplement the family income. He started work only days after leaving
school.

When the war came along, he joined the army right at the beginning
and was fortunate enough to return home at the end of it.

He met Ada at the local dance hall. She was a pretty, but shy young
girl who worked in 'service' as a maid in one of the large Victorian houses
on the outskirts of Leeds. They married and settled down in the little
house where they had lived ever since.

Peter told his parents about Nab's Head.   His dad smiled at him.

'Peter lad, Tha' knows what tha't doing. We wish you both all the
luck in the world,'

Ada didn't have much to say. She looked at Susan.

'Are you sure it's what you want to do?'

She didn't understand much of modern times, nor did she particularly want to. She was quite happy to know that her son and his nice young wife seemed to be able to cope with the pace of modern life very well.

'Next time you call, bring young Jim,'

Like most grandparents, Arthur and Ada doted on their grandchild. It seemed to Peter that they were at their happiest when Jim was around. Peter explained that they were on their way home from Widdersdale and it was getting late.

When they finally arrived home, Bill and June were sitting beside the fire. Bill glanced at his watch. It was almost time for them to go home.

'Oh, thanks for looking after Jim. We really enjoyed our evening,'

Susan told her parents about the music and about the Lancashire farmer, But Peter noticed that she seemed reluctant to mention Nab's Head.

She was indeed waiting for the right moment to mention the derelict farm.

Finally, she just had to mention it. June noticed her daughter's nervousness, but she didn't know the reason for it.

'Remember us telling you about Old Ned?'

'I know Old Ned,' her dad said.

As an agricultural engineer, he knew a lot of Dales characters.

Susan told them about the abandoned farm.

Her mother looked up sharply. The mention of Nab's Head wasn't quite as casual as it seemed. June knew her daughter perhaps better than Susan realised.

Two

June was soon to realise that her fears had been well founded.

'As you know, it's always been our dream to live in Widdersdale,' Susan said.' We have a lot of friends there and it would be a wonderful spot to raise young Jim,'

Jim's future was, in fact June's main doubt about what Peter and Susan were considering, but she had other concerns too. Was the community of Withersdale, particularly the farming community, tolerant of such novices?

Perhaps she could see into the future?

'But he'll be off to school soon. All his friends are here in Guiseley.

Nab's Head seems to be in a remote spot. Are you sure that he would handle the change?'

'You can be sure that Peter and I have discussed all of that Mum,' Susan smiled.

She knew very well how much her mother cared about them all.

She knew that June wasn't just trying to dissuade them from jumping in at the deep end. June on the other hand, knew her daughter well enough to know that she would have carefully thought about all the possibilities and talked it over with Peter.

'Don't worry mum. The village school in Billingbeck has a very good reputation. The village kids seem to do very well and, where better to live?'

There were still doubts in her mothers mind, but she trusted that Susan would not dash into anything lightly. The thought that young Jim might actually benefit hadn't occurred to her.

Bill smiled.

'Do you remember June, when we were younger, we talked of nothing else but living in Widdersdale. I must admit that I had the same thoughts once. But times were different. We didn't have the same security,'

Susan listened to what her dad had to say. She was surprised. He had never mentioned any of this before. She suspected that he was making the point now, to lend some weight to his daughter's comments. She said nothing.

Instead, she went into the kitchen. She came back with mugs of tea and a plate of fruit cake. She set the tray on a table by the fire.

Peter glanced at Susan's dad. He caught the flicker of a smile. He knew that the subject would be discussed later in some depth.

'Let's go and take a look at Nab's Head this weekend,' Susan suddenly said to Peter.

'Fine… Yes, er, good idea. I was rather hoping that you would say that. We have nothing else to do, and Jim would love the adventure,'

The smile re-appeared on Bill's face. He glanced at June. She was smiling too.

She didn't really think that Peter had serious thoughts of taking the matter any further. Nor, at that time, did Peter.

The weekend arrived, and with it came the rain! Not the cold stuff of winter. It was little more than a gentle mist really. But Peter and Susan both knew from past experience that this mist could be very different up on the moor.

'Well,' commented Susan, 'It's a good job that we have all the right waterproofs,'

Jim wasn't going to be put off by a mere drop of rain. He wouldn't have been put off by a snowstorm. It just added to the fun.

He was walking about in his boots even before breakfast.

'When are we setting off?' His little voice was impatient.

'Eat your toast,' said Peter. He tried not to smile, but he remembered his own impatience as a child.

The plate that had been set in front of Jim emptied very quickly. Seconds later, he was standing there, wearing his big waterproof jacket, buttoned up wrong, his woollen hat jammed tightly on his head. So tightly that he was having difficulty seeing.

'Are we ready?' The area around Jim's mouth was liberally coated with crumbs and his voice was even more impatient. And so, with a little more urging from Jim, they all three climbed into the van, and they were off on the big adventure.

They took the turn by the cattle market at Beddington but, instead of the usual far reaching view of the Dale, they could see nothing much of anything.

'We couldn't have picked a worse day,' Peter peered into the gloom.

'Yes we could. It could have been too hot,' Susan muttered.

'Then, perhaps we would have wanted a drop of rain?'   Peter looked at Susan,

'I can well remember some of the soakings that we got up on the moors,'

The road ahead stretched out into oblivion, winding up upwards towards Willowburn. Everything seemed to just end in a huge wall of wet white mist. Sheep ran across the road in panic, startled as the van appeared as if from nowhere.

'Lets have lunch at the Black Bull,' Susan said, 'Maybe the mist will clear up later,'

'That's the best idea you've had in years,' Peter said.

Jim, on the other hand, wanted to carry on. He was full of excitement and he wanted to be up on the moor.

'Let's keep going," he said. "Perhaps, it'll rain harder,'

In the Black Bull, there were a few damp looking hikers round the bar, and more sitting by the fire in the lounge. They discovered Ned sitting in his usual corner. This time, he was accompanied by his wife.

He didn't look at all comfortable.

His cap sat straight on his head and a tie was knotted tightly under his chin.

He looked relieved to see the young couple.

While Peter went to order the meal, and a few drinks for themselves Ned and Ned's wife Betty, Susan settled herself beside Betty. The topic of conversation was, as it often was, the weather. Jim meanwhile, became instant friends with several of the visitor's children and, in moments, he had disappeared into the games room, Nab's head forgotten for the moment.

'What brings thee into t' Dale on a day like this?' Ned asked, once the couple had ordered their meal, Peter and Susan told them of their intention to visit Nab's Head.

'Yon's not in good condition. Now, don't thee go offerin' proper money for it,' Ned shook his head doubtfully.

He glanced over to where a group of farmers were deep in conversation.

'See yon chap wi' t' blue overalls on and t' bald head, He knows all about Nabsyead,'

He pointed with his stick to a lanky individual standing with the farmers. He was wearing a cap, so his hair, or lack of it, was not an issue.

Peter thanked Ned and walked over to the group of farmers.   He addressed the tall chap.

'Excuse me. Old Ned over there tells me that you know something about Nab's Head?'

Peter's question met with suspicion.

'Happen I do. Why art thou askin'?'

Peter explained that they wanted to go up and take a look at the place.

The room was very quiet. Peter learned later that farmers never just came out with a statement about anything. It was better to gain time to weigh up your opponent. To gain time to think, to draw out the other chap. Peter had gone in at the deep end. He had unwittingly shown the farmers that he was no countryman.

'Wheer art thou from?' The lanky farmer asked Peter.

He appeared to be suspicious. 'Tha' t' not from Lancashire?'

'Guiseley,' Peter told him.

'Tha't' sure tha's not from Lancashire?'

'Oh no,' Peter reassured him. 'I'm a Yorkshire chap.'

The farmers visibly relaxed. Grins appeared. All was well.

Lunch was informally served at the table.

'Look yonder,' grinned one of the farmers. 'They've ordered Yorkshire pudding.'

Young Jim suddenly decided to come into the room and sit down. He had no problems with the menu. He ordered sausage and chips, as always.

Jim did much to break the ice by chatting with the farmers.

They were all heroes in Jim's eyes. Farmers owned big noisy things like tractors and they were allowed to get their hands dirty. Jim soon had them all laughing. The tall chap grinned too, and decided to come clean.

He turned out to be 'Young' Sam Turner, the owner of Nab's Head.

Peter wondered about the 'Young' part of his name, considering that he was in his seventies. But it seemed that no-one wanted to confuse him with another Sam Turner who was eighty five. Young Sam explained that his father had been farming up at Nab's Head.

'One day, while my Dad was mending t'roof, he fell off and killed himself,'

Sam didn't show any emotion although both Peter and Susan said how sorry they were to hear about his father's unfortunate accident.

He insisted on carefully explaining just where Nab's Head was, although Peter assured him that they already knew.

'When tha's been up yon, come and tell me what tha thinks,'

He winked, as if to show that he had never doubted that they were of good Yorkshire stock. He made no mention of price. That would come later. The one thing that he did try to impress on them was the risk from his guard dogs.

'I live at Willowburn Farm. When tha' comes to my place, be very careful o t' dogs. Damn dangerous, yon dogs,' he shuddered for maximum effect.

As Peter and Susan left the pub, Jim insisted on saying goodbye to all the farmers.

'Thee look after thy mum and dad young man,' someone said.

'Don't worry, I will,' Jim shouted over his shoulder.

The rain had not diminished. If anything, it was even thicker on the tops. The moors were shrouded in heavy curtains of white moisture.

The far away bleating of sheep was answered by much closer, but still invisible sheep out on the hillside above them, Susan found the sound quite haunting, giving an impression of wildness and distance.

The very air smelled of wet sheep.

By luck, Peter spotted a sign painted with whitewash on a rock by the roadside announcing the fact that, here was 'Appleburn Farm'.

There was a narrow gap in the high wall at this point, where the lane ran up towards Nab's Head. It was rather like entering a long dark tunnel. Even Jim had gone quiet.

There came a point where the van could go no further.

Brambles and bushes had grown together over the years; there was a tangled mass of vegetation blocking the way ahead. It couldn't even be called a lane in this weather. Rather more like a small stream. They were forced to abandon the van and proceed on foot.

Jim of course, was considerably more enthusiastic than his parents.

Under the dripping trees in a little cutting known as the 'Midge Hole', they soon saw the house ahead of them looming eerily out of the mist.

Black empty gaps that had once been windows looked forlornly out at them with an awful sadness, almost apologising for not being able to make the visitors more welcome. The soft grey stone was dark and dripping with wetness; patches of old whitewash were peeling off here and there.

It was almost as if the old farmhouse was embarrassed to show itself to humans in such a run down and abandoned condition.

The three of them held hands as they walked slowly across the mossy, cobbled yard towards the porch. The rotting remains of a heavy door hung forlornly by one rusty hinge.

Suddenly, without warning, a couple of startled sheep rushed past them, clattering wildly across the cobbled yard and away into the safety of the all enveloping mist. Somewhere, high above, a bird fluttered in the rafters. The only other sounds came from the steady dripping of water and the forlorn bleating of the distant sheep.

'Well, at least the floor's dry,' Susan was the first to speak.

'It's the only thing that is,' Peter looked at her, smiling.

'Old Man Turner mended the roof. Do you remember?'

Susan shivered.

She didn't answer because she didn't want to frighten Jim.

He was clinging onto her hand and gazing round in awe. She was thinking about the people who once lived here. Peter picked up Jim to reassure him and put his arm round Susan.

The mossy old stone roof was supported by huge oak beams.

It had certainly stood the test of time. The only clue as to where the kitchen had been was a low brownstone sink filled with dead leaves.

'Oh, the poor house,' said Susan.

In a more practical tone she continued, 'There is tons of work that needs doing,'

The lounge was surprisingly dry. A vast iron fireplace with a big oven dominated all of one wall. It had a greenish tarnished brass tap suggesting some sort of water supply, and large oven doors.

The whole thing was set inside an Inglenook topped by a massive oak beam. There were rusting iron hooks hammered into the beam, the inside of the Inglenook was built from rough stone, coated with many years of peeling lime wash.

Susan looked up at the ceiling. It was a heavy affair, supported by rough blackened beams, and the deep-set windows were mullioned, but totally devoid of glass.

A wide, quite elaborately carved staircase led to the upper rooms. There were three large bedrooms and a smaller one at the head of the stairs. The floors were quite sound, and there were heavy pine doors with iron hinges and latches.

The walls were roughly plastered and not too flaky.

They both agreed that, in fact, the interior of the house was in much better condition than they could have hoped for considering that it had been abandoned for so many years. Peter smiled and thought how it would have been described by an estate agent.

'A most charming late seventeenth century farmhouse. Retaining many original features, but in need of some renovation,'

They soon discovered however, that the barn and outbuildings were not in good condition. There were leaky roofs and piles of rubble everywhere. The barn had room for about twenty cows.

It had wooden stalls built down each of the longer walls and a loose box at one end. Wooden hay racks stood in front of each stall, fed from the loft above.

'Don't go up there Peter, It doesn't look too safe,' Susan said.

They went back into the relative dryness of the house; Jim was the first to speak.

'Can I have the front bedroom please?' He jumped up and down with excitement. Susan couldn't help laughing.

'We're a long way from that yet, young man,'

She turned to Peter.

'There doesn't seem to be any water supply,'

'There is.' Peter replied. 'I noticed a well just behind the house,'

They decided to have a final look round. The well proved to be lined with stone and in good condition. They found another decent sized building and a corrugated iron lean-to on the side of the barn.

They knew very little about the land though what they could see of the surrounding fields through the mist looked promising.

The land round the farm buildings was quite flat, with a gentle hill rising behind. But they didn't know which fields belonged to Nab's Head. The Ordinance Survey map for Widdersdale showed another farm behind with the delightful name of 'Folly Edge'.

There was nothing else to be investigated, and so, reluctantly they made their way back through the Midge Hole. At the end of the lane, they took a final look back at the house. It had vanished completely, swallowed up by the mist, as though it had been a ghost.

With some difficulty, Peter managed to extricate the van from its resting place among the blackberry bushes onto firmer ground. Without any more problems, they were soon heading back towards Billingbeck and the lower end of the Dale.

As they drove down below Willowburn, the mist suddenly evaporated. It was as though it had never been.

The sun blazed down, causing the road ahead to steam as it rapidly dried out. They looked back towards the head of the Dale, to where wispy white clouds drifted across a perfect blue sky.

The soft grey stone of the cottages blended perfectly with the dappled light among the trees: everything had changed so abruptly.

The little hollow where Nab's Head lay would be basking in this wonderful lazy warmth.

There was much discussion over the next few days. The details of what they had discovered were discussed with parents, and the opinion of friends was sought. Some of the opinions were constructive, but a few of their friends seemed to consider the very idea of moving to Nab's Head to be quite hilarious. The outcome was that Peter and Susan decided to call at Willowburn Farm, the home of 'Young' Sam and Mrs Turner.

Willowburn farm was not far off the road just above the village.

There was a point where the winding lane divided into two. The left one wandering off round a corner to a dwelling called Windy Edge.

The right fork lead towards to Willowburn Farm.

There were only two gates. The first one was easy, but the second one was a very different story. Peter and Susan looked at each other and burst out laughing.

'O.K. You are the smart guy. How do we open it?'

Peter didn't have an answer. They had come across this sort of thing all over the Dales.

Baling twine, as its name implies, is for tying bales of hay.

The problem was that farmers don't like throwing anything away. Baling twine was so useful. It was a sort of plasticy string. Bright orange in colour. It had a mind of its own and seemed to want to unwind itself just for fun.

Peter and Susan knew that Yorkshire farmers were particularly good at adapting anything to do a job that it wasn't intended for. They were indeed farmers… But above all they were Yorkshire men.

They had both seen many examples of the misuse of baling twine.

It was used as bootlaces, to hold up trousers, and to tie up dogs.

They mended their machines with it and it was to be seen tying down the back doors of Land-Rovers.

A vintage five barred gate tied up with baling twine can be a deadly weapon.

The moment that anyone attempts to untie the innocent looking neat bow that is holding the gate shut, the whole thing seems to explode into a writhing mass of uncontrollable tightly knotted orange plastic. Worse still, sometimes, baling twine replaced a broken hinge. No problem if you were a seventeen stone lad built like a dry stone wall. But most ramblers were not built like a stone wall.

A lot of them had staggered down from these high, gated places with damaged shins.

A few farmers had made the leap forwards into the twentieth century and installed cattle grids. It took a lot of the drama out of what was one of Britain's most unpopular country national sports: 'gate untying'. But, it perhaps made possible a new sport, called 'fell running'.

Peter and Susan found themselves face to face with a classic example of a rotting old gate held together with twine.

'It looks like the end of the road for the van,' Susan was looking at the mass of rusty chains and a big padlock.

Houdini would no doubt have thought twice about tackling the problem.

'I'll lift you over it,' Peter was weak with laughter.

Sam's gate was a classic.

'You just stand back,' Susan said. 'I'll show you how it's done,'

She went first. But, when she was halfway over, the gate collapsed, leaving her rocking gently, as if lying in a huge orange hammock!

'Rock a bye baby,' Peter couldn't resist saying it.

Susan couldn't reply. She was helpless with laughter.

Peter tried to do better, but he finished up in a heap on the far side of the gate.

Battered, bruised, but undefeated, they dusted each other down and grinned.

'Well, we beat it,' Susan said. They were feeling smug. They had fought a fair battle with the gate and tasted victory. They set off triumphant, on the final leg of their journey.

In their enthusiasm, they had totally forgotten Young Sam's lengthy warning about the dangerous dogs. By far the trickiest part of the journey to Willowburn Farm still lay ahead. They rounded the final corner and there they were… The dogs.

The entrance to Sam's farm was between two stone barns.

The dogs were chained to opposite barns. Long, rusty chains were attached to the dogs collars, and at the other end, to Peter's horror, orange baling twine connected the chains to iron rings set into the barn walls. This weak link filled Peter with terror.

To describe the huge beasts as dogs was perhaps, a bit misleading.

They were mean, lean looking monsters of doubtful parentage: Their coats were muddy brown in colour and they had muscles on top of muscles.

The moment that Peter and Susan came into view, the huge hounds lunged forwards, the gap between them narrowing to a mere two feet.

The surface of the yard was cobbled, coated with a layer of wet mud and cow manure. Peter did his best to look like a dog lover.

'Good dogs,' he said hopefully.

The dogs responded with a smile.

It may have been a smile? What Peter actually saw were two rows of fangs exposed between drooling lips. The dogs had red watery eyes set in great folds of wrinkly skin. They were straining forwards to the limit of their chains, claws scrabbling against the muddy cobbles. Peter now realised how the Light Brigade must have felt as they looked into the barrels of the Russian guns. But, Peter was not in the Light Brigade.

He knew his limitations. His instincts said 'Run fast'.

But, they had to get to Willowburn Farm.

There was only one possible course of action. To slide through the gap. Peter edged very carefully forwards into the channel between the snarling beasts. Susan was horrified. She didn't think that the gap was wide enough.

'Be careful,'

The gap seemed to close slightly. The dogs trembled with anticipation.

How strong was the baling twine?

Suddenly, one of the dogs lunged. It had him!

Peter was pinned firmly against the barn wall, held there by two mighty paws on his shoulders.

Susan screamed. Peter was struck dumb with fright.

'Help,' shouted Susan.

But it was a desolate spot. There was no-one to hear her. There was nothing more she could do. She was helpless. The crafty dog had kept some slack on its chain.

Peter saw a huge grinning face inches from his own. Suddenly, a great sloppy tongue swiped across his face.

The great hound had fallen in love with him!

The other dog stood, wagging its tail madly, eagerly waiting for its turn.

Susan was in shock.

Quickly, she dashed through the gap.

'You seem to have a new friend,'

Once through the gap, her confidence returned. She skipped on for a few yards, totally ignored by the lovesick dogs.

With some considerable difficulty, Peter finally managed to extricate himself from the embrace of the passionate hound. But it was a rather bedraggled Peter who finally joined Susan in her place of safety.

He wiped his face on his sleeve.

'It kisses like you do,' he ducked as Susan took a swipe at him.

'Count yourself lucky young man. You could have found yourself living with a dog. I just felt sorry for you,'

Peter knocked at Mr and Mrs Turner's door. It immediately flew open. Sam stood there, a mug of tea in his hand.   His vast brown corduroy trousers were hitched up to his chest with braces and a big leather belt. His shirt was collarless, decorated with blue and white stripes. It was of a type favoured by many of the older farmers, and was known as a 'union shirt'.

On his feet, he wore carpet slippers mended with… baling twine.

He looked surprised to see the young couple, and very wary.

'How did you get past yon dogs?' he said. 'Tha' doesn't know how close tha' came to being savaged. Very dangerous, yon dogs,'

'Did you say savaged or ravaged?' Susan grinned. 'Peter was very brave,' she explained.

Peter nodded. He was shaking a bit. Sam seemed satisfied that his guard dogs had performed their duties. He grinned and stepped to one side.

'Come in,' almost as an afterthought, he muttered, 'Paid some good brass for yon dogs,'

Three

Peter and Susan stepped into Sam Turner's lounge.

It took a moment for their eyes to adjust to the relatively dim light of the room.Susan instantly recognised the smell of mothballs and Mansion polish. It brought back a distant memory from her childhood. Her Grandmother's home, so long ago. Also, there was a faint aroma of paraffin. More wonderful memories of her childhood came flooding back to her.

Slowly she looked round the room. Almost the whole of one wall was taken up by the inevitable huge fireplace. The black iron had a deep sheen and the hinges of the oven doors were of polished steel. Susan knew that the shine could only be achieved by painstakingly rubbing the metal hinges with sand. A copper kettle and several brass pans were gleaming in the reflected light of a bright fire.

The middle of the room was dominated by a large oval table. It was covered by a very white, tasselled Irish linen cloth. In the centre of the table was a large copper paraffin lamp with a crystal shade.

The table had very heavy ornate legs and was surrounded by six

severe looking high backed chairs. A dresser full of expensive looking Victorian pottery sat along the wall opposite the fireplace, and in
a corner stood a magnificent looking grandfather clock. It was ticking
slowly.

Susan wondered how many years it had ticked away in that same
corner of the room.

There was only one picture hanging on one of the walls.   It was a
sepia portrait in a gilded frame of a young man wearing the uniform of
a soldier of the First World War.   Sam saw Peter looking at it.

'My brother,' he said quietly. 'He didn't come home,'

A door opened and a small woman came into the room. She was
wearing an old fashioned dress and a wrap around pinafore.

Her complexion was fresh and suggested a life in the Dales. She
appeared to be a quiet calm lady, well in control of her surroundings.
Susan particularly noticed her bright smiling blue eyes.

'I would like you to meet my wife Mary,' Sam spoke softly and with
great tenderness,

'Mary, I would like you to meet the young couple I was telling you
about. Mr and Mrs Barnard. They have an interest in purchasing Nab's
Head,'

'I'm very pleased to meet you,' the woman spoke with a gentle voice.

'If you will excuse me, I'll go and make some tea,'

With that, she disappeared through the low door which obviously
led to the kitchen.

Sam indicated that he wished Peter and Susan to sit at the table.

He himself, sat at the head of the table, looking rather like a Victorian
father.

They discussed many things. The weather, the price of cattle at the
auctions, 'of which Peter and Susan knew very little', and the risk to ramblers who were silly enough to approach Sam's dogs.

At this point, there was no mention of Nab's Head.

After a while, Mary reappeared carrying a tray.   She set the tray on the table and withdrew again without a word.

There was a brown earthenware teapot and three dainty china cups and saucers, a sugar bowl and milk jug. Also, a matching plate with fruit cake and a slab of Wensleydale cheese, and three little side plates.

Sam gestured to Susan to pour the tea. while he cut himself a fair sized chunk of cheese and some of the crumbly cake. He put cheese on his cake and took a huge bite with obvious relish.

The young couple followed his example and all three of them ate in silence.   They were following an old Yorkshire custom that both Peter and Susan had been brought up with.

Finally, the subject of Nab's Head could be avoided no longer.

Sam leaned back in his chair, rocking it on two legs. He looked thoughtful.

Finally, he spoke.

'Well,' he said, 'I recon tha's been lookin' round Nab's Head?'

'Indeed we have,'

Peter was trying to contain his impatience.

Sam said nothing. It was quite obvious that he was waiting for Peter to make the next move.

He didn't even bother to glance in Susan's direction.

Sam Turner was one of a dying breed of northern men who considered that matters such as property deals were for men to discuss.

Both Peter and Susan were aware of it. They quickly glanced at each other, Peter smiled.

'Sam, Susan here is my wife. We are both considering the purchase of Nab's Head, so, Susan will be wanting to know all about the place. I need her comments and suggestions,'

Sam looked rather uncomfortable. But he got the point of what Peter was saying.

Susan on the other hand, found it very difficult to show no emotion. She was trying not to laugh when she saw poor Sam's face.

'It needs some work doing,'

Peter put the conversation back on course.

'A bit o' work never hurt no-one,'

Sam was back on form.

'Thou art young, thee two. That always busy on't hills. There's always summat to do, up in t' hills,'

Susan noticed with amusement, that she was included in the conversation now that work was being mentioned.

'Well, tha's seen t' place. What does tha' want to know about?'

'We don't know exactly how much land there is, or where the fields are,' It was Susan who spoke, causing Sam to wince visibly.

He stood up and went across to a battered old roll- top desk.

He opened a draw and produced a bundle of yellowing papers which he brought over to the table. He spread them out and pointed to a large map.

'Come and look at this,' he said.

Peter and Susan looked at the map.

It was an ancient, dog eared land map of the area covering Nab's Head Farm and surrounding countryside.

'There's t' land shown in red. If tha looks at t' top end, tha'll see tha's got grazing rights on t' moor. Boundary goes o'er yon hill and all t' way down to Bert Dickinson's place. Then round yon and joins up wi' Old Ernie's place,'

The boundaries were outlined in red and easy to follow. Each field had a number and was marked with its acreage.

'Proper maps wi't' lawyer,' Sam explained.

'Have you considered a price?' Peter asked him.

'If tha thinks tha's getting t' place for nowt, tha can think again,'

Sam was quick with his answer. He stared at Peter. 'Ar't' thou thinkin' o' farmin?'

'Well,' said Peter. 'We hadn't given it much thought,'

'Tha' knows nowt about farmin'. I'll tell thee. Tha' can't learn farmin' out o' a book. Tha'd lose all thy brass,' Sam shook his head. 'I can see, tha knows nowt,'

'We rather hoped that you could give us some advice,' Susan said.

'Aye, well, maybe I could. But, tha'd have to be sharp t' learn farmin. It's summat tha's born with. It's in t' blood. Soon lose thy brass,' he repeated.

Little did Peter and Susan realise just how often they would remember Sam's remarks over the coming years.

'Fifteen hundred,' he suddenly announced.

Peter and Susan were taken aback. Sam had suddenly stated his price.

'Fifteen hundred pounds. I'll take nowt less,'

He had a look of grim determination on his face.

Peter and Susan had thought that the price would be around two thousand.

They were delighted. Susan glanced at Peter; her eyes sparkling with excitement. Sam spotted the glance. But he misinterpreted it.

'Now then young lady. Don't thee go hagglin' o'er t' price. Yon's a fair price. I'll not be bartered,' then he grinned.

'Tha'd have a good neighbour. Old Ernie o'er t' top at Folly Edge. He's a sound chap, Old Ernie,' he paused. 'I'll gi' thee a bit o' luck,' he said.

Neither Peter nor Susan knew what he was talking about. 'A bit o' luck'?

But pride didn't allow them to ask him.

Susan looked at Peter.

'What do you say?'

They both knew the answer.

'Fine,' Peter said.

It was fine indeed. They could afford to buy Nab's Head!

'Fine' Peter repeated.

"By gum lad. Tha's a lot to learn,' Sam smiled.

This young couple had indeed got a lot to learn. Sam was surprised because they hadn't quibbled about the price. But they seemed willing enough to listen to good advice.

'I'll ask Mary to make a drop more tea,' he disappeared through the low door.

When he had gone, Susan whispered to Peter,

'Well, we can raise the money. Here is where the hard work begins,'

Peter grinned at Susan.

'Thou art young. A bit o' work never did anyone any harm,' he almost got pushed from his chair.

A moment later, Mary and Sam both re-appeared.

A fresh pot of tea was placed on the table.

This time, because the business discussions were over, Mary thought it proper to sit at the table. Soon, she was nattering away with Susan.

She proved to be a very quick witted lady with a great sense of humour.

One thing was very obvious; Susan couldn't help noticing that this couple were totally devoted to each other.

'By gum. Tha were lucky to get past yon dogs,' Sam said again.

He had heard the dogs barking while he was in the kitchen.   Mary smiled. Maybe she knew something that Sam didn't?   Mary was telling the young couple about the days when Sam's dad was up at Nab's Head.

They had not known that Sam's father had lost his wife many years earlier from consumption as it was then known, and that he had continued to live alone when Sam took over Willowburn Farm from one of his uncles.

It was really the tale of the childhood of so many of the hill people.

Mary had met Sam when they were quite young. Her father had run a rented holding in Nidderdale. She was one of ten children and they all stayed in farming.

Peter glanced at his watch. Time was getting on.

Really, it was time to go. Jim was being looked after by Peter's parents. But, they would have time to call in at the Black Bull for a rapid meal before heading home to Guiseley.

They were sorry to say goodbye to Sam and Mary.

Although they had gone to Willowburn Farm to discuss the purchase of Nab's Head, they had been made very welcome. They got the impression that Sam and Mary Turner didn't get many visitors.

Soon, Peter and Susan were on the road up to Billingbeck. When they entered the Black Bull, Bert Eckersley was holding a glass up to the light.

'Well,' he smiled. 'It's the new farmers. How did the deal go?'

The couple glanced at each other. How on earth did Bert know about all that?

He was amused at their bewilderment.

'I'll tell thee how I knew. Easy. It didn't take a detective. I saw thee.

I was walking t' dog up by t' turn to Willowburn Farm. Everyone knows about thy interest in Nab's Head,'

'You are a bit of a Sherlock Holmes,' Susan laughed. 'You guessed right. You can be the first to know. Sam decided that we would make damn good farmers and yes, we are buying Nab's Head,'

Bert pulled a pint and a half of his best bitter and placed them on the bar top.

'On the house,' he said.

He lifted up a glass that he had hidden under the counter and raised it.

'Let me raise my glass to our new Widdersdalians. I want to be the first to welcome you to t' Dale,'

They all laughed and raised their glasses to the future.

Because the pub was empty, they took their glasses into the back room and sat by the fire. Bert joined them, and Susan told him about Peter's lucky escape from Sam's dogs.

Bert laughed.

'I don't even know how you got as far as the dogs. How did you get through his gate?'

Suddenly, they were interrupted by the arrival of Old Ned leading a scruffy looking sheepdog on a bit of twine. Ned was delighted to see the couple. He sat down. His dog lay so close to the fire that it was almost smouldering!

'Well, tha's gone and bought Nabsyead,' Ned shook his head.

'Tha'll be havin' a bit 'o work to do up yon,'

Peter and Susan looked at each other in utter amazement, and then they burst out laughing. How far had the news travelled? People over the border in Lancashire would know by now, no doubt!

'How did you know?' Peter asked him.

'Yon chap wi' t' shorthorns told t' chap in t' antique shop, an' he told me.' almost as an afterthought he muttered, 'It were t' milk chap as told Ernie wi t' shorthorns,'

Ned didn't see anything the least bit unusual about the way that the village grapevine worked.

What surprised Peter and Susan was the speed of it all. The news got to Old Ned in the time that it had taken them to drive from Willowburn Farm to the Black Bull. It could have been no more than an hour including time spent talking to Brian.

'Make sure tha' gets a bit o' luck,' Ned winked.

Sam had mentioned 'luck'. What was 'luck'? They didn't ask, because they both wanted to give the impression that they knew.

As they were driving back to Guiseley, They discussed the deal in more detail.

As well as paying Sam, they were going to need a considerable amount of building materials to make the house habitable.

Suddenly, Peter laughed.

'Well Mrs Barnard., how does it feel to be a farmer's wife?'

Susan looked at him with a happy expression.

'I never imagined it. Oh Peter, I can't wait to tell Jim. He's going to be thrilled,'

Peter smiled, but his face took on a more serious look.

'I have a feeling that we will have to do some convincing. We will be watched very carefully. There are so many things to learn. It isn't going to be easy to convince those Dales folk. At least, we have a few hundred in the bank, but we need to sell the flat pretty quickly,'

'I know,' Susan looked thoughtful. 'A lot depends on that. We have so much to plan. It's only just beginning to sink in. We need to know what we are doing,'

Peter was well aware that Susan was the more practical of the two of them.

He had no doubt that she would already be sorting out some plans for the immediate future in her head.

Luck seemed to be on their side. As soon as they mentioned to a few friends that they were selling the flat, one of them happened to know of a friend of a friend who was looking for just such a flat. They got a visit a few days later.

A young couple introduced themselves. They had recently married and were living with the girl's parents. Yes, the flat was just what they were looking for, and most important of all, the cash was available!

Things could move on. Peter and Susan were in a position to contact a solicitor.

Peter's parents were happy that the young couple were about to make the move to Widdersdale, but it was Bill and June who made all the difference.

June had had time to give a lot of thought to everything that had been discussed. She gave them all her support, much to the relief of Susan.

June could see, on reflection that Jim would actually benefit from living in the Dale. There was an excellent school in Guiseley and Jim had become good mates with some of Peter and Susan's friend's children, but he was absolutely committed to the move himself.

Most of the children around Widdersdale were typical Dales kids.

They seemed to know a great deal about sheep and farming matters, but they separated their way of life from school. The village school curriculum was taken very seriously by most of the parents. Their children were quite knowledgeable on most school subjects.

Susan noticed a considerable increase in June's enthusiasm for the project.

Bill actually knew a lot of the farmers personally. He worked alongside them. He knew what his daughter was capable of and he had the highest regard for Peter. But, being male, he perhaps didn't look into all the possibilities quite as much as June did? He never had a lot to say, but very little escaped his quick mind.

'You're going to change so many things,' He said. 'You are choosing to leave behind everything you know,'

Peter nodded.

'I have a feeling that the next couple of years are going to give us some surprises,'

But, the person who did most to convince everyone that everything was going to turn out fine was Young Jim. He had no doubts whatsoever.

'It will be years before I go to school,' he said to June, 'By then, I'll be all grown up.' he discussed the decor of his new bedroom with her and confided his big secret.

'Mum is going to buy me a rabbit,'

He didn't understand anything about such boring matters as banks and solicitors, after all, that silly stuff was for grown ups. It wasn't very complicated, thought Jim. Just paint his room and move in. And buy the rabbit.

What Peter and Susan didn't know was that Bill and June had been discussing how they could help out.

They called at the flat a couple of days after Jim's discussion with June.

It was quite obvious to Susan, that her parents had something to say.

Peter had been working in Bradford that day. It meant that he was a little bit later than usual getting home. Bill and June played with Jim, but it was easy to see that they had something on their minds.

Peter finally arrived home and greeted his in laws.

'It's nice to see you both. Sorry I'm late. It's been a long day. I was delayed in Bradford waiting for a delivery,'

Jim ran to his dad as he always did, and got his cuddle, but even Peter, who was not usually very good at sensing atmosphere, noticed that Bill and June had something on their minds.

A quick glance passed between the two parents. Bill nodded and June cleared her throat.

'We've been thinking about your decision to move to Widdersdale,' She looked embarrassed. 'You do realise that you are going to be really pushing it a bit, when you begin your restorations,'   Susan nodded.

'Don't worry too much Mum. We do have some talent when it comes to house repairs. After all, this flat needed practically re-building,'

Her mum smiled patiently.

'You're missing my point Susan. We know that you must be a bit worried about what you are committed to. We don't doubt that you can do the work. What I am trying to say, and not saying it very well is, Well,'

She looked embarrassed. 'We want to put a bit of money into the project. We have some savings and we would like to put a bit of brass into your new home. Let's just say that it's helping out a bit with Jim's future. The fact is, we hope that you will accept a thousand pounds. We believe that the move will be right for Jim's future in the long run,'

Susan jumped to her feet and ran across the room. She flung her arms round her Mum. Then, she reached out towards Bill. He had been keeping in the background, looking rather embarrassed. Smiling, he put his arm round his daughters shoulder.

'You are amazing. Both of you. Oh, we won't let you down,'

Peter couldn't find words.

He just gripped Bill's hand and nodded his thanks.

June picked up Jim, who wasn't quite sure what all the fuss was about, and gave him a big kiss.

'We really believe that you two wild beggars can pull it off,'

June broke into her version of a Dales accent. 'Tha'd better not let us down,'

Bill sat down with a smile on his face. He had the distinct feeling that they had, perhaps, saved the day.

The time came for Peter and Susan to pay a visit to the chambers of Messrs Ackroyd, Jones and Ackroyd, Solicitors and Commissioners for oaths.

There was a time, long ago, when the woollen industry dominated Yorkshire's prosperity. It was of the utmost importance for a Victorian gentleman of substance to provide a home for his family that would reflect his good taste and the success of his mill.

Above all perhaps, to impress his contemporaries who owned the cotton mills in neighbouring Lancashire! The way to do it was to build a mansion in the country, leaving the mill towns choking on the foul pollution that was pouring out of the mill chimneys.   The mill own-ers built their homes in Yorkshire's impressive countryside.

Peter and Susan knew that, in this case, the mansion was indeed impressive.

'Beaumont house' stood in the midst of overgrown rhododendron bushes, right alongside the road, taking up almost all of one side of the charming cobbled square at Willowburn.

There was a certain sadness about it, standing as it did among the small stone dwellings that made up the village. A monument to a time long gone. Mr James Ackroyd was the last surviving member of the partnership.

Peter and Susan climbed the wide stone steps. The door was stand-ing open. Just inside, they saw a little notice pinned to the door with brass drawing pins, inviting visitors to press the bell for attention. They saw a small window with a sliding glass panel just in front of which was a brass bell with a button on top.

Susan had an almost irresistible urge to thump the button.

'Let me press the button,' she said.

Peter stepped back and Susan gave the button a resounding thump. There was a loud 'clang'.

The result was instantaneous and startling. As if from nowhere there appeared a bright looking young lady who had apparently been sitting beneath the window, waiting for someone to press the bell.

She smiled, but said nothing.

'Good morning,' said Peter. 'We have an appointment to see Mr Ackroyd. Mr and Mrs Barnard.'

The young lady appeared in the hallway as if from nowhere and smiled sweetly.

'Ah yes. You are expected. Would you come this way please?'

She indicated a long gloomy corridor that led deep into the interior of the house. The impression was of much ornate, carved plaster and heavy oak wainscoting.

Peter and Susan followed the young lady down the gloomy corridor, looking round with interest. It was rather like being in some sort of living museum.

They came to a door with a worn brass plaque, announcing that this was where Mr Ackroyd was to be found.

The young lady didn't knock, but instead, opened the door and said,

'Mr and Mrs Barnard have arrived.'

She smiled and stood aside.

The room was large. Two walls were completely taken up by bookshelves containing hundreds of dusty looking, ancient law books.

On the remaining walls hung a few oil paintings of people wearing very shiny top hats and surrounded by packs of eager looking hounds. The pictures were large and they each had a very ornate gilded frame.

There were a couple of extremely uncomfortable looking leather chairs facing a large desk.

Or at least, Peter and Susan assumed that it was a desk.

It was almost totally hidden under a mass of documents, maps, papers, outdated office equipment and on top of everything else, several copies of 'Dalesman' and 'Yorkshire Life' and the current edition of 'Farmers Guardian'.

Mr Ackroyd was a large man. Well over six feet tall.

He was a jovial looking chap. A pair of silver rimmed half glasses balanced on the end of his nose. He was wearing a Harris Tweed suit with a waistcoat, a pink shirt and a large yellow bow tie. He had a great deal of fluffy white hair which rather gave him the look of being everybody's favourite uncle.

He peered over his glasses and beamed at the couple.

'Mr and Mrs Barnard,' his voice was as powerful as his appearance.

He reached carefully over the desk so as not to knock anything off and shook hands with Peter and Susan.

'Please sit down,' he indicated the two chairs.

'Now then,' he boomed, 'Nab's Head, isn't it?'

After a few seconds searching among the utter shambles on the desk, he held a bundle of papers aloft triumphantly.

He gave the distinct impression that he considered the worst to be over.

He had found the documents.

On his face, was the expression of a child who has just been given a 'Rupert Bear Annual' for Christmas. He waved the bundle again.

Susan almost giggled.

She felt like complimenting this big friendly chap, on his ability to find the documents.

'Yes, Nab's Head,' He looked thoughtful. 'I knew old Turner quite well you know, Silly chap fell of the roof and killed himself,' he said this quite happily as though he considered that it was an amusing and ridiculous thing to do.

'A bit of a character was old Turner. He used to ride his bike all the way to the Black Bull and fall off the damn thing, trying to get on again to ride home. He used to go to church on that bike.'

He suddenly seemed to remember what Peter and Susan were there for.

He spread the documents in front of them and produced a fountain pen. 'There are just a couple of things to look at,'

He explained all about such things as mineral rights, water rights, land drainage and agricultural registration. Acreage and rights of way were pointed out on the map, along with the common grazing rights.

'Young Sam'll be glad to see someone up there again,' he said.

Mr Ackroyd's secretary came into the room with a tray loaded with three mugs of tea and a plate of fruit cake.

Somehow, she managed to clear a corner of the overloaded desk.

'Good stuff, this cake,' said Mr Ackroyd. 'We get it from Mrs Eckersley's shop up in Billingbeck. She's Bert's sister. You know Bert, the landlord of the Black Bull,'

Peter and Susan managed to balance plates of Mrs Eckersley's excellent cake and mugs of tea on their knees. The cake was indeed very nice, even though it covered the young couple with crumbs.

A very important fact came to light as they looked over the documents. Mr Ackroyd told them that there was no 'notice of closure' on the property. If there had been, it could have created all sorts of problems.   All work would have to have had to be up to the standard required by the council and they would have had to do whatever was required to remove the notice.

It may have been that Nab's Head was considered an agricultural holding, or simply that the council considered that no-one would be daft enough to want to live in a derelict farm. For whatever reason, there was no notice of closure.

Their business completed, Peter and Susan shook hands with Mr Ackroyd and thanked him for all he had done. He smiled.

'It's how I earn my beer money,' he said jokingly.

He looked thoughtfully at the young couple, his mind obviously far away.

'Do you know,' he smiled, 'I envy you young people,'

Naturally, they could not wait to get up to Nab's Head now that they actually owned it.

Their lives were about to change forever.

The adventure that was about to unfold would exceed even their wildest dreams. But most of all, they were going to learn...'Farmin'.

And of course, Jim was going to get his bedroom and his rabbit.

Four

Peter and Susan were very much looking forward to seeing Jims face when they told him that they were going to live at Nab's Head.

Every little boys dream must be to have a whole farm as an adventure playground. He would be delighted.

As they drove along in the sunshine, they chatted excitedly, coming up with all sorts of totally impractical and ridiculous ideas. But the one thing that they both knew was the fact that it was going to be a long uphill slog.

Nab's Head was a long way from being the comfortable home that it must become in order to even survive up on the top of the moors over the long winters. But even as Susan considered the tasks ahead, she knew the answer with absolute certainty.

She glanced at Peter, concentrating on his driving as they followed the winding road that wound its way down the Dale

She snuggled a little closer and smiled to herself.

'As our parents say, we have our age and lots of enthusiasm on our side. And I must admit, a little bit of madness too,'

'Better hang on to the madness darling. It's our best asset,' Peter laughed. He glanced down at her, 'Don't think the madness had gone un-noticed,'

'I learned it from you,' Susan threw back at him.

'Joking apart, we have each other. The chance has been given to us and we never thought it was going to be easy,'

Peter fell into silence. He was thinking about his parents.

Arthur and Ada had just quietly accepted that everything was going to turn out alright. They saw in Peter, a son who had been given a chance in life.

They were proud of him. He had been the first one in the family to get to Grammar School and now, he had what they considered to be a good job.

They had made sacrifices because they didn't want Peter to follow his Dad into the mill. Now, they were sure that it had all been worth while.

Susan's parents, on the other hand, saw it all rather differently.

Perhaps, deep down, they were slightly envious. They would both have loved to have had the chance to do exactly what Peter and Susan were doing.

When they heard the van pull up outside the flat, Bill opened the door.

'How did it go?' he asked.

'All done. Signed and completed. We are now the owners of one derelict farm, up on the top of the Yorkshire dales,'

Susan didn't say anything. She didn't need to. Her happy face said it all.

The last one to get the news was Jim. At the moment, he was fast asleep, tucked up in his warm bed and no doubt dreaming about rabbits.

'You had better get that room ready for Jim,' laughed June

'There are quite a few rooms that need to be got ready,' Susan found her mothers remark amusing. 'Or perhaps we only need to put a lick of paint on the walls?'

They had told Sam that they were going up to Nab's Head on the following Thursday. Peter had managed to get a few days off work, and so, they had a long weekend.

The warm mid-morning sun gave the weathered limestone walls a bleached look. The hedgerows and little sheltered places among the trees were full of the fragrance of wild flowers. Buttercups had changed whole fields into carpets of gold and the fragrance of meadowsweet was heavy in the shaded glades beside the beck.

Mixed with the heady scents of early summer, was the faint aroma of warm sheep. Eyes closed, the ewes stood, nibbling away at the grass, surrounded by their growing lambs.

'Isn't everything just so beautiful?' Susan never ceased to be in awe of the beauty of her Widdersdale.

Jim looked most like a worker. Jim was a practical guy. He was sitting comfortably in the back of the van, impatient to begin work on his room.

As they turned into the lane past Appleburn Farm, it was very noticeable that there was absolutely no trace of mud. The surface was hard and dry. It smelled rather of cow dung. There must still be some field drains working somewhere.

As they drove through the Midge Hole, suddenly the old farmhouse came into view.

'Oh, I can almost imagine that the old place is pleased to see us,' Susan said.

Peter laughed.

'How can a house be pleased?'

'Oh Peter. You are so practical. I can really see that old house smiling at me,' Susan was determined to believe in her little dream.

'I think its smiling too Mummy,' Jim of course, had the vision of a child. 'It feels happy,'

'There you are you see. Two to one. All you can see is stone and wood,' Susan winked at Jim.

The sun was hotter up where they were on the top of the Dale.

Peter and Susan began to carry things into the cool of the house.

Brushes and shovels, saws and hammers and a couple of cans of creosote, plus of course, the most important things… Mugs and a flask of tea.

Somewhere out in the fields, they could hear the sound of a diesel engine. It was a common enough sound and neither of them took much notice, but the sound drew closer. Suddenly the engine stopped and, as if from nowhere, Sam appeared.

'Tha't' making a late start,' he commented. 'I see that young Jims doin' all t' work,'

He winked at Jim and Jim screwed his face up in an attempt to wink back.

'I've put some wood in t' barn,' he said. 'Mebbe tha' can use it?'

He looked rather embarrassed. 'An' a couple o' rolls of wire an' some tar.

Tha'll be needin' a good dog up here,'

Sam seemed to be on edge. It was quite obvious that he didn't want to hang about. Soon, he said his farewells and strode over to his Land Rover.

As he was opening the door, he paused and looked over his shoulder.

Almost as an afterthought, he said,

'Oh, by the way. I left thee a bit o' luck on t' price o' t' farm. Its in t' back field,'

With that final comment, he started the Land Rover engine and was gone. Bouncing over the field in a cloud of blue smoke.

Susan looked thoughtful as she gazed after the rapidly disappearing vehicle.

Luck? Something to bring good luck. A custom that ensured good luck to someone as part of a deal. A gesture of goodwill.

She had remembered the meaning of 'luck'. It was so typical of the way that the Dales farmers went about their business. Always sticking to the old ways.

She was suddenly both curious and excited.

'Come on Peter. I know what 'luck' is. Let's go and look in the back field.'

Jim, who had been listening to what his parents were saying, suddenly pulled his hand free from Susan's grip and ran on ahead. He wanted to be the first to look into the field.

'Mummy. Oh, mummy. Come and look,' he cried.

He was jumping up and down.

Peter and Susan ran to the corner of the house and looked into the field.

There, tugging at the rich grass stood two young black and white cows.

They were too big to be described as calves. 'Teenagers' was how Susan later described them.

The young cows glanced up at their new owners, tails swishing.

But they showed little interest. They wandered off and recommenced tugging at the grass.

'He's given us some cows,' Susan jumped up and down with delight.' Sam's given us some cows. Don't you see Peter? That's what luck is. Sealing the deal with a gift to bring us good luck,' Jim was totally overwhelmed. He stood, gazing at the young cows in awe.'Are they *our* cows?'

Susan picked him up and explained that Sam had given them the cows because a farm wasn't a farm without any animals.

'Slow down,' Peter laughed.'You two are leaving me behind. I think that you are a farmer now Jim.'

He remembered that Ned had mentioned 'Luck'.

The custom went right back to the days when few farmers could read or write.

Even fewer could afford a lawyer. So, to complete a deal, they would shake hands or slap their palms together and the seller would give the buyer a bit of

'Luck' money. 'May you be lucky with your new cow.

Rather like signing a document. He should have realised.

Jim helped Susan to sweep and scrub the floors. The windows were made safe and temporarily fitted with plastic in wooden frames. The heavy door was put back on its hinges. Each evening, they drove home exhausted but happy.

The most exhausted was Jim. He managed to struggle with his little tasks. He was kept going by the thought of his rabbit.

It wasn't long before friends began to appear. Word got round and everyone wanted to be in on the act.

They soon proved to have an amazing amount of talent for restoring old buildings. Cement was thrown into holes and smoothed over, gaping holes were blocked with rocks and even a crude form of the ancient craft of 'wattle and daub' was used.

Sam carried most of the items of heavy furniture for them with his Land Rover and hay trailer.

Finally, with some ceremony, a paraffin lamp was placed in the middle of the well scrubbed table. Susan stood back to admire it.

'Let there be light,' she said.

It wasn't long before the young cows started to become inquisitive.

They took to strolling round to the front of the house to see what was going on. Very soon, they realised that Jim was bringing carrots from home.

Sometimes, they would gently nudge him, to remind him that they were waiting for their carrot.

Jim wanted to play in the field with the cows... He didn't see any danger from his new friends. Susan explained to him that a half grown cow was heavy, and that, if they decided to play with him, he would get knocked down.

'Oh, but they are my friends. They would be careful,' He said.

But life was not all work. They managed to drive over to Harrogate on a few occasions.

They usually had tea in a smart restaurant and brought back a few items that they discovered in some antique shop. Things that they couldn't really afford, but that they decided that no country house could be without.

One such item was a 'Calor' gas smoothing iron. They were sure that no country house without electricity could be habitable without a Calor gas smoothing iron.

＜

Finally, the time inevitably came, for the young Barnards to say goodbye to their families and friends in Guiseley.

It was time to move on. Time indeed, to become 'Widdersdalians'.

It was with mixed feelings that they looked round the little flat for the last time. It looked so empty and abandoned now.

They had been happy there. A young married couple building a home.

How excited they had been. They remembered the time when they had made the spare room into a bedroom for Jim.

How everything had changed when Jim was born.

They held hands in the empty room. Susan laid her head on Peters shoulder.

'Do you remember how scared you were when Jim arrived?'

Susan laughed. 'A grown man. You big softie,'

Peter picked Jim up and ruffled his hair.

'It comes as quite a shock, suddenly being a dad,' He rubbed his nose against Jims, 'No-one told me what to expect,'

Jim was totally unimpressed by all this talk.

He wanted to be off. He had some carrots in his pocket.

'Let's go,' He tugged at Susan's jumper.

They couldn't have chosen a more perfect day. There was a soft haze among the trees and the whole Dale seemed to be at peace with itself, basking in the warm sunshine.

Surely, time moved more slowly here?

Obviously, the first thing to do when they arrived at their new home was to put the kettle on. It meant that water had to be carried from the well. 'I'll help,' Jim was laughable in his enthusiasm.

Peter carried two buckets and Jim carried his toy bucket. But, most of Jim's water disappeared down the tops of his Wellingtons.

Susan saw what was happening. She firmly sat Jim on the step of the porch and took his wellingtons off.

Smiling, she poured the water out onto the grass.

'Perhaps we have enough water now,' She tousled his hair playfully.

With Jim in charge, the unloading of the van proceeded smoothly.

Finally, the busy day drew to a close. Jim was tired. Without protest, he allowed Susan to get him ready for bed.

As she laid his jacket on a chair, she felt something bulky in his pocket.

It was the cows' carrots! He had been so busy, he had forgotten all about the carrots. She showed them to Peter.

'I wonder who the carrots are for?'

Jim was not quite asleep.

'Oh, I have to take them for the cows,' he muttered.

He was about to climb out of bed and head for the door.

'Go to sleep little one. There's always tomorrow,'

Jim had waited so long for this moment. He was struggling to stay awake.

He smiled and put his arms out to cuddle his Mummy.

He had planned to stay awake and watch the trees gently swaying against his bedroom window. Only he knew that there were fairies in those trees.

He would soon make friends with the fairies.

But, in spite of his plans, he was very soon drifting off into the secret world where children go, and adults, if they are very lucky and have long memories, may just vaguely remember.

Susan gently kissed the top of his head and tucked his Teddy Bear under his arm.

'Goodnight little one,' she whispered.

Neither of then knew it, but just under the window of Jim's bedroom, two young cows had settled down for the night.

Meanwhile, Peter had turned down the wick of the lamp and settled down on the settee. The day had gone well.

The dying embers of the fire cast a flickering light that danced across the ceiling. He cast another log onto the fire. Instantly, flames and sparks flew up the wide chimney, highlighting the beams and casting shadows into the far corners of the room.

He saw the light of Susan's lantern as she crept back down the stairs.

She hadn't been able to resist a last look at Jim as he lay in his bed, cuddling his Teddy Bear.

She put the lantern on the table and settled down beside Peter.

'Well, he's fast asleep. He's had a hard day,'

'He certainly has. After all, he did most of the work,' Peter muttered,

'No wonder he's flaked out,'

Gradually, the old house became silent. Susan sighed. Peter looked at her face, glowing in the firelight. Without a word, he drew her closer.

'We've come a long way,' he whispered.

'It might as well be a thousand miles,' Susan said.

She was still thinking about Jim, up in his cosy bedroom. She looked at Peter. He had a sooty smudge on his nose. She giggled.

'What's so funny?'

'Oh, nothing really. I was just thinking. It's our first night in our new home. It's all the things we dreamed about as children,'

'No. For me, it's more than that. My sweet wife and young Jim,'

Susan looked thoughtful for a moment.

'I have a feeling that we are only at the very beginning of a big adventure. There is so much that we don't know. Dales life has so much to offer, but also, it demands a certain attitude,'

'I agree,' Peter said. 'Let's look back on this moment a year from now.

I think we'll have learned some surprising things,'

Gradually, the room seemed to close in round the young couple. Whatever was in the future, this moment could never be taken away.

The following morning dawned bright and sunny.

Peter sat at the breakfast table, wondering just what their new neighbours would be doing, right at that moment. He had no doubt that they would not be enjoying a leisurely breakfast.

One thing that they knew about the rugged hill folk was the fact that, in time of need, there was always help close at hand.

Peter was to experience it sooner than he expected.

The attitude of the farmers towards the new arrivals was, for the most part, one of amusement. A lot of them had, by now, come into contact with the young couple.

One of the biggest problems that they encountered during those early months was the fact that it didn't always stay dry.

Mud… Greasy, slippery mud. Because of the slopes and ruts, and the rocky smooth parts of the lanes, they could be transformed from the dusty pleasant by-ways of summer into something resembling the battlefields of France during the First World War.

Slowly, it became more and more obvious that the long suffering van was finding the going difficult. It was a good friend, but the springs were sagging and the body was beginning to shake loose.

Mud was everywhere. Peter was fiddling under the bonnet of the long suffering van, trying to clear out a flooded carburettor with cold muddy fingers. He wiped his eye and in the process, wiped mud from his frozen fingers, blurring his vision.

Then, he dropped his spanner into the mud.

His eye was smarting and he had no hope of finding his spanner. He gave the van a hefty kick out of sheer frustration. It wasn't really Peters van. It belonged to the company that employed him.

Peter sighed. Perhaps he wasn't being fair. After all, it hadn't been provided to be used as a tractor. His eye was sore and his hands were coated with the thick glutinous mud. But his kick hadn't gone un-noticed.

'Nay Lad. Tha'll kick a hole in it,'

Peter recognised the voice. It was Sam.

'I feel like kicking it all the way to the scrap yard,' Peter was feeling very sorry for himself. 'I've had enough. I could always stick it in a field and keep hens in it,'

At this point, Susan stuck her head out of the kitchen window.

'Tea's brewed,'

'By heck. Tha' knew I was coming,' grinned Sam.

He followed Peter into the kitchen. A bright fire was burning and the teapot was on the table. Susan got three mugs from the cupboard and poured the tea.

Jim was sitting by the fire, holding a mug of milk in both hands.

'Hello Sam. I thought I heard someone muttering out there,' Susan said.

'It were that husband o' thyne. He were talking to t' van,'

'Oh, he loves the van really,' Susan smiled sweetly at her disgruntled looking husband.

'If that's how he loves thee, I'll run off wi' thee. He were kicking it,'

'He's all talk. He wouldn't last a week with you,' laughed Peter.

Sam pulled an old blackened pipe from his pocket.

He rarely smoked, but he stuffed the pipe with tobacco and lit it. He sat back, watching a curl of smoke drift towards the ceiling. Peter knew that he had something to say, but he was showing the typical Dalesman's reluctance to come right out with it.

'What tha' needs is a decent vehicle as'll stand up to t' moors. Yon van could stay o'er at Appleburn and only get used for thy job,'

He looked round as if to be sure that he wasn't being overheard. As though the next bit was in strictest confidence. Disregarding the fact that the nearest person would be at least half a mile away.

'See now. I know a chap who's getten a Land Rover for sale,' then he delivered his masterstroke… T' price is right,'

Susan was instantly interested. She turned to Peter,

'Go and look at it Peter. I'm fed up with seeing you struggle to keep the van running. All I ever see of you these days is your backside sticking out from under the bonnet of the van,'

Peter wasn't so sure.

'I'll run thee down if tha' wants t' look at it. It'll not be there forever.' Sam offered. 'Remember, t' price is right,'

Peter scrubbed some of the oily mud off his hands and wiped them on a towel. Glancing at the resulting oily streaks on the towel, he quickly hid it behind the kitchen door. But he wasn't quick enough. Although Susan wasn't looking directly towards Peter, she detected the move.

'What have you done with that towel?' she asked suspiciously.

Peter knew he hadn't got away with it.

'Its behind the porch door,' he muttered.

Susan retrieved the grubby towel and pulled a disgusted face.

Sam couldn't help smiling. As a farmer, dirty towels were a familiar bit of his life.

'Nice try,' he whispered to Peter, 'I try that one, but I always get caught,'

Peter climbed into Sam's Land Rover and off they went, sliding over the mud.

Over the bridge and across the cobbled square in the middle of Willowburn, just beyond the chip shop, there stood a rather dilapidated looking garage made of corrugated iron. There was a rusty sign advertising 'Shell lubrication', and another, advertising to the world that this was 'Kestrel Garage' and that it was where repairs to all types of vehicles were undertaken.

It also informed the general public that the establishment was in the capable hands of Mr. William P Benson.

The door stood open.

In the gloomy interior, Peter saw several cars and an assortment of engines and spare parts that took up a lot of the floor space. There was a large box full of carburettors and assorted bits and pieces plus a pile of old batteries. In the corner stood an impressive looking red toolbox. It looked rather out of place.

Then, he saw the Land Rover.

It was green and it had a rather shabby looking 'rag top'. It had acquired the average number of small dents and scratches over its years as an agricultural vehicle. The back was rolled up. Inside, the usual stuff.

A bale of hay and a pair of ancient rubber boots, plus a large knotted bundle of orange baling twine.

The place seemed to be deserted. There was no sign of the proprietor of Kestrel Garage.

'Put the kettle on,' the voice seemed to come from under Peter's feet.

Sam seemed to know exactly what to do. He walked over to an old desk that was piled high with old invoices, torn buff envelopes and rusty spanners.

There was also a bottle, half full of milk and a tin full of crumpled tea bags and a packet of sugar. Sam filled a battered electric kettle at a brass tap in the corner and plugged it in.

Peter looked carefully round.

Suddenly, he spotted a pair of boots sticking out from under the Land Rover. He had found the proprietor.

'It's not too bad under here,' commented the disembodied voice.

'Just puttin' a new exhaust on it,'

Sam grinned and gave a broad wink to Peter.

'Chap here looking for a Land Rover,'

Suddenly, the voice under the Land Rover changed beyond recognition.

It acquired a tone of deep sincerity and honesty.

'It's like new under here. No oil leaks. It's been very well looked after, this one,'

Sam laughed,

'Tha't wasting thy time Percy. This chap's from up in t' hills. Tha'll not pull one over on this chap,'

The feet started kicking. Out popped a lanky individual wearing an oily German army tank suit. There was a big grin on his friendly looking face.

'Looking for a good Land Rover are ye, laddie?'

Finally, he stood up, grumbling about his aching back, and staggered over to the steaming kettle. He produced three cracked mugs from a tiny cupboard and threw a tea bag into each.

'Brew time,' he announced happily.

Peter couldn't help hoping that 'Kestrel Garage' wasn't the official Rover car agency for the Dales.

Percy poured boiling water into each mug and dripped in a miniscule drop of milk. He stirred the resulting orange coloured liquid with a pencil and handed the best of the mugs to Peter.

'What's thy name laddie?' he asked Peter.

'Peter,' said Peter.

'I'm Percy. But most people call me Wishbone,'

Wishbone seemed to have the talent, as so many Dales folk do, of being able to drink very hot tea rapidly. Draining his mug, he walked over to the Land Rover.

'Well then Peter. Let's have a look at this Land Rover,'

He opened the door and climbed in. He turned the key and pulled the starter knob. There was a puff of white smoke from the exhaust pipe and then the engine burst into life with a good, healthy diesel clatter.

'Nothing wrong under t' bonnet,' He pressed the cut-off button and the sound of the engine died away. He jumped out.

'I've been playin' with her over t' moor. She's good on t' rough stuff.

Good gears and nowt wrong wi t' four wheel drive,'

He patted the bonnet,

'The brakes were a bit floppy, but I fixed that,' He poked at a hole in the rag top. 'As you're a mate of Sam's, I'll throw in a new rag top. I've got one in t' back o' t' garage,'

Peter walked round the Land Rover. It stood, square and solid looking. The wheels were rather larger than average and they were fitted with 'off road' tyres. He noticed new grease on the spring shackles.

'How Much?'

Sam was visibly shaken. This lad had a lot to learn.

Wishbone patted the bonnet with affection, as though he were patting a favourite grand child on the head.

'It's got six months tax on it. To you… Six hundred pounds,'

He glanced hopefully in Sam's direction.

Sam shook his head.

'Oh, you farmers are all the same,' Percy shouted. 'I'm not running a charity for hard up farmers,'

He paused for a moment, trying to look like someone who was about to lose a large amount of cash.

'Alright. Give me five fifty,'

Peter wrote out a cheque and handed it to Wishbone, who seemed to be well satisfied.

'Yon rag top counts for luck,' he said.

They spent an hour swapping tales of the dale and its inhabitants over another mug of tea. Finally, it was time for Peter to climb into his 'new' Land Rover and head for home. He backed it out into the road and, with a final wave; he headed off up the Dale and towards home.

Everything seemed to be working properly, but he noticed that the fuel gauge was showing 'empty'. Naturally it would be. Who would give away free fuel?

No matter. He was passing the Black Bull on the way home. He would call at Bert Eckersley's pumps and fill her up.

He drew in round the rear of the pub and pulled alongside the diesel pump. Mrs Eckersley came out to serve him.

Mrs Eckersley was a thin woman. She had a severe hair style, cut very short.

She raised her eyebrows in surprise when she saw Peter standing beside the Land Rover.

'By gum Peter. Tha's getten a new Land Rover. Tha must have come into a bit of brass?'

She stood there grinning, hoping that Peter would tell her where it had come from and, better still, how much he had paid for it.

Mrs Eckersley rarely helped out in the Black Bull. Usually, she looked after the shop or served petrol. But, she had her place in the village gossip chain whenever she got any information.

She unhooked the nozzle of the diesel pump and put it into the Land Rovers fuel filler. As the tank was filling, she stuck her head into the cab and glanced at the recorded mileage on the speedometer.

'Nice,' she said, 'Tha'll be set up for t' winter,'

As Peter drove away, Mrs Eckersley stood in the yard, staring at the disappearing Land Rover. Then she dashed back into the shop to spread the news about the Barnard's new found wealth.

⁘

Susan and Jim had been waiting impatiently for the arrival of their new vehicle. It was Jim who heard it first. He was out of the house even before the Land Rover got clear of the Midge Hole. He was closely followed by Susan.

The two of them stood in the yard, staring at the approaching Land Rover.

'Oh, isn't it sweet,' Susan was ecstatic.

Peter climbed out and looked at the muddy and rather battered

Land Rover.

How could anyone describe it as 'sweet'? The interior was musty and had a distinct aroma of sheep and wet dogs. It was very rare for Jim to be stuck for words, but he just stood there gazing at the muddy vehicle with a look on his face that said more than words ever could. Totally mesmerised, he slowly walked all round it.

'There's a new hood in the back,' Peter said.

He refrained from using the name 'rag top'.

Susan's grin widened.

'Let's put it on,'

She started to undo the brass buckles that held the canvas top in place and dragged it off. The Land Rover looked quite naked without its top.

Soon, the new top had been unfolded and they dragged it over the frame and into place.

There was an immediate transformation. The new hood was a wonderful olive green colour with gleaming brass buckles. Peter half expected Susan to produce a tin of 'Brasso'. Instead, she went into the kitchen and emerged carrying a bucket of soapy water and a cloth and brush. She began to wash off a few years of accumulated cobwebs, old hay seeds and muddy cow dung that, in Peter's opinion, gave the Land Rover much of its character. Underneath all the agricultural gunge, it was a nice shade of green.

Soon, it was a very different looking Land Rover that stood proudly in the middle of the farmyard. Everything was cleaned and polished.

They stood back to admire the effect.

'By gum,' said Jim, much to the amusement of his parents.

'Now… Yon looks pretty,' Peter put on the Dales accent. 'We could turn up at t' farmers ball in yon,'

Jim was placed in the cab. He grinned as Peter put his cap on his son's head.

'You look just like a farmer Jim,' Susan laughed and lifted him from the cab. 'It's tea time young man,'

He didn't sit at his usual place at the table. Nor did he chatter away as he normally did. Instead. He placed his chair where he could see through the window and sat in silence, staring out at the Land Rover.

Peter now parked the long suffering van under the trees beside Appleburn Farm. The plan worked very well because he could easily walk the short distance through the Midge Hole in the mornings.

Now, the steep and rocky corners of Nab's Head Farm became easy to get to. Peter and Susan could use the Land Rover to carry such things as fencing posts and wire to wherever they wanted them to be.

After years of neglect, the remote corners of Nab's Head began to benefit from improved fences and a lot of the stray sheep became deprived of some free grazing.

The local sheep farmers had come to regard the semi abandoned farm as 'no mans land' as far as roaming sheep were concerned. But now, they respected the fact that the Barnards were trying to make something of the place.

The word was passed round at the Black Bull.

'Fair play,' one of the sheep farmers had said. 'We had a good innings lads. Yon young 'uns up at Nabs Yead'll be wantin' all t' grass they have soon. Good luck to 'em. They don't want our sheep all over t' hay medders,'

Sam explained all about how the hill farm subsidy worked, and how the high land was suitable for rearing what he described as 'T' beef stock.'

Peter and Susan listened fascinated, to everything that he told them.

Suddenly, he laughed.

'I'm talking a foreign language to you two. But what I'm telling you is what most kids in the village school know. If tha's in any doubt, ask old Ned when tha't in't Black Bull. He'll put thee right,'

Some stray sheep were still getting past their carefully constructed defences, and they didn't know why.

But it wasn't a farmer who told them where they were gong wrong.

It was Wishbone! He arrived at Nab's Head Farm, one morning, supposedly to make sure that the Land Rover was running O.K.

But in truth, he had found himself driving past the entrance to the farm lane, at Appleburn, and decided to call in the sure knowledge that he would be offered a cup of tea. Of course, the kettle went on the stove.

Jim was in awe of Wishbone, because he knew all about tractors and Land Rovers. Wishbone placed him on his knee and held out his clenched fists.

'Which one do you choose?' he said to Jim.

Jim pointed to Wishbone's left hand.

'How did you know?'

He opened his hand and revealed a toy Land Rover. Jim's eyes opened wide.

'Look Mummy. A Land Rover,'

Wishbone winked at Susan.

'I know Father Christmas. He decided to send that a bit early,'

Jim looked at him with awe.

'Better still, he sent you a trailer too,'

He opened his other hand, to reveal a matching toy trailer.

Jim didn't forget to say 'Thank You,'

Very soon, he was on the rug, pushing the toy Land Rover across imaginary fields, totally absorbed in his little world.

Susan told Wishbone about the problems that they were having with stray sheep. To her surprise, he pointed out the obvious.

'Tha's got to be crafty,' he said, sipping his tea. 'If thy puts a strand o' wire across top o' thy wall, on't outside, about nine inches higher than't top o't' wall. They can't get a grip,' He laid on the accent.

They had seen it all over the Dales. Why hadn't they realised it?

She couldn't wait to point it out to Peter.

'How could we have failed to realise what the wire is for?' Peter said

' Really, it doesn't need a brain to work that one out. Just shows how you can see something every day and still not see the significance of it.'

By weekend, they were loading fencing posts and wire into the back of the Land Rover, under the supervision of Jim.

'Don't forget the big wooden mallet and the pick Dad,'

He was becoming very knowledgeable about such matters because he always accompanied his Mum and Dad on working trips around the farm.

Peters skill as a dry stone waller was improving with practice, but the few sheep that were still determined to live at Nab's Head, were crafty.

Peter often found that, as he opened a gate to drive the Land Rover through, a few sheep would make a dash for it before he could close the gate.

But his efforts were not going unobserved. One day, Peter, Susan and Jim were doing a repair to a wall up by the boundary between Nab's Head and their neighbour at Folly Edge. Jim was bringing small stones from the grass alongside the wall. Suddenly, he stopped what he\ was doing and looked carefully up the hill.

'Mummy, There are some dogs sitting in the grass up there,' He pointed to a point a bit higher up the hill.

Susan brushed a few stray strands of hair from her eyes and looked carefully.

She could just see the dogs, ears erect, lying very still, in the long grass.

'Look up there Peter. There are some dogs watching us,'

Peter stopped what he was doing. He too could see the dogs.

Then, he spotted the owner of the dogs. He suddenly appeared over the summit of the hill. Even from that distance, they could make out a cloud of smoke as he puffed on a pipe. It was their neighbour.

Peter waved to the old man. He got a raised hand in return.

The dogs suddenly stood and dashed off towards their master and they all disappeared back over the hilltop.

'That was old Ernie, our neighbour,' Peter said, 'I think he wanted to know if we can mend walls,'

They didn't know too much about their neighbour.

He had been farming at Folly Edge for longer than anyone could remember. Peter and Susan had seen some of his cows. Fine looking beasts but not the usual type to be found on the hilltops around the Dales. He had asked old Ned about them.

'Dairy Shorthorns,' Ned had informed him. 'Very fine cattle, but they have been out of fashion for many years,'

They knew that Ernie lived alone. He never visited the Black Bull,

He was very well respected among the farming community, but he was a loner. Not only were his Shorthorns unusual but his farming methods were out of date. He had been left behind by time.

But, he missed nothing.

Five

It wasn't long before Peter and Susan met their new neighbour from Folly Edge Farm. It was early morning; the sun was bright in the eastern sky, showing promise of a glorious day. Peter was up near the top of the hill towards Folly Edge, mending a storm damaged wall.

Just as he was lifting the last of the large stones into place onto the top of the wall, laying it across the wall to form a strong bond known as 'toppers', he suddenly realised that he was surrounded by dogs. There were three of them, typical farm dogs. Two stood and stared at Peter, but the third one, obviously younger and less sophisticated, was making a complete fool of itself. Dancing about eagerly and doing a great deal of panting.

A few moments later the owner of the dogs appeared over the brow of the hill. Peter immediately recognised their neighbour from Folly Edge.

He was a white haired chap, who seemed to be in his late sixties.

His weather beaten face had a jovial, but mischievous expression;

There were a few days growth of white whiskers on his chin. He was wearing an old fawn raincoat and grey moleskin trousers, a pair of stout boots on his feet.

He waved the stick that he was carrying in greeting.

'Good morning to thee, young 'un. Tha'll be t' new neighbours from down at Nab's Yead?'

'Yes,' Peter wiped his hands on his trousers.' And you'll be Ernie from Folly Edge?'

The dogs abandoned Peter and strolled over to sit beside their owner.

'Aye,' Ernie's next comment surprised Peter, 'Tha doesn't smoke a pipe, dust tha?'

'No. I don't smoke,' Peter said.

Ernie looked rather crestfallen.

'No. I didn't think tha did,'

The two men stood for a moment in silence, quietly observing each other.

'I just thought, if tha did, tha might have a bit o' baccy about thee,'

Ernie took an ancient pipe from his pocket and a tobacco tin that had at one time been bright red, but now was battered and aged with rust. He opened the tin and pulled out a small amount of rough looking black tobacco.

Very carefully, he put it into the pipe and produced a box of matches.

Shielding himself behind the wall, he crouched down and managed to light the pipe. A cloud of foul smelling smoke drifted over towards Peter, causing him to cough and splutter. After a few moments, Peter spoke.

'If tha wants a brew, t' kettle'll be on,' he surprised himself by using the local accent. 'I'm Peter,' he said.

"Aye, I knows thy name. And yon lass o' thyne and t' little lad. Tha knew my name. Tha gets to know everything down in t' village,'

He paused to take a puff at his pipe. Once again, Peter was enveloped in smoke, causing him to cough. Then, his face broke into a broad grin.

'Did tha say tha were making a pot o' tea?'

There was little doubt that Ernie knew a lot more about his new neighbours than he was telling.

The two men walked down the hill, the three dogs staying at Ernie's side.

When they arrived at the farmhouse, Peter opened the door and invited Ernie inside.

Ernie took off his cap and followed Peter into the kitchen but the dogs stayed in the porch.

Susan was using the smoothing iron.

She looked surprised to see their neighbour. She held out her hand.

'Hello. You'll be the chap that lives over at Folly Edge?' she said. 'We caught a glimpse of you the other day, up on the hill,'

'Aye'''

Ernie left Susan wondering which of her remarks were answered by 'Aye,' maybe both.

'Sit down by the fire,' said Susan, 'I'll put the kettle on,'

Ernie looked uncomfortable.

Not asking if anyone minded if he smoked, he puffed away at his old black briar. He gratefully accepted a steaming mug of tea, grasping it with both hands. Once in possession of his tea, he seemed to settle slightly.

'Thanks, young lady,' He looked up at Peter. 'Will tha be havin' enough hay for yon two stirks?'

He puffed on his pipe. 'It's a long winter up here. Nine months winter and three months bad weather,' He wagged his finger at Peter. 'Tha's been havin' a spot o' bother wi't' stray sheep?'

'Yes,' said Peter, 'They are all over the place,'

Ernie was about to speak, when in came Jim. He had been playing with his toy Land Rover in his bedroom, but, hearing voices, he came down to investigate.

Jim gazed at Ernie. He wasn't sure, so he stood beside his mum. She picked him up,

'Jim, this is our neighbour from Folly Edge,'

They knew that Ernie's second name was Collingworth, Only because the solicitor had pointed it out.

'Hello,' Jim said very quietly. 'We saw you up on the hill last week.

I saw your dogs,'

Ernie solemnly said.

'I'm very pleased to meet you young man. I even know thy name. Thou art called Jim,'

He had just been about to solve the Barnards sheep problem when Jim had come into the room. Suddenly, he realised that he had an ally.

He addressed himself to Jim.

'Thy mum and Dad have been gettin' a lot of stray sheep,'

'I know,' Jim said. 'We were mending the wall when I saw you,'

'Aye. Well young man. Ask thy Mum and Dad if they are interested in a good dog,'

He knew very well that Jim would do his selling for him.

'Oh, Mummy,' Jim knew who would weaken first. 'A dog,' he was jumping up and down with excitement.

Ernie grinned at Susan because he, quite rightly knew that she would be on Jims side. She would find a dog irresistible.

Winking at Jim, he went out into the porch, took hold of the young dog and led it into the kitchen.

The young dog stood with its tail between its legs, looking very sorry for itself. Indeed, it looked every bit as uncomfortable as Ernie had when he first came into the house. The other two dogs didn't move.

'See, I've fetched young Meg,' said Ernie. 'She's got't makin's of a grand dog, she is. Bold enough for t' cows an' crafty enough to send yon woolly jumpers back where they came from,'

He stroked the head of the shivering young Collie.

'She'll cost thee five pounds. But she'll save thee hundreds,'

Ernie explained that a decent dog very quickly learned where the boundaries were, and would be eager to work.

Peter Susan and Jim looked down at the young dog. Meg looked up at them and flicked the tip of her tail.

'Born out o' Lassie, my best dog,' Ernie put the pressure on.

'Got brains, yon dog has. Tha'll get nowt like young Meg for five pounds,'

Meg looked at Jim with soft brown eyes. She seemed to be aware that her future was in the balance.

Susan had put Jim down and he was sitting on a three legged milking stool. Suddenly, Meg crept up to Jim and started washing his face with her tongue.

There was nothing else to be said.

Peter pulled his wallet from his back pocket and produced a crumpled five pound note, whilst Ernie pulled a scrap of baling twine from his pocket and expertly made a collar and lead in seconds. He slipped the collar over Meg's neck and handed the makeshift lead to Jim.

'Tha can be t' boss o' Meg,' he said, seriously. 'She might as well know who t' boss is,'

He touched his forelock. 'Got to be on my way. Chap from t' A.I is coming,' Peter and Susan glanced at each other. They didn't know what the A.I was, and they didn't ask.

Ernie had one thing more to say to Peter.

'Tha' thinks that tha's goin' to be a farmer. Tha forgot to ask for a bit o' luck,' he put his hand deep into his pocket and handed a couple of coins to Jim. He winked and said, 'Thy luck money, young man,'

He went out into the porch, followed across the yard by his two remaining dogs.

Lassie, the mother of Meg, made no effort to look back and Meg made no effort to follow her. She just sat, looking up at Peter with utter devotion.

Peter looked at Susan.

'I often have this effect on women,' he explained.

'I hope that you two will be very happy together,' Susan stroked Meg.

Meg was allowed into the house right from the start.

An old rug was placed beside the fire, and Jim sat alongside the new member of the family, gently stroking her silky head.

Peter smiled to himself as he watched his son. It was perhaps, not the best start for a dog that was going to become a farm worker.

But, Meg seemed to really enjoy her new role. She soon developed an intense dislike for stray sheep that were on the wrong side of the gate and ran swiftly round them, her belly close to the ground and ears erect.

The sheep looked totally startled. They saw an end to their supply of free food.

Both Peter and Jim watched with considerable satisfaction as the sheep took off at top speed, back through the gate.

Peter was amused at Meg's way of handling the situation.

She obviously loved her new role as top dog. She wanted to keep going, but a severe warning from Peter stopped her. She would come reluctantly back to his side. He always made a fuss of her and muttered a few words of encouragement. She would roll over on her back and wave her feet round in the air... It was not quite how a sheepdog was supposed to behave.

Jim's idea of rewarding Meg was to join in the rolling about.

It was Meg who decided where her place was to be in the pecking order. She soon decided that Jim was her best friend; Susan was her provider of food, water and comfort. But, Peter was God...!

Meanwhile, Old Ernie kept very much to himself.

Sometimes, a faint glow was to be seen coming from his window in the late evening, or they would catch a glimpse of him walking across his yard.

Sam sold Peter a few bales of good hay for the coming winter and advised him to go down to the 'provin'merchant' at Beddington to buy some feed and mineral supplements.

All too soon, June was nearly over. The Barnards had been at Nab's Head for more than three months. So much had happened in that short time.

The 29th of June was Jim's birthday.

A family gathering was called for. Peter went to Guiseley to pick up his parents, Arthur and Ada, in the Land Rover.

Arthur came out of the neat little terraced house, carrying a small box. Peter noticed how carefully he was carrying it.

'There is something very fragile in that box,' he said.

'Aye, well it's for Jim,'

Arthur put the box down very carefully in the back of the Land Rover, and then he climbed in alongside it and sat on the padded wheel arch. Peter was intrigued.

Suddenly, the box moved.

'Whatever have you been up to?' Peter said.

'Well, Jim was supposed to be getting a rabbit. So, we bought him one,' Arthur held the box very carefully.

'It'll keep thee busy. Tha'll have to build a rabbit hutch,'

Susan was told about the contents of the box. She put it into a corner by the fireplace, where Jim couldn't help but notice it.

They didn't have long to wait.

A car was coming through the Midge Hole. It was a Green Ford Anglia. That could only be Bill and June. Jim ran out to greet them as the car pulled into the yard.

June swept him off his feet and gave him a big hug.

'Sorry we're a bit late,' she said. 'There were some sheep blocking the road just above Beddington,'

Arthur pointed to the box by the fireplace behind Jims back. He put his fingers to his lips, and winked. As Bill and June looked at the box, it suddenly moved again. It was obvious that there was some sort of animal in it.

They ignored the box.

It was Meg who finally brought Jims attention to it. She had seen it move, and, she could smell rabbit.

She ran over to the box and pushed it over with her nose. Then, she stood, front legs wide apart, wagging her tail and staring at the box.

'That box moved,' said Jim.'Look. It's moving again,'

Susan grabbed Jim and put him on Arthur's knee.

'I think that Granddad knows something about what's in the box. Better ask him,'

Arthur smiled at Jim.

'Well, do you remember, when you came to live here, you wanted a rabbit?'

He could say no more. Jim flung his arms round his Granddads neck.

'It's a rabbit,' Jim's eyes were sparkling as he ran to Susan.'There's a rabbit in the box,'

Arthur carefully opened the box and reached inside.

He lifted out a young black and white rabbit.

Everyone pretended to be surprised. Peter carried the baby rabbit over to Jim and put it carefully into his arms. There was a moment of panic when Meg dashed over to Jim.

But, all that Meg did was lick the rabbit. Susan laughed at its reaction. It didn't seem to be at all amused.

It was late when everyone went home. Peter ran Arthur and Ada back to Guiseley. At last, he arrived back at Nab's Head, and parked the Land Rover in the yard.

Jim had been put to bed, so Peter crept quietly up the stairs and found him fast asleep. The rabbit had been carefully placed on the floor in a big wooden tool box full of hay. It had some wire netting over the top and it too was asleep, surrounded by carrots.

Jim was up very early the following morning. So was Peter.

Luckily, he didn't have to be at work until lunch time. And so, the morning was spent with Jim in the barn, sawing and hammering until

'Big Teeth' had a new home.

Jim had decided on the rabbit's name. So, Big Teeth it was.

⤸

Bill had mentioned to Peter that he had called at a farm over at Ottershead He had noticed some old machinery tucked away in a corner behind a barn.

'I took a look at it,' Bill told Peter. 'There was some stuff that I thought you could use, so I asked the farmer what he was doing with it,'

'Scrap,' the farmer had told him. 'Yon's old stuff. It's nowt but scrap,'

Bill had nodded, If it was scrap, it wasn't doing anyone any good, so he explained to the farmer that his son in law had a little place over at the top of Widdersdale.

'He only has a few acres. He could make good use of those machines,' he had said.

The farmer had put his hands into his pockets and said,

'If thy son in law wants any o' yon machines, he can come and gi' us a bit o' brass,'

Suddenly the machinery wasn't scrap. 'A bit o' brass' had been mentioned.

Bill had smiled.

The following Saturday, Peter drove over to Ottershead, to take a look at the vintage machinery.

A small chap wearing a brown smock and a tweed cap pulled well down over his ears, met him at the farm gate.

'What kept thee? Tha's late. Cows in t' barn,' he opened the gate and Peter drove into the yard.

He got out of his Land Rover.

'I think you are mistaking me for someone else,' .

'Tha't not t' chap from t' A.I. then?'

'No. I'm Peter Barnard. I came to look at your old machines,'

'Oh. An' I'm Joe Worthington. Thou art t' chap from top o' Billingbeck. Thy dad's t' engineer. Has tha brought some brass wi' thee? By gum, I wasn't thinkin' o' sellin' t' machines. I could have used them myself,' he blatantly lied.

He walked over to the house.

'Come an' have a cup o' tea,'

Peter knew that the question of 'brass' would be mentioned, but he had not expected it so soon. He followed Joe into the house, removing his cap and stooping under the low porch doorway.

Joe introduced his wife to Peter.

'This is my wife, Jenny; this here is Peter from t' top o' Widdersdale. He's come to look at yon machines,'

Joe's wife, Jenny appeared to be a happy woman. She had laughing eyes and a welcoming smile. She wiped her hands on her 'Pinafore', and held out a hand in greeting.

She looked very much a farmer's wife. She was quite small and bouncy.

She was wearing a mans tweed cap, but otherwise she was dressed fairly normally in a flowery patterned frock. The two men sat at the table and, very soon, Jenny set down three mugs of tea along with the inevitable plate of crumbly fruit cake.

Peter was asked a lot of questions about what they were doing up at Nab's Head. Joe asked him what sort of cattle they owned and how many. When he replied that they owned two stirks, Joe and Jenny laughed.

'What dust tha need machines for? Tha can cut all t' grass thy needs wi' a pair o' scissors,' Joe said.

Mugs emptied, they all three went out to look at the machines.

Peter didn't know exactly what their purpose was. They were obviously quite ancient, but not all that different to the machines being used by Peter's neighbours.

'Nowt wrong wi' 'em,' said Joe. "I recon tha could make good use o' 'em. They're a bit slow these days, an' time is brass,'

He pointed to what was obviously a mowing machine.

'Yon mowing machine. My dad used to use it, wi' horses. I put yon shaft on, so that we could tow it wi't' little Fergy. Tha knows. Little grey Ferguson tractor,' He explained what the rest of the machines were used for. There was a 'wuffler' for shaking the hay, a huge iron wheeled rake, a drum shaker and a machine that put the hay into rows behind the tractor.

Peter had nothing to make hay with. He saw a glimmer of humour in Joe's eyes.

There wasn't much paint left on any of the machines, but, there wasn't a lot of rust either. Joe smiled to himself. He was impressed by this young lad's enthusiasm and his honesty. But, Peter's lack of experience was obvious.

When it came to the price, Joe knew how much he would have got from the scrap merchant.

He didn't ask for anything more.

'I'll be honest wi' thee. I was going to send all t' lot to t' scrap chap,'

He paused for a moment. 'Tha can give us a fiver for each of t' machines as tha wants, and a tenner for t' mowing machine. I've got some spare blades for yon machine,'

Peter handed the money over. Joe smiled.

'Tha forgot to ask for t' luck money,' He handed a five pound note back to Peter. Peter muttered his thanks and stuffed the five pound note into his pocket.

It was agreed that Peter could borrow Joe's big hay trailer to carry the machines back to Nab's Head. Soon, they had three of the machines, plus the mower securely roped down on the trailer.

Peter headed back towards Widdersdale with Joe's trailer behind the Land Rover.

As he was driving through Billingbeck, he spotted Old Ned and Betty. They both stopped and stared at the trailer with its load of machinery.

Peter smiled to himself. Very soon, news of the machines would reach the Black Bull.

Susan and Jim were very excited about their new machines; Peter unloaded them alongside the barn. Then, all three of them inspected their new purchases. Levers were pulled and pushed. It was all a wonderland to a little boy who was just five. Jim was full of questions about how everything worked.

'All the other farmers have machines like these,' Jim said.

'But Ernie hasn't got any,'

Susan pointed out that the other farmers had machines that were a bit newer than the ones that he was admiring.

'Ernie doesn't want any machines,' she told Jim. 'But, I think that we will be able to help him to cut his grass?'

Jim was very impressed.

'We can cut some hay for Big Teeth,'

Peter heard what Jim said.

'We can cut enough hay for hundreds of rabbits Jim,'

It didn't take long for the news of the Barnard's machines to reach Ernie. The next morning, he paid Peter and Susan a visit. He didn't seem to be very impressed.

'Tha can cut better wi' a scythe,' he muttered. 'Waste o' time, all these new fangled machines,'

Peter and Susan had hoped for a better reaction from an expert.

'Don't you approve?' Peter asked him.

'I cut wi't' scythe. Tha loses half 'o' thy grass wi t' modern machines. All t' good grass is in t' bottom,'

He stared into the fire. 'Cut a bit and get a bit,'

Then, he played his ace card.

'Anyway, tha' can't cut nowt. Tha's getten no tractor. What are t' thou going to do? Drag all thy new fangled machines all over t' meadow wi' yon Land Rover, or whatever thou calls it,'

He pulled his old briar from his pocket and carefully stuffed it full of his strong black tobacco from the red tin. He took a few puffs and waved his pipe in the air to emphasise his point.

Peter was slowly beginning to realize that Ernie was something of a doggedly determined chap who would always stick with the farming methods that had served him very well in the past.

'You youngsters. Tha never thinks before tha jumps in,' Ernie disappeared in a cloud of smoke.

He finished his tea and left, muttering something about the world being full of machines.

Meg was rapidly growing up. She would sit beside Peter and gaze out over the fields eagerly. One morning, a couple of days after Ernie's visit, she suddenly dashed off up the slope like a greyhound.

Peter saw nothing. But, Meg knew something that he didn't. Her mother and cousin were standing at the top of the hill.

That could only mean one thing.

Ernie was paying them another visit.Meg dashed up to the other Collies, only to be treated with contempt because she was playing the idiot.

Suddenly, Ernie appeared from behind a small hillock. He was obviously amused by Meg's antics.

He waved his stick and shouted to Peter,

'Tha's not getten much control over thy dog,'

Meg was gazing up into Ernie's eyes with obvious devotion.

'Here Meg,' Shouted Peter.

Reluctantly, Meg slowly trotted back to him.

Ernie's grin broadened as he fumbled in his pocket for his battered red tin.

'Nay. Don't look so glum lad. Tha's getten a good dog. Needs a bit o' experience at t' job,' Peter realised that Ernie was being too diplomatic to mention the Barnard's lack of experience.

'Howdo Jim,' Ernie said. His tone had altered again.

Now he was talking man to man with young Jim.

'I wonder if thy mum will have t' kettle on?' Ernie held out his hand

and Jim ran eagerly towards him. He looked up at his Dad.

'Do you think that Mummy will have the kettle on?'

Peter was more contented now.

Meg was at his heels and looking very guilty.

'Let's go and find out,' he said.

The three of them set off down the slope. Peter at the front accompanied by the grovelling Meg and Ernie close behind, gripping Jim's hand.

'How's young Big Teeth coming along?' Ernie asked Jim.

'Oh, alright thank you. He may need a bit of provin' for the winter,' Both men laughed.

'I'll tell thee summat,' Ernie said, 'Young Jim here has got t' makin's of a farmer,'

As they approached the house, the door opened.

'Don't bother to ask. I saw you coming. The kettle's on,' Susan called out.

'Grand young chap, Jim is,' Ernie addressed Susan.

'Oh, there are two sides to him,' she answered.

'I wonder where he gets that from,' Ernie grinned at Peter.

In spite of the late spring warmth, it was cool in the kitchen.

Soon, Susan had a pot of tea on the table and three mugs.

She found a smaller mug and filled it with milk for Jim.

'This farmer husband o' thyne has been showing me how Megs coming along,' Ernie's face was the picture of innocence.

'Well,' Susan was quick with her answer. 'We are doing O.K. The sheep have all disappeared. Meg does a good job, Peter will, no doubt, soon be having Meg doing sheep dog trials,'

Ernie settled more comfortably in his chair.

'I've been thinking young man. Tha's getten no muck-spreader. And tha's not getten much muck either,'

He sipped his tea. 'Willy Nelson has just getten himself a new muck-spreader. His old one will be going cheap. It's a Bamford. I reccon tha could get it for ten pounds,'

Peter did some rapid thinking. The little amount of manure that they had would easily fit into a wheelbarrow.

Ernie appeared to be very enthusiastic about Willy Nelson's muck-spreader. Why?

It dawned on Peter that Ernie had to take his muck out in a wheel-barrow, and spread it with a pitchfork. The result was that, over the years, a vast amount of this 'black gold' had accumulated behind Ernie's barn.

It was worth giving Peter some of the manure, in order to get some spread on his own land.

'Crafty sod,' thought Peter.

All that Ernie was doing was using his good old Yorkshire talent for spending nothing of his own money.' Peter would gain, but at the same time, Ernie got his muck spread for no cost. And for years to come no doubt.

'Now young man. I've found thee a tractor. I know where thou can get one cheap,' Ernie's talent for spending other people's money was admirable.

He told Peter of a little known place which he described as being 'Just by t' side o' t' trig point.'

'Tha goes up to t' Trig point and tha turns down by t' old quarry. Lees Farm, it's called,'

There was no doubting their need for a tractor, Susan, who up to now, had said nothing, looked thoughtful. Suddenly she said,

'Daddy's going to buy a tractor,'

So it was decided.

Jim thought that the most important thing on any farm was a trac-tor. His eyes shone and he looked up at Peter.

'Will it be a red one Daddy?'

As soon as Ernie had set off for home, Peter jumped in the Land Rover and drove up towards the Trigonometry point. The lane beside it was almost invisible. Peter had not even noticed it before. At one time, it had led to a quarry, long since abandoned.

Even the Land Rover struggled to find a grip on the loose mossy surface. Water that was draining off the moor ran down the lane, so that it was more like a small stream in places. It was certainly in need of repair, but short of a major construction project, it was doubtful if it could be repaired.

The long winding track led into a little known valley at the top of Widdersdale. The area was known as 'Top o' t' Dale'.

It was indeed, a desolate place. Nothing but wet rocks and stumpy, dead looking bushes. Peter was in some doubt. Could there be a farm down there?

Then he spotted a large rock with the words 'Lees Farm' painted on it with lime wash.

Driving lower, suddenly he saw the tiny farm. Nestling among some ragged old trees, right at the bottom of the valley.

There was a rotting gate at the entrance to the yard.

Orange baling twine had certainly arrived at Lees Farm. It looked as though it had been many years since anyone had lived in the house.

The rotting windows certainly did have some dirty looking glass in them, but there were squares of cardboard, where the glass was missing. Peter could hear a radio playing; He lifted the gate out of the mud and allowed it to swing open on its one hinge.

In the cobbled yard, he was met by an odd assortment of small pigs, several ducks and a mangy cat the colour of marmalade.

In the middle of all the desolation there stood a very intelligent looking black and white Collie dog. She was regarding Peter with bright eyed interest.

She looked totally out of place among all the other animals.

She was flicking the tip of her tail in greeting. Peter instantly had a feeling of comradeship with that dog. They were both completely out of place in the middle of such a shambles.

The house was at the far end of the yard.

It stood among a strange collection of buildings. It was small and low and had, at one time, been whitewashed. Its rotting gutter hung down and rested on top of a mossy, greenish barrel containing foul looking water. The flaking door had, at one time, been painted bright red. A rusty horseshoe hung over the door, which was wide open.

The music was louder now.

Nettles grew in great profusion all round the yard, well fertilized by the manure from the strange assortment of wildlife that seemed to exist in a sort of communal lifestyle. Domestic, agricultural, wild: all seemed quite happy to reside here.

Peter was not sure that the dog was quite happy about the accommodation arrangements: the expression on her face was almost one of apology.

The out-buildings were constructed of rusting corrugated iron and rotting timber. Windows, where there were any, were coated in a thick accumulation of old cobwebs. Here, a rusty pitchfork, there an old cart with grass growing around its rotting wheels. The long gone Victorian farmers who once inhabited this place had, no doubt, been a different breed.

But, where were the people who lived here now?

'Hello,' called Peter.

Silence. 'Hello-ooo,'

Nothing… Then, he heard the rattle of a bucket. The sound came from the open door of one of the buildings, and, yes, he could hear a human voice.

'Gid'oer,' Peter walked over to the place where the sounds were coming from.

He saw an amusing sight.

A small chap was standing with a bucket in one hand and a three legged milking stool in the other. He was pushing a reluctant cow out of the way with his elbow, trying to make a space on the floor for the stool.

'Gid'oer,' cried the man again. All the cow did was swish its tail.

Peering more carefully into the gloomy interior, Peter could make out the small man better. He was a strange looking individual.

He had a greasy farmer's cap on his head, but it was on backwards.

His wild, overlong hair hung round his collar and several days' growth of stubble dotted his chin. He wore a mud coloured waistcoat over a thick woollen shirt, and a pair of old fashioned riding pants. But, the most startling thing was his socks: they were red and yellow football socks. And, on his feet he wore a pair of clogs. They had, at one time been black, but over the years, they had taken on a mossy green colour.

Suddenly, this strange looking man spotted Peter.

'Howdo,' he said though the gaps in his teeth. 'Bloody cow!'

He dropped the bucket with a clatter and came out into the light. Peter was astonished to see that the chap was only in his mid thirties.

'What are t' after?'

'Howdo,' Peter said. 'I'm from Nab's Head. Peter is my name. I was told that you may have a tractor for sale,'

The chap with the green clogs narrowed his eyes,

'Tha' t from Nabsyead. Young Geoff told me that thou were lookin' for a good tractor,'

Peter had no idea who 'Young Geoff' was. But obviously, 'Green Clogs' was well informed. He offered no name. Green Clogs stared at Peter."

'Never thowt as Sam would sell yon place. It'll be good for a bit o' hill subsidy. Tractors over in yon shed,'

'Good. We certainly need a reliable tractor,' Peter said.

Green Clogs hobbled over to the house and disappeared inside.

He re-emerged carrying a yellow plastic bucket full of water.

'It'll need a drop o' water in t' radiator,'

They walked to the tractor shed, joined by the dog, which walked alongside Green Clogs, gazing up at him with love in her brown eyes.

The farmer fiddled about with knotted baling twine wrapped round rusty nails, eventually he managed to pull the creaking doors open.

Dozens of outraged hens flapped out into the yard. The air inside was thick with dust and floating hen feathers. Peering into the gloom, Peter got his first view of the tractor.

It was standing in the middle of the shed, propped up by an assortment of shovels, brushes and other semi- retired agricultural tools.

An old army greatcoat rested across her bonnet and a couple of dusty hen eggs sat on the iron seat.

Green Clogs dived into a gloomy corner and emerged carrying a battered can. He removed the brass cap and sniffed the contents.

'Paraffin,' he announced triumphantly.

He proceeded to pour some of the rust coloured liquid into the tractor's fuel tank.

'Not been run for a couple of days,'

More like years, thought Peter. Or even decades.

The little farmer poured some water into the radiator.

Carefully, he climbed up onto the iron seat, almost sitting on the eggs.

He spotted them at the last moment and put them carefully into the tractor's tool box.

He smiled sweetly at Peter and pulled the choke knob. It came away in his hand.

'No need for t' choke. A couple of swings and she'll be away,'

Undaunted, he jumped down and swung hopefully on the starting handle.

He had a look of extreme concentration on his face.

Some time later, after removing the plugs and washing them in the rusty paraffin, removing the magneto, putting it in a vice and freeing it up by hitting it with a big hammer, fiddling with various screws on the carburettor, he gave the handle one last desperate swing.

There was a deafening, shattering roar. Clouds of blue smoke filled the shed.

Green Clogs leaped up into the saddle and fought with the throttle lever in an effort to keep the engine running. Somehow, he managed to put the tractor into gear and, with a loud grinding sound; it lurched out of the shed into the blinding, bright sunshine.

She was a quaint old lady.

She stood there, resting on her soft, worn tyres. Orange water dripped from her leaking radiator and black oil collected in a pool under her sump. She was painted a shade of blue. At least, most of her was. The rest was rust, with darker areas where oil leaks stained the paintwork.

Everything was faded by the sun of many summers. Across her bonnet in large white letters, Peter read the word 'FORDSON'.

'Best tractor they ever made,' shouted her proud owner, patting her bonnet as if he was showing off his new girlfriend.

'Me Dad bought her from a farm sale in Preston. Drove her all t' way home,'

As he patted her bonnet, he gradually disappeared in a cloud of steam. Peter could smell burning Paraffin; it lay heavy in the air.

Peter hadn't said anything. There was really no point. The noise was so loud, that he wouldn't have been heard.

The sweating farmer backed the tractor into its shed, fearing, no doubt, that it may seize up. The crackling roar died away as he pulled the stop knob. Peter saw oil and water dripping onto the floor.

At last, Peter could speak.

'How much do you want?'

He had no intention of buying the tractor.

'Eighty five,' came the immediate reply. Surely Green Clogs was not serious?

'Eighty two?' asked Green Clogs hopefully.

Peter shook his head.

'I've getten another round t' back,' Green clogs was unabashed. 'A real good 'un. I didn't want to part wi' it,'

He clattered across the yard and disappeared behind a mound of vintage manure, dog at his side. Peter hurried after him.

'There she is,' announced Green Clogs with pride.

All Peter could see was a great pile of junk with nettles growing everywhere.

In one corner, the nettles grew high and undisturbed.

In the middle of a pile of rotting timber, rusty wire and long discarded junk, Peter saw the exhaust of a tractor protruding above the nettles.

He brushed the weed aside, and there she was.

Even to Peter's inexperienced eye, it was obvious that this relic of times gone by was beyond restoration. It had the greenish covering of moss that usually grows over things that have lain for years in damp corners of farmyards. Its tyres were flat and worn. Its seat was missing and its radiator had nettles growing through it.

'Yon were a damn good tractor,' said Green Clogs. 'My dad used it when he were a lad. A German prisoner let t' frost burst t' radiator in t' winter of 1944,'

Peter knew that German prisoners had worked on farms during the war. He couldn't help thinking that this particular prisoner of war should have been awarded the Iron Cross for his attempt to sabotage Britain's wartime food production.

'I'm not a scrap dealer,' laughed Peter. He found himself amused by this chaps optimism.

'Forty?'

'No,' said Peter. ' Not even forty shillings,'

As he walked towards his Land Rover, away from this little corner of rural England, Peter could hear once again, the rattle of the bucket in the cow shed and the clatter of clogs, as Green Clogs, once again pitted his wits against the reluctant cow. Peter had no doubt about which of the two had the most intelligence, and it wasn't the farmer.

Peter's last memory of the farm in the hollow past the 'trigonometry point' was a very sad one.

There, in the middle of the squalor and rot, stood the little Collie dog.

She stood very still, her head on one side, regarding Peter with her intelligent eyes. She watched as Peter chugged back up the hill in his Land Rover until he had gone round the corner, and out of sight.

Six

News quickly got round… As news usually did in Widdersdale.

A few days after the 'green Clogs' incident, there was a knock at the door.

'I'll get it,' Susan called, and went to the porch.

A young man, about Peter's age stood there.

'Hello, I don't think you know me. My name's Geoff. I live in Billingbeck. I've been told that you are looking for a tractor?'

'Better come in. I'll call Peter,' Susan stood to one side.

The young man thanked her, took off his cap and stepped into the porch.

'Peter,' Susan called out. 'We have a visitor, Geoff. He knows where there's a tractor for sale,'

Peter had been fixing a broken cupboard in the lounge.

He looked closely at the young man. He was sure that he had seen him before. Yes…Usually accompanied by a scruffy looking dog.

He carried a stick and often wore an old waxed jacket, whatever the weather.

Peter had seen this chap around the village, and occasionally on the moor.

Susan explained to Peter that the visitor might know of a tractor for sale in the area. Peter smiled.

'You aren't from Lees Farm are you?'

The lad laughed.

'I heard about your visit to Lees Farm. No, I'm nothing to do with that chap. I happen to know where there is a decent tractor for sale,'

'I hope it's better than the last one that Peter went to look at,' Susan said.

The lad seemed to be very amused.

'Most of the farmers round the Dale know me. I do a bit of work up on the tops. A bit of walling, lambing, shearing, hay time. Lots of things over the year,'

Geoff... Hadn't Green Clogs up at Lees Farm mentioned someone called Geoff?

'Be sure that I would never tell you about anything for sale at Lees Farm. He's a strange chap. If you don't mind me asking, who told you that there was a tractor for sale up there?'

'As a matter of fact, it was Ernie from Folly Edge.' Susan said.

Geoff burst out laughing.

'He would. Perhaps he thought that you would be able to do some mowing for him?'

'As a matter of fact, he said that he would rather use his scythe,' Susan said.

'Oh, he would say that. Don't you believe it. He always says the opposite to whatever you expect him to say. He can be a cantankerous old chap, but he's the salt of the earth. It's just his humour really,'

Peter and Susan glanced at each other. They had begun to suspect it.

'Will you excuse me for a moment? I just want to check on my dog,'

'Where is your dog?' Susan frowned.

'Oh, he's in your yard. He's a bit wary of strangers,'

Up to now, Jim had said nothing.

'Will you bring him in please? He can play with Meg,' he said.

Geoff looked at Jim.

'Tell you what I'll do young man. I'll ask him. Perhaps he doesn't want to,'

Geoff went out into the yard, and the Barnard family plus Meg followed.

Geoff's dog was sitting in a corner of the yard looking very bored.

It was a scruffy, friendly looking dog of doubtful parentage.

It jumped up at the sight of Meg, and the two dogs walked round each other, tails wagging.

'What is it called?' Jim asked.

'She's called Scruffy. Best name I could think of,'

Reluctantly, Scruffy allowed herself to be led into the porch, but no further,

She lay down in a corner. Meg lay down too.

Jim was about to join the dogs, but Susan told him to leave them alone.

'You aren't a local lad are you?' Peter could detect no trace of the Dales accent.

'Yes I am. I was born in Billingbeck. My parents sent me away to be educated,'

He seemed to see the funny side of that.

'I'm most happy up on the tops. Really it was all a waste of time,' he looked thoughtful. 'No. Perhaps it wasn't. One day, I'll take off to the city and change my way of life,'

Susan couldn't quite imagine this lanky, windswept individual working in the city.

Geoff glanced at his watch

'Got to be off,' he said.

He put his cap on his head and picked up his stick. Scruffy could see him from the porch. She immediately jumped up, wagging her tail.

He explained where the tractor was.

'Holly Bank Farm. It's just opposite Driggs Farm on the road down to Beddington. Tell them that Geoff told you about it.'

They thanked him and accompanied him to the door. As he was leaving, he winked and bent down to speak to Jim.

'You will be meeting my wife soon young man,' he said.

With that, he was gone.

Holly bank Farm was a very neat well kept place. The buildings were in good condition, they were round a large concrete yard that had obviously just been swept.

Peter turned the Land Rover into the yard and a lad came out of one of the buildings. He looked at Peter.

'Hello. You're Peter from Nab's Head, aren't you? What brings you down to Holly Bank?'

Peter knew the young man. He had seen him at the Black Bull on several occasions. He was one of the group of farmers who collected there, discussing the goings on around the Dale.

Peter explained that he was looking for a reliable tractor.

'Geoff told me that you may have something,' he said.

He told the young farmer about his experiences up at 'Green Clogs' establishment. It caused considerable amusement.

'Aye, Tha'd get a load of rubbish up yonder. He'd try to sell thee a bucket with a hole in it. You've come to t' right place. Dad's Thinkin' o' selling t' David Brown. I don't think you know my name? Bill Jarvis,' he stroked his chin. 'I'll get my Dad.'

'I think I have seen him in the Black Bull,' Peter said.

Bill nodded.

'Aye, tha' would do.'

Bill went over to the house. He opened the door and shouted to let his father know that they had a visitor. In a moment, out came Bill's father.

Peter recognised him from the Black Bull. He was an older version of his son.

'My Dad, Tony, he said. 'Did you get yon Land Rover off Wishbone?' he said. 'It used to belong to my brother,'

Peter told him that the Land Rover had indeed come from Wishbone's garage.

As they were talking, another chap appeared from the house.

He was obviously Bill's brother. All the family looked very much alike.

'Anyway young man. Tha's come to look at yon tractor. Come on, I'll show it to thee,'

They all followed Tony to a big shed. Peter couldn't help noticing that the two lads were trying not to show amusement. He wondered why.

Tony opened the shed door. Inside, Peter saw a very new looking tractor with a cab. It was green and obviously little used.

'Just what tha'll be looking for? Tha'll have no trouble wi yon,'

'I don't think I could afford that,' Peter said.

Father and sons burst out laughing.

'I'm only teasing thee. Look round t' corner,'

Peter went to the side of the shed and there he saw another tractor.

Tony could see that Peter was impressed.

This one had two seats. It was bright red and had the word 'Crop Master' painted on the side. On the front, there was a little badge announcing that it was a 'David Brown'.

Tony turned on a tap underneath the fuel tank, and a glass bowl filled with yellow liquid. Tony explained.

'It uses petrol to start up. As soon as it's warm, you turn the tap over to T.V.O.,'

'What's T.V.O.,' Peter was out of his depth.

'Tractor Vaporising Oil,'

Tony seemed to think that everyone knew what T.V.O. was.

He swung the starting handle lightly.

There was a puff of smoke from the exhaust and the tractor came to life.

Bill swung up into the drivers' seat and lifted the throttle lever. The tractor responded immediately. It moved obediently forwards.

'Thee take it out onto t' field and try it out,'

Bill climbed down and Peter climbed up. Bill showed him where the gears were.

'Off tha goes,' he said.

Peter let out the clutch and he was away.

The sky was blue and life was good.

Peter could smell the heady aroma of burning tractor fuel.

If they bought the muck spreader, he thought. They would be ready for anything.

Peter knew without any doubt, that this beautiful tractor was going to live at Nab's Head Farm.

By now, he had her in second gear and was chugging happily over the lush grass. He waved to his little group of onlookers.

Another son had joined the group. They waved back. Very enthusiastically, Peter thought.

Gradually, he was slowing down. His daydreaming ended fast. Looking ahead, he saw water. He had driven right into the duck pond!

His little group of admirers had stopped waving. Now, they were holding each other up, helpless with laughter. Finally, the water reached up to Peter's knees. Then it began to recede. The tractor was climbing slowly out of the evil smelling water. Foul bubbles burst on the surface of the pond.

The smell was indescribable. Rotting vegetation and well fermented cow dung. Worse. There was something else in that water that caused Peter to smell faintly for days afterwards.

He wasn't out of trouble yet, not by any means.

Black mud flew up all round the tractor. The wheels began to spin, finding no grip in the soft greasy mud. He could go no further. He had reached the end of his journey.

Then he made the fatal mistake of pulling the 'stop' button.

The silence was astonishing!

No… There was noise.

A few popping bubbles and the distant sound of great merriment.

The four farmers came staggering across the field, propping each other up. They couldn't wait to get to the Black Bull.

'By heck lad. If tha wanted a boat, tha's come to t' wrong place,'

All four were red faced. The three sons were wiping their eyes.

'Tha'll not get out o' yon pond. Tha'll need another tractor to pull thee out,'

Peter wiped mud from his eyes. He couldn't think of anything to say.

The green tractor was carefully backed up to the edge of the pond and Bill threw a chain out to Peter.

'Tha'll have to fasten that to t' front o' t' tractor,'

All Peter could think of to say was,

'Thank you,'

His politeness caused the men to double up in fresh gales of laughter.

Only one person had to wallow about in the mud, attaching the chain to the tractor. It was of course, Peter.

He wasn't exactly willing, but, no-one else would do it. Gradually, his boots were being sucked into the mud.

He grabbed the chain and wrapped it round the front axle. Now, he was coated in the evil black stuff right up to his elbows.

That was when he got the irresistible itch on the tip of his nose.

He climbed back into the drivers seat. The end was in sight.

To Peter's intense relief, the Red tractor started to slowly emerge from the mud. Peter was towed back to the shed, alongside a hosepipe.

Tony stood well back.

'You can use yon hosepipe t' clean t' tractor. Thee too,'

It took some time to clean Peter up. In spite of his best efforts, it was obvious that he wasn't going to be invited into the house.

Eventually, after much effort, Peter and tractor were reasonably free of the worst of the clinging, black goo.

Finally, it was time for Peter to ask about the price of the tractor.

He wasn't in any mood to haggle. Tony knew that. But, there was no haggling to be done. The price that he wanted was fair, and that was it. Take it or leave it. He could not resist a final dig at Peter.

'Tha can have t' tractor for a hundred and fifty pounds, an' t' fertilizer that's on it; tha can have that for nowt,'

Peter was quite happy about the price; he knew that they had found a serious working tractor at last.

'Great,' he said. 'It seems like a sound tractor,'

'Well, tha's given it a good test,' Tony muttered.

More seriously, he said,

'The Crop Master. It's a good all rounder. It'll do everything that tha'll need a tractor for,'

Getting it back to Nab's Head was no problem.

Bill Jarvis had to pick up a couple of cows from Appleburn Farm.

He decided to take one of his brothers along, who would drive Peter's Land Rover back for him. Luckily, there were not too many people about.

Peter was well aware that he would be seen by someone around Billingbeck. He was also aware that both he and the tractor showed signs of their recent adventures. Fortunately, it would be lunchtime for most of the villagers, thought Peter.

The few motorists that he did encounter, seemed very amused by the sight of a farmer driving a tractor that looked as though it had been mud wrestling.

When he finally arrived home, Peter didn't get as far as the porch. Susan and Jim heard the tractor, and ran out of the house to see it.

Jim burst out laughing at the sight of his damp dad sitting on a distinctly muddy tractor. If Peter had been hoping for sympathy, he didn't get it.

Susan had her hand over her mouth, trying to hide her amusement.

'You were supposed to come along the road,'

Her eyes showed her amusement. 'It looks as though you drove all the way from Holly Bank in the Beck. How on earth did you manage to get covered in mud?'

Peter climbed down from the tractor seat.

Jim backed away.

Peter didn't know how to explain what had happened without sounding like an idiot. He did try.

'I accidentally drove into a pond while I was having a trial run,' he muttered.

He had to tell Susan the truth because the whole story would soon be common knowledge at the Black Bull.

'I like the new tractor,' Jim spoke at last.

Naturally, it was clean up time.

Peter was told to go into the barn while Susan brought hot water, soap and a towel. She also found a complete change of clothing.

Peter's job kept him busy up to the weekend.

He was finding it increasingly difficult to keep on top of everything these days. Of course, his job with the T.V. Company had to take priority.

It was their bread and butter. But, he often found that he was dashing about, trying to botch something about the farm.

Susan was doing more than her fair share. She managed to do a lot of work and make sure that Jim got put ahead of everything. He was, after all, growing up. He had an inquisitive mind.

There were so many questions that needed answers.

Then there was the house to look after and, because Peter was away most days, she found herself going round the fields several times each day, accompanied by Jim and Meg. There were often a few sheep about.

Peter had noticed that Susan didn't read as much as she used to.

She loved nothing more than curling up in the big chair, with a 'brew' and a good book. Peter would be playing with Jim in the evenings, and notice that Susan was asleep in the chair, the book that she had been reading, fallen to the floor.

The time had come to do some serious thinking.

How had he been so blind? He knew that Susan would say that everything was fine, but Peter knew that it wasn't.

One evening after Jim had been put to bed; Peter brought two mugs of cocoa from the kitchen and put them down by the fire.

Normally, Susan would be tidying the room, picking up a few toys, or putting cushions back on the chairs. It had become something of a luxury to curl up on the settee together. This evening, Susan picked up her mug and sat beside Peter.

'That's nice,' she smiled at Peter. 'I needed this. Thanks,'

She put her head on Peter's shoulder. Peter put his arm round her. He smiled to himself. 'I'm a lucky beggar,' He thought.

'You work too hard,' he suddenly said.

Susan smiled at him.

'No-one ever said it was going to be easy,' she whispered.

'No. I'm not joking Susan. I am concerned. You are trying to be everything. A mother and a wife, a builder and a farmer and all the other things. When you should be relaxing in the evenings, you still don't stop.

When you are showing Jim how to spell, or drawing a picture for him, it isn't resting,'

Susan laughed.

She had been just as concerned about Peter working all day, and then doing so much around the farm in the evenings.

'We both act like idiots. Just let's keep sight of the fact that we are a family. We need a bit more time for each other. Then, we can manage fine. Jim'll be at school soon,'

Peter realised that what Susan was saying was perfectly true.

He had been looking at it in the wrong way.

Susan's concern was that the little family should always share love and appreciate what they had.

How right she was. But, he still had a nagging thought that he could do something to make things easier. He sipped his cocoa and looked into the dying fire. When he looked at Susan again, she was fast asleep.

They talked over the question of Ernies enthusiasm for spreading manure. Now that they had a good tractor, they would see if Willy Nelson still had his redundant 'muck Spreader'. It wasn't too late to do a bit of muck spreading.

It was supposed to be done in the early spring, when the ground was loosening up after the winter frost. But, a bit of muck would freshen up the summer grass as soon as it washed into the roots.

Ernie knew little about any sort of machinery, but he was well aware of the advantage of manure on the land.

Peter took Susan and Jim with him to Willy Nelson's farm.

Meg was allowed to ride in the back. She always loved the chance to ride in the Land Rover.

It was a perfect day. The gentle summer sun lay across Widdersdale, bathing everything in its soft warm caress. The sweet smell of the Dale was indefinable. It was a mixture of so many things. Of lazy summer warmth and the gentle English countryside.

Everything was so perfect for a trip to Bradley Fold.

It was just across the Dale. Hidden from view in its wooded hollow.

The farm lay in a very picturesque spot. The woods were heavy with the pungent aroma of wild garlic. High mossy rocks lined the track, with the trees towering above. Ancient oak trees and majestic ash and horse chestnuts with a rich carpet of Wood Anemone and Primrose colouring the ground from early spring. Bright white and yellow flowers sprinkled among the rich leafy grass.

There were always rabbits to be seen in the hollow below Bradley Fold to the delight of young Jim, and the warm air was alive with the song of many woodland birds.

Willy Nelson was a jovial chap. A regular visitor to the Black Bull.

He saw the Land Rover approaching the farm. The smells here were very familiar to the Barnards, as with all Dales farms. Cows, sheep, and tractor oil. Creosote and warm stone, hay and dogs. Willy was pleased to see his visitors. He laid the sweeping brush that he was holding, against the barn wall.

'By gum. What brings thee o'er t' this side o' t' Dale? Young Jim too.

It must be important. Tha's brought t' boss wi' thee,'

Willy looked very hot. His cap was pushed well back on his head and his shirt sleeves were rolled up. His jovial face was red.

Peter told him that they were interested in the old muck spreader.

'Ernie told us that you had a redundant spreader,'

'Ernie's hoping to get some of his muck spread,' laughed Billy.

'That's exactly what we have already been told,' Susan said.

'I'll tell thee what. We've got some elderflower pop for t' young man and I'll put kettle on. I'm t' boss today. It's a wonder tha didn't see Betty in t' village. Gone doin' a bit o' shopping,'

Willy led the way into the cool farmhouse. He filled the iron kettle and lit the Calor gas stove.

'Betty's been bakin'. Would ta like a scone wi' butter on? Good butter.

Betty made it from a drop o' milk from t' Jersey cow,'

Jim was told to sit at the table,

Willy put a huge enamel mug in front of him. He brought a bottle of home made Elderflower pop from a shelf under the cool stone stairs.

As he filled Jim's mug, the kitchen filled with the wonderful aroma of elderflowers. Carefully, Willy cut a huge scone and put butter on it.

'Well, that's got t' little lad sorted out. I'll only be a moment wi' t' brew,'

Willy was the perfect host. He didn't use the usual everyday mugs.

He laid out dainty china cups and saucers and matching side plates.

Willy seemed to do things in style.

'Good baking,' remarked Susan,

'Aye. Betty does things proper. Her mother were a good 'un at baking too,'

They gossiped for a bit.

Willy was an amusing character. He had a way of seeing the funny side of everything.

Jim listened to the adults conversation as he struggled with his huge scone. He knew a lot of the people who were being discussed.

Peter noticed that he was smiling at Willy's funny stories.

The muck spreader proved to be in excellent condition. It had big rubber tyres and it was painted a bright yellow with 'Bamford' in large letters on the side. Willy wanted thirty pounds for it. He explained that he had bought one of the new side delivery spreaders.

The outcome was that the Bamford duly arrived at Nab's Head.

Ernie didn't need to be told about events. The following morning, he arrived at the Barnard's door.

'I saw t' Bamford in t' yard,' he said. 'If tha brings it 'oer, we can load it up,'

Peter laughed at Ernie's casual enthusiasm.

'It'll have to wait till weekend Ernie. I have to go to work sometimes,'

Considering Ernie's lack of enthusiasm for new fangled machinery, he seemed to show a keen interest in the Bamford. He seemed to be on edge, he didn't want to hang about. Susan offered him a brew; he thanked her but refused the offer.

'Thanks lass. But I've getten a chap coming up to t' farm. Happen he'll have some ducks for me,'

He looked round. 'Where's my mate Jim?' he asked

'You're a bit early Ernie. But if he hears your voice, He'll be down,'

As Susan spoke, she heard little feet coming down the stairs.

A sleepy looking Jim wandered into the room. He looked at Ernie.

'We got the muck spreader,' he said.

Ernie looked at Peter.

'Your Dad will be bringing it o'er t' get some fertilizer off me on Saturday,'

Peter was rushing about. He had not got much time left. He was working in Ilkley, so he could afford to be a bit later than usual.

But he wanted to be off. He picked Jim up and gave him a cuddle.

'Be a good boy for Mummy. I'll be home soon,' Jim flung his arms round Peter and gave him a kiss.

'I'll be good,' he promised.

Peter gave Susan a kiss and looked at Ernie.

'If tha thinks that tha' art' getting' a kiss off me, tha can forget it,' Ernie grinned as Peter dashed out of the door.

'Well, I'd better be gettin' back too,' he said.

Susan and Jim accompanied him to the door.

She watched as Ernie walked over to the Bamford. He carefully inspected the chains and cogs.

'Aye, it'll do. Tell Peter to put some oil on t' chains,'

With that, he was off.

Filling the muck spreader took a long time.

Ernie, in spite of his age, was loading three times as much as Peter. Most of the crumbly black manure was falling off the end of Peter's fork and dribbling down the tops of his wellingtons.

Susan and Jim had walked over to watch the new machine being loaded.

'Nay lad,' Ernie stopped working and smiled at Peter's efforts "Tha'll not do it like that,' Ernie was trying not to laugh. 'If tha swings t' fork and throws it 'oer thy shoulder, tha'll fill t' box, not thy Wellingtons,'

He showed Peter how to work more easily and with much less effort.

After that, things proceeded much more efficiently. Peter was grateful.

Now that he had acquired his new skill, it didn't take long to fill the box of the Bamford.

Peter climbed onto the tractor and put it in gear. Now, it was doing what a tractor was intended to do.

Peter was sweaty and had a distinctly rural aroma, but he was satisfied that everything was going to plan. He chugged towards the field that was going to be fertilised. Susan and Jim had gone on ahead.

They were leaning on the wall, ready to offer moral support. Peter was pleased.

There was nothing wrong with a bit of showing off.

He waved to his little audience and pushed his cap onto the back of his head. He had thought of everything. Nothing could possibly go wrong. The moment of truth had arrived.

Peter reached behind him and hauled on the lever that put everything into gear. He had selected second gear because he worked out that it would be about the speed that would give maximum efficiency. He had lined everything up to follow the edge of the field right down to its lowest point. Out with the clutch. The tractor lurched forwards obediently; it was growling and sending little puffs of white smoke high in the air,

Down the side of the field Peter went. Susan was impressed.

Her husband looked every inch the farmer.

Jim was jumping up and down with excitement.

'It works,' he clapped his hands together. 'Look Mummy. It works. Isn't Daddy clever?'

Susan saw the wall of finely chopped manure being thrown high into the air.

As soon as Peter got the feel of things, he looked over his shoulder.

All was not well! Even to Peter's inexperienced eye, it was obvious that all was not as it should be.

He could hear the clanking of the chains and the thrashing of the blades as they chopped the manure, and did what they were supposed to do.

But, he couldn't see anything at all. His view was obstructed by a thick mist of manure. Not only that… he was 'in' the mist.

Gradually, both the tractor and Peter were turning into a nice shade of brown. He peered through the mist.

He could vaguely see Susan and Jim. They had been joined by Ernie, accompanied as always by his faithful dogs. They all looked very amused, even the dogs. Some quick thinking was needed on Peter's part.

It was the merriment of his audience that saved the day.

Dignity and pride were involved.

He knocked the machine out of gear and the evil cloud that had been surrounding him, instantly subsided. He had time to consider where he had been going wrong.

He had been working with the wind coming from behind. He should have noticed before he even set off. Hadn't the puffs of white smoke been blown away in front of the tractor?

He simply drove across the wind. Really, it was obvious.

Peter managed to salvage what was left of his dignity and do the job without any further unsavoury incidents. Two of the fields at Folly Edge were completed that day.

Soon, it would be the turn of Nab's Head. It was obvious that there would be a vast amount of the wonderful, black manure left over.

Of course, at the end of that first day, Peter was not allowed into the house. After he had parked the tractor and swilled everything down, he knew from past experience, what was expected of him. A smiling Susan brought a couple of buckets full of hot water from the house and poured them into the tub. She also brought out a complete change of clothes and laid them across a cow stall. Up to now, she had said nothing.

'Scrubbing time again,' she said. She burst into laughter. 'Getting to be a bit of a habit. I feel a bit sorry for the tractor,'

Jim was watching from the barn door. He too, had a big smile on his face.

He looked at Peter, standing there in his underpants.

'Mummy told me that you might be going to live with the cows,'

The only one who had said nothing was the dog.

But, Peter had the distinct impression that even Meg was trying not to laugh. But then, Collies are very good at looking unimpressed, with their big soft sad eyes.

That evening, Peter, Susan and Jim went down to the Black Bull.

The first thing that they noticed was the smiling farmers.

Ned was sitting in his usual corner.

'If tha t' thinkin' o' sittin' wi' me lad, I hope tha's had a bath,'

He spoke loud enough for the farmers to hear. They all laughed.

'I'll tell thee what lass,' one of them spoke to Susan. 'Yon chap o' thyn'll grow a foot taller, wi' all yon fertiliser,'

Even young Jim had realised that news gets round pretty fast in Widdersdale.

He dashed off to the games room to see if any of the kids knew the story of his dad's misfortunes.

As soon as he got into the room, a couple of the farmer's children spotted him.

'Owdo Jim. What did thy dad do? My dad told my mum that he got covered in muck,'

Jim saw the funny side, he wanted to defend Peter, but even at his age, he knew that these kids were just asking what had happened.

'My dad was using our new muck spreader,' Jim laughed.

'He got covered in muck,'

The children thought that it was hilariously funny.

'I'll bet that thy mum wasn't pleased,' one of the girls said.

'No, he had to wash it all off in the barn,'

This was a bit more news. They couldn't wait to tell their parents, but as is the way of all children, the subject was soon forgotten.

Jim took his place in the queue to use the slide.

Both Peter and Susan took all the leg pulling as it was intended.

It had a side that was complimentary. They both knew that it was a way of showing that they had been accepted into the community.

Peter started to relax. But, it is a mistake to relax when one is learn-ing 'Farmin'. All went well with the muck spreader. Susan was pleased to see that Peter stayed relatively clean. It all went wrong when he saw a chance to practice another of his rural skills.

'Come on Jim. We've got a job to do,'

Jim followed his dad across the field. There was some very steep land along the edge of the field. Peter had decided to show his good old Yorkshire upbringing. 'Waste not, want not.'

He filled a wheelbarrow with some of the manure and he planned to spread it where the tractor couldn't go.

Jim followed his dad, accompanied by Meg.

It was yet another lovely morning. The sun was shining and the still, warm air was intoxicating. Peter pushed the wheelbarrow, fork sticking out of the manure

Jim had decided that he wanted to learn to whistle. He was walk-ing along, blowing hard, but he only succeeded in making a 'shooshing' sound Meg recognised it as an attempt to whistle though; she was look-ing round for stray sheep.

'Right lad. Stand back,'

It had been hard work pushing the wheelbarrow, but Peter had man-aged to push it up the steep slope. The next bit was easy. He had seen Ernie doing it many times. He lifted a forkful of the crumbly muck, just as Ernie did it, but he only managed to lift about half as much as Ernie would have

What did it matter? There was plenty of time.

With grim determination, he swung the fork round in a graceful arc, but what should have happened didn't. There was no beautiful spread of manure. It just went where it wanted to. Mostly down the neck of his shirt and inside his wellingtons. A small amount did indeed fall among the grass, but it was only a small amount.

Perhaps a more scientific approach was called for?

'Swinging from the hip', that was what Ernie had said.

By now, both Jim and Meg had realised that all was not well.

They were both sitting down in the tall grass, watching Peter with interest. Meg was panting and wagging her tail, but as usual, her expression gave nothing away. Jim had abandoned his attempts to whistle.

Peter made several more attempts to get it right, but with no success.

He decided at that point, to abandon the idea. The steep bits remained unfertilised.

Slowly, the three of them trudged back to the farm. Jim had resumed his attempts to whistle, and Meg had just lost interest in everything.

When they got back to the farm, Peter knew the routine.

He told Jim to go into the house, but, he sneaked into the kitchen and grabbed a bucket of warm water from the boiler beside the fire. He quietly got some clothes from the drying rack and crept out into the barn. Just as he was pulling off his socks, Susan's head popped round the door.

'Been muckspreading again love?' she asked innocently.

'If one word of this gets to the Black Bull, I'll know where it came from,' Peter muttered, red faced.

This time, the secret stayed within the family.

There was however, one member of the family who had the last laugh.

It was Susan who noticed it first.

'Did you leave your wellingtons in the barn Peter?'

'Certainly did,' Peter said. 'I must admit that they are a bit pongy,'

They all three noticed that there was a distinct smell of manure creeping round the house. It was Jim who first discovered where it was coming from.

'Oh. Go away Meg,' He was holding his nose.

Meg had crept in unnoticed. She thought that she had been improving her status in the dog world by rolling on her back in the manure.

The source of the awful smell had been discovered.

Meg didn't think that anything was wrong. She just stood there, wagging her tail, but it wasn't long before she was in the barn, getting the hosepipe treatment.

The wonderful summer progressed without any serious mishaps.

The fertilised grass began to look lush and green. Peter couldn't resist commenting.

'I did a good job with the muckspreading,'

Er, Yes. After a few false starts," Susan muttered.

'Soon, we will be cutting some grass. Then, after hay time, it'll be getting near time for Jim to be off to school,'

'I know,' Peter was serious. 'I wonder where time goes,'

'I don't like the idea of Jim going to school,' Susan said. 'I don't want to lose my baby,' Peter put his arm round her.

'I know you've been thinking that, but he'll only be in the village. He wants to go, doesn't he? After all, he knows a lot of the village kids now,'

Susan smiled at him.

'I know it's silly. I'm just being a mum,'

Peter did understand how Susan felt.

'Just think,' he said. 'Jim joining the ranks of the educated masses,'

'I like it best, when you come home from work. Then, we are a little family,' Susan said. 'With Jim gone too, the house'll seem so empty,'

They were interrupted by the arrival of Ernie. His weather-beaten face appeared at the door.

'I brought thee a couple of duck eggs,' He held up a brown paper bag.

'Come in Ernie. I was just going to put the kettle on,' Susan said.

Ernie took off his cap and walked over to what had become his seat by the fire.

He sat down and produced his battered tin and his pipe.

Susan made the tea and the three of them sat by the fire. Jim got his cup of milk. He was in the porch, playing with the dogs, but Susan brought him in to drink his milk.

'Leave the dogs alone. Come and sit on your stool. I brought you some milk. If you don't drink it, Meg will steal it,' His mum told him.

Ernie watched Jim with an amused expression on his face.

Suddenly, he spoke.

'Tryin' hard to make a go of it, thee youngsters,'

Peter and Susan were astonished. Ernie usually grumbled in a humorous way about most things. But, outright praise... Ernie sounded sincere.

It had just been said out of the blue. Peter didn't quite know what to say. But,

Susan said,

'Praise indeed Ernie. Coming from you, it is appreciated,'

'I'll tell thee summat,' He puffed on his pipe for effect. 'I'll be honest wi' thee. I'd not have got yon fields spread wi' out thy help. How dus't tha recon tha'll do with hay time?' He had a twinkle in his eye, 'After all, tha's got all yon new fangled machines,'

'Oh, we'll do alright with a bit of good advice from you,' Susan said.

'Don't forget. Hay in t' barn's money in t' bank,' Ernie said.

He applied another match to his pipe. 'If tha's getten any spare time, I'd appreciate a bit o' grass cut wi' yon tractor o' thyne,' He muttered.

Susan poured another cup of tea. The three of them talked for a time about the weather and swapped bits of gossip. Jim went over to Ernie and gave him a demonstration of his latest talent, a high pitched whistle.

'Tha'll need yon whistle to work wi t' dogs,' Ernie laughed.

'Well I can't sit here all day wi' you youngsters,' He paused and looked thoughtful. 'If tha's got a moment Peter, I'd appreciate it if tha' could come o'er to my place,'

Before Peter could reply, he was gone, followed by his dogs.

'What was all that about?' pondered Susan.

'I don't know. I'll call round tomorrow as soon as I get home. Then we'll know,' Peter looked thoughtful.

Peter was home early on the following day. He had hoped to do some work in Brighouse, but the job had been cancelled on the last minute.

He was impatient. Ernies request had been in the back of his mind all day.

'I think I'll go over to Folly Edge and see what Ernie wants,' he told Susan. She laughed.

'I knew that was coming, I am as curious as you. Don't hang about nattering like you usually do. I want to know what it's all about,'

'He probably wants me to whitewash his cow shed,' Peter laughed.

'We do have one of those new fangled paint brushes,'

'Don't be silly. Go and find out,' Susan pushed him towards the door.

'You bully me,' he grumbled.

Peter walked over the fields towards Ernie's farm. As he was walking down the hill, he spotted Ernie coming round the side of the cow shed.

He had a sack of cattle food on his back. He saw Peter coming down the slope.

'I didn't expect thee over so soon,' he said.

Peter explained that he had got home sooner than he had expected to.

Ernie disappeared into the cowshed and emerged without the sack.

'Come wi' me,' He beckoned Peter to follow him.

He disappeared back into the gloomy, cool interior of the shed.

There was a smell of cattle feed and hay.

Pulling a knife from his back pocket, Ernie cut the string around the neck of a sack and tipped a measured amount of cattle nuts into each of several battered buckets lined up along a wall.

The effect was startling. The cows that were in the main part of the shed heard the rattle of the nuts falling into the buckets and started mooing and getting very restless.

'Thee take t' buckets down t' side by t' door,'

Ernie didn't wait for an answer. He picked up two buckets and pushed his way between two of the young cows, placing a bucket in front of each of them. Peter did the same at the other end of the cow-shed. All was silent as the contented cows ate their meal.

'We'll let 'em out when they've finished,' said Ernie.

Soon, the dappled red and white cows were making their way across the yard to the water trough. From there, they would wander out to join the other cows in the field.

The old man was in no rush. He pulled his battered old pipe from his pocket, filled it from the red tin and lit it. Then, he closed his eyes and puffed away. He knew that Peter was dying to know what this was all about.

He was making the most of the moment.

'What dus t' think t' weather'll do tomorrow?' Ernie glanced up at the sky.

Peter was confident. He had heard the forecast on the radio.

'It will be fine in the North But with scattered showers moving in from the West later. Wind force three,'

'Where did tha get thy showers from? There'll be no damn showers,'

He pointed with his pipe.

'Winds comin' o'er t' top and t'cows are goin' o'er yon hill. There'll be no showers,' Surely Peter could see what he was talking about. There would be no rain.

Peter could contain his curiosity no longer.

'I came over because you asked me to. It wasn't to help you to give those cows their supper,'

Ernie was amused.

'Oh aye. I knew I wanted thee for something,' He acted as though he had just remembered. "Come wi' me oe'r to yon shed,'

He walked over to a small stone building across the yard and opened the top of the door.

'What dus't tha think o' yon?' He pointed with his pipe into the gloom.

Looking inside. Peter saw two tubby little black calves. They seemed to be about three months old.

'They look nice,' Peter said.

'Oh aye, they are,' said Ernie. 'That's because they've been done right. Just see if thou can raise yon young beggars. I got 'em for thee,'

Peter was speechless.

'I'll keep t' young beggars here till tha's getten a place for 'em,' Ernie rubbed his stubbly chin.

'Tha'd better get readin' yon agricultural books. Don't think tha't a farmer yet,'

Peter didn't know how to thank the old man; he couldn't express how he felt.

'Get back to yon lass o' thyne. Maybe she knows more about rearin' young 'uns than thee,'

Peter almost ran back to Nab's Head. He told Susan what had happened. She was quiet for a moment.

'I think it's his way of he's trying to say thank you for helping out with the muckspreading and offering to help with hay time,'

Peter nodded.

'The thing is, I can't say much. He has his own way of handling things,'

'He certainly wouldn't offer us money. He is just grateful for a bit of help,'

'Well,' Peter said.' Our herd has doubled in size. They are really good calves,'

Jim had said nothing up to now. He was studying his 'Beano' annual. He looked up at Peter.

'Can I come and help you to bring the calves to Nab's Head?' he asked Peter.

'Better still, you help me to make a little pen for them, and we can all go,'

Of course, Jim wanted to make the pen right then.

Jim was chief architect and Peter was the pen builder. Susan was the supplier of Tea, milk and sandwiches.

'Put more straw in,' Jim instructed.

'It looks so comfortable, I could live in it,' Susan admired the finished pen.

The calves were closely watched by Susan, she looked after the babies very carefully. Peter watched her mixing the 'calf milk' with a small amount of glucose. As she did so, she was talking to the new arrivals.

'You greedy little beggars. It won't be long now. Your milk is a bit warm,'

Jim was delighted because he was allowed to hold one of the buckets.

Peter whispered in Susan's ear.

'It wasn't long ago; you were mixing milk for Jim,'

Susan nodded and smiled.

'It seems like a few months ago,' she sighed. 'Where does time go? We were living in Guiseley then. We never thought that our lives would change so much. Who would have believed that we would be doing all this, one day?'

Seven

Susan was sitting at the kitchen table, reading a book with Jim.

As always, he was impatient. He wanted to know the ending.

'Well Mummy, Tell me what the dragon does when it has caught the witch,'

'You must try to read the story to find out,' Susan smiled to herself. She well remembered sneakily looking at the last page of her story books when she was a child.

It was a damp dismal sort of day, not the kind of weather to be out and about. Peter would be home soon.

Just as she thought it, she heard the Land Rover pulling into the yard.

'Hello darling,' Peter ran into the porch and quickly closed the door.

'Gosh, you are home early,' Susan said,

'I finished the job that I was doing; my last call of the day was in Shipley, so it didn't take me long to get home. What miserable weather,'

he took off his wet coat. 'I'll put kettle on,'

He walked over to the table and put his arms round Susan and Jim.

'What's my little genius doing? Reading a book?'

Jim saw his chance.

'Does the dragon catch the witch in the end?'

'You'll have to read some more, and find out,' He winked at Susan.

Soon, it was time for Jim to be off to bed. He did however; insist on reading some more of his book.

'The witch jumped down a rabbit hole and escaped,' he finally announced.

Susan picked him up and playfully shook him.

'Young man, time for your bath and then, it's off to bed,'

Jim was sleepy and happy now that he knew what had happened to the witch.

Peter went out to the barn.

The cows had wandered in because they had some nuts in their buckets and the barn was dry and comfortable.

He put a small armful of hay into the racks and topped up the water buckets. There was little else to do, just take a look over the fields.

Everything seemed to be fine. So, it was back into the comfort of the house.

While Peter had been doing the outdoor jobs, Susan had lit the fire in the lounge.

The evening was settling in fast and where better to be than curled up by the fire. Peter gave the long suffering radio a couple of thumps and it responded by bursting into life, it began to produce some pleasant, relaxing music. Soon, they were sitting in the comfortable old settee with mugs of coffee. The lamp was lit and the fire was flickering brightly.

Meg had made herself very comfortable. She was lying on the rug with her paws across Susan's slippers.

Peter noticed that the log pile was getting low. He knew that he should have brought some more in, but he had thought that maybe he could just get away with it. After all, it was summer, the wind shouldn't be moaning in the trees and the rain shouldn't be rattling against the windows. But, it was.

They both heard it at the same time. Someone was knocking at the door. Who would be about on the moors on an evening like this?

Peter went to the porch and slid back the bolts on the door.

He peered out into the gloom.

There stood a figure wearing a wax jacket and a cap pulled well down over his ears. A very wet, bedraggled looking dog stood by his side. Peter only knew who it was because he recognised the dog.

'Geoff! What a night to be out and about. Come in lad,'

Geoff muttered his thanks and stepped inside. His dog stepped into the porch and stood there, dripping and shivering. She didn't consider that a dog should go any further without permission.

Susan was surprised to see Geoff.

'Get that wet jacket off Geoff, there's a peg just inside the door.

You go and sit by the fire and I'll bring you a mug of coffee,'

Then, she noticed poor shivering Scruffy sitting in the porch and called her in to lie beside Meg on the rug by the fire. It was a grateful, but still reluctant dog that finally walked over to the fireside.

Geoff laughed.

'She's nervous because she isn't allowed into the house 'till she's been dried off with her old towel,'

Susan gave the wet dog a rub with Meg's towel.

'What brings you out on a night like this?' Peter asked.

'Well,' said Geoff, 'I was over at Windy Edge about tea time. Ted Rowlands was having a bit of trouble with a difficult calving, so I stayed on to give him a bit of help,'

'You should be farming yourself,' said Peter.

Geoff gave no answer. He bent down and stroked Scruffy. Then he said,

'Hillary has far too much to do to be a farmer's wife,'

'I suppose that Hillary is your wife?' Susan said.

'Sorry. I thought that I had told you, yes. She teaches at the village school,'

Susan remembered Geoff telling Jim that he would meet his wife.

'That's why you said what you did to Jim,'

'Yes. I assume that everyone knows everything in and around Billingbeck. Sorry. My wife is Mrs Winstanley. All the children know her obviously,' he looked thoughtful. 'Jim'll do well at the school,'

It was obvious that Geoff hadn't just come across to Nab's Head, just to discuss Jim's future prospects under the guidance of Mrs Winstanley.

He seemed reluctant to leave. Susan looked at the rain running down the window. She would be reluctant to leave the comfort of their fireside.

'What I came to tell you,' he addressed Peter, 'I was doing a bit of work at the felt mill down at Willowburn yesterday. Ralph Jones, 'he's the boss', was telling me that there is a vacancy for a tractor driver. I though I would come and mention it. The hours are flexible. If you were interested, it would give you more time to be here when you really need to be,'

'Quite honestly Geoff, I never considered a move. I've been with my firm since I left college,'

Geoff smiled.

'That's what I thought. But, if you want to find out more, Ralph'll be in the Drovers Arms tomorrow night. He's a brilliant dominoes player. I wouldn't expect you to just throw the towel in, and change jobs. I just thought I'd tell you. I'll be in the Drovers tomorrow. If you like, I could always get Ralph to let you know more about the job,' He glanced at the window. 'It's not going to stop raining,' Reluctantly, he stood up. 'If this is summer weather, I don't want to think about winter.'

Scruffy on the other hand, didn't seem to care about the weather. She was standing at the door, eager to be off. Peter went out into the porch too. He reached for his jacket and cap.

'You aren't walking down to the village on a night like this Geoff,'

Geoff didn't agree,

'It's no problem Peter. I'll be home in half an hour,'

'You'll be home in ten minutes in the Land Rover Geoff. I won't take no for an answer,'

The two men and the dog dashed across the yard and jumped into the Land Rover. Susan watched them from the shelter of the porch.

She saw the Land Rover chug out of the yard and watched it until it had disappeared among the swaying trees of the Midge Hole. Then, she closed the door and went back to the warmth of the cosy settee beside the fire.

Smiling to herself, she laid the last of the logs carefully on the fire.

As she watched the fire slowly coming back to life, she reflected on the evenings events.

Geoff had, no doubt, come all the way over from Ted Rowlands farm to tell them about the vacancy at the felt mill because he thought that Peter might be interested. She knew that jobs at the mill were highly prized in the Dale.

Most of the people who worked there had never done anything else in their lives. In fact, they usually followed their fathers and even grand-fathers into the job. But, she knew nothing about what they actually did there.

It was such a big step. She thought about the security of Peter's job with the T.V. people. They had never considered anything else, but on the other hand, If the job at the mill offered so much flexibility and relative freedom from fixed hours, it may well be worth looking into.

Such were Susan's thoughts as she listened to the wind moaning among the trees.

In what seemed like a few minutes, she heard the Land Rover pull into the yard. A dripping Peter burst in through the door and closed it, to shut out the storm.

'I'm back,' he announced.

'I can see that,' laughed Susan. 'You delivered Geoff safely home then?'

'Yes. I think he was glad of the lift. And, I met his wife, Hillary.

She seems to be a very nice woman. Typical teacher. When Geoff introduced me, right away she mentioned Jim. In a few weeks now, he'll be one of her pupils,' He took off his coat and hung it back on its peg. 'I didn't go in to their house; I wanted to be getting home,'

Peter was soon sitting before the fire, clutching a mug of coffee in two hands.

'What do you think about the job offer?' Susan asked him.

'It sounds like a possibility. The idea of flexible working hours sounds great, but we know nothing about the job. Why would a mill need a tractor driver?'

They discussed the evenings events at some length. Finally, Peter decided that he would go down to the Drovers Arms and meet the boss of the mill in order to find out more.

The Drovers Arms was in Willowburn.

It was not at all like the Black Bull. Rather, it was a very old fashioned sort of typical northern pub. Just a long grey stone building sitting back among the trees to the side of the village square.

Peter arrived shortly after eight o clock and he was struck by the lack of Land Rovers, or even cars on the side of the square. The Drovers Arms didn't boast a car park of its own.

On entering the pub through it's one and only entrance, a low door, he found himself in a gloomy passageway with a serving hatch just inside the door. Several men stood in the passage, holding pint glasses of beer.

There was a lot of smoke in the air. Peter made his way down the passage.

No-one gave him a second glance; everyone seemed to be deep in conversation. He stuck his head inside the first door.

It was a small, crowded room, rather gloomy. It had a bench running along two of its walls, they were rather like church pews, upright and uncomfortable looking with no padding on the seats, Apart from that, there was no other furniture except a few cast iron tables with circular wooden tops, and simple chairs. The walls were papered with old fashioned wallpaper, tobacco stained and totally devoid of any sort of pictures.

The occupants of the room looked up to see who had just arrived.

But, not recognising Peter, took no further interest in him.

The second room however, was different. The people sitting round the room were mostly men. There was total silence; everyone was watching what was going on in the middle of the room. There was a dominoes match in progress.

Four men sat, holding their dominoes, and watching each other very carefully. One of the men placed a domino down on the table, with a self satisfied look on his face. He sat back in his chair looking very smug.

The two men sitting opposite glanced at each other.

'Can tha do owt about yon?' one of them said.

The other one slowly laid down his dominoes, face up, and pushed his cap onto the back of his head.

'Tha's beaten me,' he said.

There was much clapping and laughter. Suddenly, the room burst into sound, everyone was talking at once.

Then, Peter saw Geoff. He was sitting over in a corner of the room. Geoff indicated that there was a space for Peter to sit down.

It wasn't easy to cross the room. Tables were close together, and all the chairs were occupied, but, finally, Peter managed to cross the room and squeeze himself into the seat in the corner.

'Didn't think you'd make it,' Geoff shouted.

The conversation in the room was still loud, following the end of the dominoes game. Peter nodded.

'I came to find out a bit more about the job vacancy,' Peter said.

'I've never been in here before. Does it always get this crowded?'

Geoff laughed.

'No,' he said. 'It's dominoes night. That's why the whole village is here, the only other time it gets crowded is when there is a darts match on, particularly, when the ladies team is playing. On those nights, there is usually a coach from one of the other villages, full of supporters,'

As the two of them were talking, they were suddenly joined by a third man. He was quite small and he had an intense and serious expression.

He nodded to Peter.

'I imagine that you are Peter from Nab's Head?'

'I am indeed,' Peter said. 'You must be Ralph?'

'I saw you waving to Geoff so I guessed who you were, I brought an extra pint,'

He carefully put down the three pint glasses that he was holding, on the table.

Geoff picked up one of the glasses.

'Ralph's in a good mood. His team won the dominoes match,'

Peter looked round the room.

'Do you know, it's just like going back in time in here.'

Ralph smiled,

'Well, we can't compete with Billingbeck,' he said seriously,

'You get all the visitors up at your end. Bit like Blackpool at weekends,'

He winked at Geoff. Then, his voice took on a more serious tone. 'Geoff tells me that you want to know about the job at the mill,'

'I certainly do,'

Peter told Ralph about his job with the T.V.company, and the need to be closer to home in the winter. He pointed out that he knew nothing at all about the mill, but that he imagined that he was a quick learner.

Ralph laughed.

He explained that the job involved moving rolls of felt from the mill to the warehouse and checking on stock.

'That's where the tractor is involved,' he explained. 'As long as the job runs smoothly, I'm not too bothered about how and when. The machines have to be cleared and the records need to be kept properly.'

It sounded ideal to Peter.

'Why don't you come down on Friday morning? I can show you round and explain the job better.'

It was agreed that Peter would be at the mill at seven thirty on the coming Friday, to be shown the job in more detail.

Peter told Susan all about his meeting up with Ralph, when he got home.

'I can look in at the mill on Friday morning,' he said. 'I don't need to be in Shipley until about ten o clock.'

Susan was quite happy to go along with Peter's plans.

They had discussed the whole thing in some detail; it was beginning to sound as though the job could be the answer to many of their problems.

Friday morning dawned wet. Not really raining, but with the familiar white mist hanging over the fields and hiding the steep sides of the Dale.

Peter was up and about early. He wouldn't see Jim this morning.

Susan made a hurried breakfast, and it was time for Peter to climb into the Land Rover and face the unknown. It was too late now for second thoughts.

As he turned off the road and drove down the steep lane leading to the mill, his thoughts were mixed.

The tyres of the Land Rover crunched on the loose stones.

Close by, on his left side, he could just make out the familiar silhouette of the hills through the mist, to his right; the ground fell away towards the rushing water of the beck. Below, he saw the outline of the mill through the mist.

Peter's first impression was of time standing still.

He saw a long stone building in among the trees with rows of small windows, some of which were lit with a soft yellowish sort of glow.

Everything seemed so gloomy among the dripping trees. To the side of the mill, he saw the rotting remains of what had once been a water wheel.

There was practically nothing left now but a few mossy bits of wood and rusty iron cog wheels hanging over the deep, dark water of the beck. It was a very strange looking place indeed. It all seemed to Peter rather like something taken from the world of Charles Dickens.

There were two men clattering over the wet cobbles towards a low green painted door with a naked light bulb over it, the only external illumination. They were wearing raincoats and caps; each was carrying a tin box which Peter guessed contained their lunch.

They didn't look at the Land Rover. They both just disappeared through the green door.

Peter parked the Land Rover and, taking a deep breath; he quickly strode over to the green door and lifted the latch.

He found himself in quite a large room. The walls were of rough stone covered with many years of whitewash. There were wooden racks containing tools and various bits of machinery. In the middle of the room was a long table. Seated round the table on low wooden benches were about a dozen men, some smoking and some reading newspapers. Each one had a large, steaming mug of tea in front of him.

Ralph was sitting at the head of the table, wearing a grey smock.

He looked up and smiled.

'Glad you could make it Peter. We'd better find you a pot of tea,'

It was obvious that the men were expecting him. They looked up and muttered a greeting. One of them went over to a corner of the room where there was an earthenware sink with a brass tap, and, on the wall, a copper gas operated water heater. It was obvious that the room was used as a canteen by the people who worked at the mill. He filled a pint pot with tea, from a very large brown pot.

Little further interest was shown towards Peter,

There was little conversation. The newspapers seemed to absorb the interest of the men sitting round the table. Suddenly, one of the men did speak to Peter,

'Can tha play dominoes?'

'Yes,' said Peter.

'Tha'll do,' The man seemed to be quite serious. He had nothing else to say. Ralph laughed.

'You should be careful Jack. Mebbe Peter can beat you,'

There were smiles round the table, but nobody else had anything to add to the conversation. Finally, one of the men pulled a huge watch from his waistcoat pocket.

'Come on lads. Time for t' start,'

They drained their mugs and folded their papers. One by one, they disappeared through a door at the back of the room.

Nothing had taken away Peters first impression of a Dickensian atmosphere.

Ralph went over to a grey steel locker and put his mug into it.

'Well Peter, I'll show you what the job involves. I realise that you need to give a weeks notice to your firm, but we can't cover the job for much longer than that. I would really appreciate it if you could make a decision as soon as possible,'

He led Peter through the main part of the mill.

It was a huge open space containing very big machines, obviously for weaving felt. Bales of raw materials were stacked up, and in the middle of the floor, rolls of felt were waiting to be removed. They walked up a low wooden ramp onto a higher level. There, in the middle of the floor, stood a grey Ferguson tractor with a low trailer attached to it.

There was only one man in the room.

'How do. I'm William. I'm t' warehouse manager,'

William was a very large chap in every way. Peter guessed his age at about thirty. Peter got the impression that William took life as it came.

'William loads the lorries,' Ralph explained.' What you would be doing is, bringing the finished rolls from the mill and stacking them according to size and type, and recording everything in various stock books. Sometimes supervising and helping out with loading lorries. Rarely, that needs to be done late, or even over weekend. That's about all there is to it,'

Peter had already discussed everything in detail with Susan. He knew what his answer was. He turned to Ralph.

'There's nothing to say Ralph, except that I like the look of everything.

Susan wants it to be my decision. It's a week on Monday if that's O.K,'

'You come well recommended. Geoff has told me about your efforts up at Nab's Head.' Ralph grinned, 'Week on Monday it is then. The job is yours,'

Peter settled very well into his new job. He soon found that he could work very much to a pattern that gave him much more flexibility.

He found that he was popular among the lads. He also discovered that there was some rivalry between the two Dale villages that he hadn't suspected.

Willowburn considered itself superior because it had a cricket team.

A couple of days after Peter became one of the 'mill lads'; he was checking the walls, accompanied by Meg and Jim.

These days, there was rarely any sheep damage. The wire had improved things a lot, plus, the sheep were slowly beginning to realise that there was a dog to be considered as they enjoyed the grass over the newly repaired walls. There was however, just one solitary sheep grazing near the top of the hill. It didn't notice Meg until she was well up the hill,

Meg ran fast, tongue out and ears up. She enjoyed her job.

The unfortunate sheep suddenly looked up, startled, and dashed for the only way out, a slight dip in the wall. Jim laughed.

'Meg nearly rounded that one up didn't she?'

Peter didn't answer him

The four young cows had caught his attention.

They were lying in a sheltered corner of the field, enjoying the morning sun.

But, Peter was concerned. For some reason, something didn't seem quite right.

He took hold of Jim's hand and walked towards the young cows.

Three of them lazily stood up and started to wander slowly down the slope.

But the fourth one didn't move. Even Jim had, by now, noticed that something was wrong.

'Why isn't Daisy standing up?' he said.

As they got closer, Daisy did try to stand. She struggled and kicked, but she couldn't get to her feet. She was breathing much faster than normal. Peter picked up Jim and hurried down the house. Susan was pegging out some washing and saw them coming down the slope.

'What's wrong?' she said.

'Something's wrong with Daisy, she can't stand up,' Peter was breathless. 'I'll couple up the trailer and take it up the hill,'

He coupled the trailer to the Land Rover and put Jim in the cab. Susan quickly put her washing in the porch and jumped into the Land Rover.

They pulled up alongside the struggling cow.

Peter pulled on the handbrake and jumped out. Daisy seemed to realise that help was at hand, she just lay still, looking at her rescuers with big sad eyes.

Peter and Susan discovered strength far beyond anything that they would have thought possible. They quickly had the poor helpless creature on the trailer. Susan stayed on the trailer to steady the young cow. She stroked its head and spoke to it softly. It seemed to reassure Daisy. She didn't struggle.

Peter Put Jim back into the cab and very slowly, drove down towards the barn. Poor Jim was very upset. He had a tear running down his cheek as he ran to his mum.

'Is Daisy going to be alright?' He clutched her leg and looked up at her,

'Of course she is,' Susan picked him up and reassured him.

'Daddy will go to the phone and tell the vet, Very soon, Daisy will be alright again,'

Jim was doubtful.

He sat on the barn floor with his arm round Meg's neck.

Meanwhile, Peter was back in the Land Rover. They had done everything that they could do. Daisy was lying on a thick bed of straw

She had been offered a drink and a handful of calf nuts, but she seemed uninterested.

'Ill be back as quickly as I can,' Peter said. 'The vet should be here soon,'With that, he put the Land Rover into gear and shot off through the Midge Hole. It took him only a matter of a few minutes to get to Appleburn Farm. He knocked on the door. Bert was away at the auctions, but his wife Annie invited Peter in, to use the phone.

'I'll tell Bert as soon as he gets home,' Annie said. 'He'll be over right away,' Peter thanked her. He rang the number of the vet's surgery. The phone rang for a few moments. To Peter, it seemed like for ever. Suddenly, a voice at the other end said,

'Good morning. Dobson's surgery, can I help you?'

Peter explained what the problem was. The voice at the other end of the phone said.

'Yes sir. If you can just tell us where you are, my partner will be along shortly,'

It all sounded very 'matter of fact'. Peter had expected that there would be a note of urgency in the vet's voice. But he didn't detect any.

Back home, everything was much the same.

Jim was sitting beside Daisy, offering her a handful of 'calf nuts', but she wasn't interested.

Susan was sitting with Jim. Her hand on his shoulder and Meg, sensing that all was not well, sat in a corner of the barn, her nose resting between her paws.

Time seemed to stand still, but, after what seemed like forever. In actual fact, it was no more than half an hour. Eventually, an old Morris

Minor came rattling along the lane through the Midge Hole. It pulled up in the yard and out stepped a young man.

He reached into the back of the car and produced a bag.

He walked across the yard giving the impression that he had all the time in the world. Peter, Susan and Jim met him at the barn door,

'Morning,' he called out. 'Pretty rough lane you've got there,'

He was a lanky fresh faced young man with a mop of curly fair hair.

He had laughing blue eyes and a friendly smile. He was wearing a tweed sports jacket and faded corduroy trousers. His tie was carelessly fastened in a loose knot. He was carrying a pair of green wellingtons.

'Well, where's the patient?'

Peter indicated the barn door,

'In here,'

The young vet paused to step into his wellingtons.

He winked at Jim.

'Let's have a look at this cow of yours. You show me where it is,'

Jim nodded and walked ahead of the vet.

The young man opened his bag and produced a thermometer. 'Bit of a temperature.' he muttered. He felt the cow's stomach.

'Has she been on grass?' he asked Peter.

Peter nodded. He glanced at Susan. She was looking worried.

The vet asked if the patient had access to any vitamin supplements. He felt the young cow's legs and pressed his fingers on the sides of her neck.

'Not been up here very long have you?'

Susan told him that they had only been at Nab's Head for a few months.

She had the distinct feeling that they should have known what was wrong with Daisy.

The vet seemed to be able to read her mind. 'Oh, it's nothing that you would have spotted. Nothing to worry too much about,' he muttered.

He opened his bag again and took out a disposable syringe and a small glass phial. He held the phial to the light and pushed the needle into it. He drew out the syringe to expel any air.

'Got to warm this slightly,'

Susan held Jim close as the vet injected Daisy in her neck.

Jim chose to bury his face in his mother's woollen jumper. He put his arms round her.

'That's it,' The young man put everything back into his bag and glanced at his watch. 'I'll come again in the morning,'

He tousled Jim's hair.

'Soon have her out and about,' he said. 'Don't worry,'

'Would you like a cup of tea?' Susan said.

'Thank you, but, no. I do have a busy schedule this morning. I appreciate the offer though,' He smiled at the little group. 'See you in the morning then. I'm off to Ottershead now,'

'Can you tell us what's wrong with Daisy?' Peter asked.

'As I say, you wouldn't have known. A spot of magnesium deficiency. But, you got me out in time; it would become serious if it wasn't treated fast. But, I am confident that she'll be fine by morning,'

He almost gave the impression that Peter had cured the cow.

As he was leaving, he stooped down and said to Jim,

"If tha't' thinkin' o' becoming a farmer young man, tha's getten a lot t' learn,'

Jim laughed at the vet's attempt at putting on a Dales accent.

The following morning, Daisy was standing again.

Her eyes were bright and she was soon chewing a few nuts. The young vet came to visit them and gave Daisy another injection. He gave

Peter a small packet.

'Put a spot of this in their drinking water,' he said.

This time, he took up Susan's offer of tea. He washed his hands and sat at the kitchen table.

'Good tea,' he said. 'Let me know if you have any more sick cows,'

Just as he was speaking, in rushed Ernie's dogs.

Susan knew that Meg would be unable to resist jumping up to greet her friends.

The vet was laughing at the behaviour of the dogs, when Ernie arrived at the door. He stepped into the room, pipe glowing as usual.

When he saw the vet, he scowled.

'Morning, young vetinary,' he muttered.

'Good morning Ernie,' the vet smiled.

It was obvious that he had had dealings with Old Ernie in the past.

'Well, I must be off,'

The young man was obviously trying to hide his amusement.

'Thanks for the tea and biscuits,' He winked at Ernie. 'Just been looking at a sick cow,'

'I know what tha's been doin' young man,'

He turned to Peter.

'If tha'd come to me, I've summat in a bottle that'd have had thy beast back on its feet in a day,'

The young vet was really trying hard to keep a straight face.

'It's on its feet Ernie… In a day,'

Peter went outside to see the vet off.

When he got back into the kitchen, Ernie was sitting, stroking Megs ear. He was holding a mug of tea.

'If tha' wants to go chucking thy money away on yon vetinary, it's up to thee. I've getten summat in a bottle,'

He was sucking on his pipe, but it had gone out. He picked up a scrap of newspaper and held it to the fire, and then he applied the blazing result to his pipe, sucking furiously. Susan was exasperated.

'We didn't even know what was wrong with the cow Ernie,' she explained.

'Well, tha' should have,' He fiddled with his cap. 'I don't hold wi' yon vetinaries,'

The expected bill from Dobson's vetinary surgery never arrived.

Peter and Susan called at the surgery several times, but the young vet was never in residence.

The senior partner, who always seemed to be there, showed little interest.

'Nab's Head? Oh yes. Young Richard attended. How is the cow?'

He seemed very concerned that Daisy had made a full recovery, but once reassured, he lost interest.

'Leave it with me,' he would say.

Still, no bill arrived.

A few weeks after Daisy's illness, the Barnards were driving past the Black Bull. Suddenly Peter swung the Land Rover onto the car park.

'We've got him,' he exclaimed.

'Got who?' Susan was alarmed at Peter's sudden, unexpected behaviour.

'Yon young Vetinary,' He pointed to a battered Morris Minor in the corner of the car park. 'I won't be a moment,'

He dashed into the pub.

.The Black Bull was quite crowded. In the long gloomy interior several farmers were having a break, standing round the bar.

There was no sign of the vet.

Over in one corner, a rather attractive young lady was sitting alone.

She looked across the room with an expression of devotion on her face.

Peter looked in the direction of her gaze.

There was the vet. He was carrying a brimming pint glass and a smaller glass full of some greenish liquid. He returned the young lady's smile, and set down the glasses carefully. It was quite obvious that no-one else in the room existed.

They just gazed into each other's eyes.

Peter walked over and coughed politely.

The couple looked up.

'Mr Barnard. What a pleasure. Won't you join us? How's my friend Jim? The future of farming in the Dales,'

'Thanks, but no. Susan is outside in the Land Rover. What I called in for was to settle our debt. We owe you some money,'

'Not too good at paperwork I'm afraid,' Muttered the vet. 'It was only a small cow. Anyway, I got a lot of pleasure from my encounter with Ernie,'

Still, no bill arrived.

Two young people struggling to survive, Young Jim's charm, a sick cow...

It all added up. Peter and Susan knew that no bill ever would arrive.

Eight

Haymaking was only a matter of days away.

Peter was worried because there were so many things to consider. Untested machinery and total ignorance about when to start cutting or when the hay could be taken into the barn. Then there was the weather, the great uncontrollable factor.

Both Peter and Susan had heard of barns burning down because hay had been got in too damp. Internal combustion worried both of them.

Surely, if it could happen to experienced farmers, they were so much more likely to get it wrong.

'I'm sure that everything will be alright,'

Susan had faith in Peter, despite his unfortunate episodes with the muck spreader.

'So am I,' Peter was really trying to convince himself.

It was all so complicated.

Peter Susan and Jim had each inspected their two meadows and they agreed that they looked like everyone else's.

Jim was worried though.

He had spotted a rabbit among the grass and he thought that it was in danger. Peter reassured him that the rabbit would be frightened by the noise of the tractor, and it would run away.

The skies were blue and the Dale had once again taken on its wonderful hazy warm feel so typical of mid July.

The stone of the farms and the endless field walls had a bleached look, and everything was basking in the gentle warmth. Tall grass was swaying in the breeze, but, to Peter and Susan, it wasn't just a breeze, it was a 'drying' breeze.

Little was seen of Ernie.

All his time was taken up by his endless scything.

Although he knew that he could rely on help now, he never slowed down.

As soon as the dew was off the grass, Peter and Susan saw him out in his fields, endlessly swinging his scythe. It may have been that he didn't entirely trust his inexperienced neighbours to get it right, his instincts told him to 'cut a bit and get a bit', as he often said to Peter.

Bill and June came to visit, just before hay time.

Bill handed Peter a heavy parcel wrapped in brown paper.

'Thanks Bill. It's just what I always wanted. Must I not open it 'till Christmas?'

Bill laughed.

'"You'd better to open it now Peter. It's something that you are going to need,'

Susan was curious. She watched Peter unwrap the parcel. It contained several big files. Peter realised that they had some connection with haymaking.

'What are they for?' he asked.

Bill explained that they were known as 'farmer's friends'.

'You'll need them. They are for sharpening the blades on your mowing machine, but, be careful, it's a tricky job. Most farmers manage to cut themselves,'

Peter hadn't thought of having to sharpen the blades. He thanked Bill and took the files out to his workbench in the barn.

Bill and Jim followed him into the gloomy building.

'There,' Peter said. 'I think that everything is ready,'

He pointed out his tools and oil can. 'Now I have some Farmers Friends, I don't think I left anything out,'

Bill couldn't help smiling at his son in laws enthusiasm.

He saw the insecurity.

As soon as they were back in the house, Jim began pushing his toy Land Rover across some imaginary fields; Meg was lying right on top of one of his fields. Why should she move? She was comfortable, and not in the least concerned about Jim's farm. Everything was so 'normal'. But Peter felt as if he were on the brink of disaster. How could everything seem so calm and peaceful in here?

The following morning, Susan was browsing through the 'Farmers Guardian'.

'Listen to this Peter," she said,' Items for sale. Assorted hand tools. Hay rakes, forks, scythe and other items,'

The address was a farm in Haworth, not too far from Widdersdale. Susan decided to ring the number when they were in Billingbeck Later.

'It sounds as though some of those items would be very useful Peter,'

'It's well worth finding out. We only have one fork and one hay rake,'

He laughed. 'If you could describe it as a hay rake. I made some new pegs, but it's held together by bits of wire. Ernie only has one rake, I think. It must be a bit like sweeping a football pitch with a yard brush,'

'OK, it's decided then. We'll ring while we are in Billingbeck,'

Jim was excited at the prospect of travelling all the way to Haworth.

'A witch used to live in a cave in Haworth,' he said.

'No Jim. That was in Knaresborough. She was called Mother

Shipton,'

'Oh,' Jim was disappointed. 'Can we go to Knaresborough please?'

'One day,' Susan winked at Peter, 'There is a well there that can turn things into stone,'

Jim looked doubtful, Grown ups believed some strange things.

Peter parked the Land Rover in Billingbeck High Street and the three of them walked to the Post Office. Susan was holding the scrap of paper with the phone number written on it, so it was Susan who went into the phone box.

Jim squeezed. in too. Peter wanted to listen, so he put his foot in the door.

Susan rang the number.

'Yes…Fishrake Farm,' boomed a voice.

Susan was taken aback. She held the phone at arm's length.

Peter didn't need to have worried about not hearing both sides of the conversation. The chap at the other end must have decided that Susan was very deaf.

'Hello, I understand that you have some haymaking tools for sale?'

'Haymakin' tools? Aye, lots of 'em,'

If the chap in Haworth had been able to shout a bit louder, there would have been no need for the phone.

'Rakes, Forks, Scythes n Sickles, all the lot,'

Susan grimaced. She thought that she was actually going deaf.

It took time, but it was arranged that the Barnard's should go over to Fishrake Farm, to look at the tools on the coming Saturday. Susan put the phone back onto its hook and stepped out into the comparative silence of the high street.

'Saturday,' She shouted.

Peter stepped back in alarm.

'Why are you shoutin'?' shouted the voice over the phone.

Jim still had his fingers in his ears.

The journey to Haworth was interesting.

Neither of them had ever been in this part of Yorkshire before.

It was very different to the Dales. A vast area of wild, sombre moors.

There were small farms and tiny hamlets clinging to the rocks, and miles of black dry stone walls stretching out over the bleak boggy land.

They had both read 'Wuthering Heights.'

Looking out over these desolate moors, it was easy to imagine that Heathcliffe still roamed abroad in the mist. Would they discover the Bronte sisters, still living in the village?

Slowly, they realised that they were lost.

Fishrake Farm seemed to be hidden away somewhere out on the moors. Then, they spotted something that looked totally out of place.

A bright red telephone box.

Susan laughed,

'You can ring Fishrake Farm. I am still a bit deaf,'

Peter got out of the Land Rover and fumbled in his pocket for change.

'I'll stay in here with Mummy,' Jim said.

'Aye. Tha't not far away when tha' sees t' bridge. Turn down by t' railway sign,'

Peter shouted his thanks down the phone.

'Why art thou shoutin'?' The owner of Fishrake Farm asked him.

Peter ran out of the phone box.

They drove on, and soon came to a black and white sign that announced 'Railway'. There was no bridge and no lane.

The only thing to do was ask somebody, but they had not seen anyone for miles. The place seemed deserted.

'Perhaps no-one lives here,' Susan announced.

Just as she spoke, they both spotted the couple with the dogs.

'There you are,' Peter said. 'Someone must live here. Who feeds the dogs?'

The couple were walking along with some difficulty.

A woman and a small girl. Each had two large, big footed, nondescript dogs on the end of long leads.

The dogs were obviously enjoying their walk, each of them pulling enthusiastically.

The woman wasn't having much of a problem because she had the advantage of weight. She was wearing a long blue coat and a headscarf that hid most of her face. Her dogs were gasping as they heaved on taut leads.

The girl however, was hanging on to her leads in sheer desperation!

Her dogs set the pace. She was red in the face and looked very angry as she cursed the eager hounds.

Peter slowed the Land Rover.

The dogs seemed to be interested. They began milling round the vehicle and putting their paws up on the door.

Susan pulled the window aside and tried to speak. She quickly ducked out of range as a wet tongue tried to wash her face.

'Excuse me. Would you happen to know where Fishrake Farm is?'

'You daft sod,' screamed the young girl. 'Look what tha's done. Tha's gone and tangled t' damn dogs up,'

The woman, who was obviously the irate child's mother, was standing to attention. She had little choice because her dogs had run round her several times, effectively tying her ankles together.

They both spent some time trying to untangle the long, leather leads.

'You damned idiots. It's thy fault,' shouted the red faced girl.

'Nice dogs,' said Jim, trying to be helpful.

The girl was now bent double, trying to pull the leads over her head.

She glared at Jim.

'Tha knows nowt about damn dogs,' she shouted.

Jim rapidly pulled his head back into the Land Rover.

Eventually, order was restored. Dignity however, was not.

The large dogs had become passive, tired of the game. They were sitting happily on the pavement, gasping and looking innocent.

The woman was enjoying her freedom and the girl was sitting down in the middle of the dogs. It was as if none of it had ever happened.

The woman looked apologetic.

'Sorry, I don't know where Fishrake Farm is,'

'Oh yes tha' does,' The girl spoke up.' It's Billy Watson's place,'

'Oh yes. Billy Watson,'

The woman pointed back in the direction they had come from.

'Just round t' bend. If tha goes down t' lane on t' left, tha'll come t' Billy Watson's farm,'

Susan thanked her, and they drove on to the next place where it was possible to turn round. On their way back, they passed the couple with the dogs. Again, they were struggling with the enthusiastic animals.

The girl glanced at them as they passed and muttered something unrepeatable.

They soon found Fishrake Farm.

They drove along the lane and, as they topped a small ridge, there it was in front of them. A neat farm, set in the middle of a clump of trees.

A boy who seemed to be about Jims age was standing in the farmyard.

He ran into the house to announce the approach of the Land Rover.

As they pulled into the yard, a large, jolly looking chap came to the door.

'Tha'll be t' folk from Widdersdale?' He spoke with a soft, gentle voice.

Peter jumped down and held out his hand.

'Right,' he said. 'This is Susan, my wife and this little chap is Jim. I'm Peter,'

'I'm Billy Watson. Come on inside. Tha's had a long run down from t' Dales,' the man said.

They followed him and, at the porch door, he stood aside and indicated that they should enter. The room was obviously the farm kitchen.

There were lots of well polished copper and brass ornaments round the fireplace. The wallpaper was rather old fashioned, with large pink roses intertwined with green leaves. As is usual in most Northern farm-houses, the focal point of the room was the inevitable big pine table. A friendly looking lady stood beside the Aga, holding the hand of the boy who had announced their arrival.

'This is my wife Mary Ann and yon little chap's Benjamin. But tha can call him Ben. We've getten two more. Girls, but they've gone t' Keighley on t' train, doin' a bit 'o shopping,'

Mary Ann spoke to Jim.

'Ben here'll take you into t' back room and tha can play wi' his toys if tha wants,'

'Come on Jim. I've getten a new fire engine,' said Ben.

Jim was extremely interested in seeing Ben's fire engine. The lads needed no further encouragement; they wandered off as though they were lifelong friends.

Peter and Susan got the impression that the couple didn't get many visitors. Mary Ann laid the table with what was obviously the best china.

She made a large pot of tea and brought some homemade scones from an earthenware container with a wooden lid.

'We make our own butter,'

The farmers were always proud of their butter and keen to hear the comments of visitors. Susan bit into her scone.

'Wonderful baking,' she said and the butter. 'It has to come from a Jersey cow. Just salted right,'

Billy Watson was delighted.

'Have another scone. Help yourselves. Don't wait to be asked lass,'

Susan found Mary Ann delightful to talk to. She knew so much about the lives of the Haworth folk and, of course, she was talking to another farmer's wife.

'Women,' Billy laughed. 'They can talk forever. Never short of summat t' talk about,' Susan laughed.

'We didn't think you'd notice. You were so busy nattering your-selves,'

Billy became serious.

'What was it you were after? You can be sure we have it, Come and look in t' barn,'

Peter and Susan followed him across the well swept yard to the largest of the stone buildings. Billy switched on the lights.

Peter and Susan glanced at each other... Electric lights!

Everything was laid out in a very orderly fashion along the far wall.

There were several good hay rakes with spare pegs, a few assorted pitchforks, a box of triangular mowing machine blades and rivets, buckets, wellingtons... even a complete electric fence. There were coils of barbed wire, posts and lots of other things.

'Wow,' Peter was impressed.

Soon prices were agreed upon and the Land Rover was loaded with a lot of stuff that would be useful back at Nab's Head.

Jim was reluctant to leave Fishrake Farm. He had found a good mate in young Benjamin.

There comes a time when decisions must be made. Things just cannot be put off any longer. A time when excuses just run out.

It was hay making time.

The meadows had been inspected and the machines were oiled and ready to go. But it hadn't been easy.

Several of the triangular blades on the cutting arm had needed replacing. Peter fastened the arm tightly in a vice and drove out the old rivets. Putting in the new blades was uncomplicated. The problem came when the whole arm of blades needed sharpening with a farmer's friend.

The angle of each blade was important. The arm full of blades resembled a row of shark's teeth.

The trick was, to complete the job, while keeping most of your fingers more or less intact. Peter had four blades to sharpen, each containing about thirty cutting edges. He managed to complete the job while still retaining five fingers on each hand, but with lots of plasters and lint on most of them.

He could do no more.

Conditions would never be better. It was now or never.

Peter coupled up the mowing machine to the tractor and drove up to the chosen meadow. He had the moral support of Susan and Jim of course.

He lined up very carefully along the edge of the meadow and grabbed the handle behind him.

He set the tractor to its favourite speed,

Old Ned had told him that a tractor was really like a horse when it was being used for towing any of the old machines.

He carefully and slowly lowered the blade into the lush grass. The blade was swishing as it bit into the grass, and it dropped smoothly, right down to the level it had been set to.

Glancing back, Peter saw, to his utter amazement, a long swathe of cleanly cut grass stretching away behind the machine.

The swishing had settled down into what Susan later described as a 'clacking' sound. It was music to her ears. When the tractor reached the far end of the field, Peter turned gently, so that he was running along the edge of the far wall, He felt almost a part of the machine. When he was about halfway down the field, he turned at right angles, so that he was running more or less across the middle. He didn't know why he did it. But, what he was doing, was mowing the top half only.

Row upon row of the sweet grass fell neatly before the swishing blade; it was turned neatly inwards by the wooden board at the end of the cutter.

As the work progressed, the air became heavy with the sweet, heady aroma of cut grass. Susan and Jim had, by now, come into the field, and were sitting in the silky grass, with their backs to the wall. Jim felt so proud of his dad. He watched as the top of the field was gradually transformed into a pattern of neatly cut swathes.

Susan knew that hay time was going to be a success. She watched Peter, his sunburned face serious as he concentrated on doing the job properly. His cap was pushed onto the back of his head and his faded tartan shirt was undone at the front, no doubt, it was because he was feeling the heat of the tractor engine.

She marvelled at the way in which everything came together. The old machine that would have been considered worthless on many farms, and the red tractor, working in perfect harmony.

Peter was so immersed in what he was doing, that he failed to notice that he had another spectator.

Old Ernie had heard the sound of the tractor and guessed that hay time had begun over at Nab's Head. He was leaning on the wall at the top of the field, watching the whole proceedings with a grin on his face.

Finally, he gave his presence away by lighting his pipe.

Even over a fair distance, and in spite of the sweet aroma of the cut grass, Susan detected the bitter smell of Ernie's tobacco. She waved to him, and he walked over to where the two of them were sitting.

'Seems t' be getting t' job right, young lady,'

'Yes Ernie. Peter does try hard. There are some things in farming that need many years of practice, but we both try you know,'

Ernie didn't answer her.

He was watching, as Peter finally cut along the last bit of standing grass, and brought the tractor to a standstill. Peter jumped down from the tractor and lifted the cutting arm, so that it clicked into its socket, in the upright position.

He waved at the little group of spectators and gave them a very over-done theatrical bow. Then, he threw his cap into the air and shouted,

'Yippee,'

Susan and Jim laughed at his silly antics. Even Ernie grinned.

There was Peter, standing in the middle of a field of hay, acting like an absolute idiot. It was sheer exuberation; Susan thought that her husband was allowed his moment of madness.

Ernie, on the other hand, puffed on his pipe and watched Peters antics without comment. Jim joined his dad, by doing his own version of the celebratory tomfoolery.

Peter walked over with a happy smile on his face.

'Who said we couldn't do it?' he said.

Ernie was inspecting the field. He bent down,

'Tha's wasted some,' he muttered, 'Tha could have set thy blade lower,'

To Peter and Susan, everything looked perfect. The stubble seemed to be shorter than the stubble on Ernie's chin.

'I just knew that it wouldn't be right by your standards,' Peter said,

'I think it was a damn good effort. There's tons of hay out there,'

He bent down and picked up an armful of hay.

Ernie finally allowed his face to break into a smile.

'Oh, Tha's not done badly. I see that tha took notice of what I were telling thee, and tha's only cut half o' t' meadow,'

Peter couldn't remember what Ernie had told him,

'Oh yes Ernie. I only cut half of it,'

'It'll rain in a couple o' days. Tha'll just get yon hay into thy barn,'

Peter looked up into the perfect sky. The wind direction hadn't changed, everything was exactly as it had been for the last few days.

'How do you know it's going to rain?' Peter asked him.

'Because I'm a farmer,' Ernie winked at Susan. 'Thy should know too,' He looked carefully at the meadow, 'Tha should have cut lower,' he muttered, 'Tha's wasted some. Anyway, I'm wastin' time; I've plenty o' work to do,'

Without another word, he walked off across the field.

He didn't even look back. Just a wave of his stick, and he was gone.

'Well, at least you knew about the rain,' Susan said.

They both laughed. It was time for lunch. All three set off towards the farm, Jim in the middle, holding hands with his mum and dad and being swung along.

After lunch, Peter was out in the meadow again. This time, using another of their wonderful machines. The job of this monster was to shake up the cut grass and turn it over, so that the warmth of the sun and the wind could begin the process of 'making' the hay.

The grass was thrown up behind the machine, and formed great fluffy rows of loose grass behind it. Susan picked up a handful of the drying grass and threw it at Jim. He responded by chucking such big armful at Susan, that he tripped over it, and fell, laughing, into a heap of grass. Soon, a sort of pillow fight had developed, with Susan cheating, and burying Jim under great heaps of grass.

By teatime, it was obvious that everything was drying out.

The meadow gradually changed colour from the bright green that it had been. into a soft sage colour. There was nothing more to be done that day, so, after supper, they walked through the Midge Hole to the place here they could see across the Dale. Everywhere, the fields were changing appearance.

The slope down towards the village was gradually being transformed from the acres of tall, swaying grass that they had become accustomed too, into a patchwork of colours.

There were the soft greens of cut grass drying, and even pale yellows, where hay had already been gathered in. One big difference that was very noticeable was the fact that, most of the bigger farmers used baling machines, and so, a lot of the fields contained, what looked like hundreds of green bricks, from above.

The following morning, it was Peter's intention to get down to the mill early so that he could clear any backlog of urgent work and get home in time to do some more hay shaking. But, he found that Ralph and William had already done all the urgent jobs.

'We didn't expect you to come today Peter,' said Ralph. 'Go home and don't come back until that hay's safely in the barn.'

He put his hand on William's shoulder.

'William here knows about the importance of getting your hay in.

You can always do him a good turn some time. He helps his brother out with his pigeons sometimes.'

William nodded violently in agreement.

Peter was surprised, because William had never mentioned that he even had a brother.

'I could wait in t' pigeon cote an' clock a few in, comin' back from t' race.' He had a happy smile on his face.

Peter felt guilty because he could easily have got to know more about William's interest in Pigeons.

'Of course William. I'd be happy to cover for you,' he said.

By eight o' clock, Peter was home, and, after explaining to Susan that he had the next few days free, he was out in the meadow again.

After lunchtime, they were using the huge, iron wheeled rake to drag the hay into 'cops'. Row upon row of dry, sweet hay was soon transformed into large heaps that they had heard Old Ned describe as 'cops'.

After teatime, the trailer was coupled up to the tractor and it became a means of carrying the hay to the barn.

Jim was placed in the middle of a large mound of hay.

He soon scooped out the middle and made himself a natural nest. Meg jumped in with him and the two of them were safe while Peter and Susan forked the hay onto the trailer. They soon discovered that some skill was involved. If they didn't get it right, as Peter moved the tractor along the rows of cops, large amounts of hay kept slipping off the trailer.

'We keep losing it,' Susan was laughing. 'By the time we get back to the barn, we'll have an empty trailer.'

Peter laughed too.

'If we keep on losing it, we'll be hay making at Christmas.'

But they soon got the hang of it. When the trailer was ready to be taken down to the farm with its loads of hay, Susan would stay on top of the load and Peter would grab Jim and pass him up to Susan, so that the two of them could ride all the way into the barn.

The huge cool barn looked rather like a gloomy cathedral.

Surely, it would hold all the hay in Widdersdale?

It proved to be a hot, dusty job unloading the trailer. Jim was taken to a safe spot, well out of the way of the swinging pitchforks.

'I'll play with Big Teeth,'

He was well aware of the danger of being anywhere near the hay area, and he was happy to cuddle his rabbit.

Load after load was moved into the barn, but they needed to dry some areas a bit more.

Slowly, darkness crept in across the Dale.

In some places, farmers were still working in the light of the head-lamps of tractors and Land Rovers, but up at Nab's Head, they didn't own one of those wonderful tractors with lights. As they brought down the last load, they suddenly realised that they were relying on the light of the moon.

And so, finally, job was abandoned.

Jim had his bath and a late supper. It was a very sleepy, but happy, red faced little boy, who finally clutched his teddy bear and instantly fell asleep. While Susan made supper, Peter put the trailer alongside the overhanging roof of the barn. His final job was to refill the fuel tank.

He noticed that, in the moist, still air of the evening, his senses seemed to be sharpened. Somewhere in the distance, he could still hear the snarl of a tractor. The aroma of the 'cooking' hay and the background smell that was always around the barn, Cows and creosote, nettles and old wood, and the warm tractor engine, with its unmistakeable sweet smell of tractor fuel. Peter smiled to himself.

It was pure nostalgia. If he could bottle those smells, surely he could sell thousands of bottles?

In the kitchen, they sat and ate their big chunky sandwiches and sipped hot tea in the glow of the oil lamp.

'Not much to get now,'

Susan's face glowed in the light of the lamp. 'Tomorrow, we should have the field cleared by lunchtime. Then, it all begins again,'

Peter reminded her about Ernie's weather forecast.

'Old Ernie can't be right all the time,'

Susan laughed, 'Oh, I'm so tired. My hair is full of hay seeds. A good scrub is what I need,'

She went over to the stove and filled the kettle because there was no hot water. It had been far too hot a day to light the fire.

The following morning dawned bright and clear, with the promise of yet another glorious day. Susan decided to catch up on a spot of housework because Jim would be in his land of dreams for some time. Peter, on the other hand, was out very early.

After a final shaking, he soon had the last of the dry hay collected up into cops and, by the time that Susan and Jim arrived in the meadow, he had the trailer coupled up. By lunch time the very last of the hay was on the trailer. They both looked over the meadow, now looking almost shaved, the very last of the hay had been gathered up using the wooden rakes, and thrown onto the top of the last load.

'It's a satisfying feeling, isn't it?' Susan said.

'I don't ever remember doing any work that gave me such satisfaction,' Peter put his hand on her shoulder.

"Cheeky beggar. Who do you think you are, Mr Farmer? Jim and I did most of the work. Anyone can sit on a tractor,'

Peter picked Jim up and gave him a hug.

'I must agree. Jim here ran the farm while, all we did was a bit of hay making,' Peter drove down the slope with the final load, while Susan and Jim followed, Susan carrying a couple of rakes.

As Peter backed the trailer into the barn, he suddenly felt the first of the huge cold spots of rain on his back. By the time he had shut down the tractor engine, Susan and Jim came running across the yard,

They were laughing as the heavy rain soaked them both.

Peter looked up, and saw a large, black cloud creeping across the sky.

'What did Ernie say?' Susan laughed as she pulled Jim into the shelter of the barn, 'Cut a bit and get a bit,'

After lunch, Peter put on his old waxed jacket and, accompanied by Meg, he went over to Folly Edge, to see how Ernie was getting along.

Ernie was standing in his cowshed doorway, looking up at the dark sky when Peter arrived at the farm. He was, as always, puffing away at his pipe.

'Well, young man. Did tha get thy hay in?' he greeted Peter.

'Aye, we did. You certainly got the weather forecast right,'

Ernie just smiled.

'Hay in t' barn's money in t' bank,'

It was some days before the rain relented, and the hot sun returned.

It gave Peter time to catch up on his work at the mill and do some extra work that he wasn't expected to do, as a sort of 'thank you', to Ralph and William.

The rest of the hay was gathered in with no further problems, the barn did in fact fill to the very top of the rafters, But, over a few weeks, as the hay dried out, the level dropped under the weight of the stack. Much to the relief of Peter and Susan, it also cooled down very considerably.

Now, it was time to assist Ernie with his haymaking. Peter put a new blade into the mowing machine and oiled all the moving parts. The old baked bean can was removed from the top of the tractor exhaust pipe. It had been put there to stop rainwater from going down the pipe. Peter gave a couple of swings on the starting handle, and the engine instantly burst into life.

Meanwhile. Susan had been busy too; she had prepared a packed lunch of ham and Wensleydale cheese sandwiches, which she placed in a wicker basket, along with two large flasks of tea and several bottles of beer.

She went on ahead of Peter, with Jim and Meg.

Ernie was, as she had expected, Busy with his scythe, working just as he had done all his life.

He knew that Peter would be along with the mowing machine, but, right to the end, he followed his instincts.

When Peter arrived with the mowing machine, Ernie walked over to his barn and laid down his scythe.

'So, tha's come wi' yon new fangled machine to cut some grass, has tha?'

What was really happening, perhaps without Ernie realising it, was that he was being brought into the mid twentieth century!

He didn't trust it at all.

'Getten some lunch Ernie. Come on. Stop what tha's doing and let's get summat to eat,' Susan used the local dialect sometimes, for fun.

Ernie knew that, because after all, he wasn't a local man himself.

He grinned at Peter,

'By gum Peter lad, t' main thing about hay time is havin' a good woman about,'

They sat on an old bench outside the barn and Susan handed round huge ham and cheese sandwiches.

The dogs looked on in hopeful anticipation.

'There's a jar of pickles somewhere in the basket Ernie,' Susan said.

'By heck lass, tha't a good farmer's wife,' Ernie muttered with his mouth full. When all the food was gone, a bottle of beer was produced.

'Nay. Tha'll not work wi' that inside thee. What tha wants is a drop o' cold tea,'

Peter pointed out that there was no hard work to do.

The tractor that thought it was a horse and the 'new fangled' 1920s mowing machine would do all the work.

Ernie would have none of it. He had an old cider bottle full of cold tea. So be it. Jim was offered some cold tea, but he declined the offer because he had seen his Mum put a bottle of lemonade in the basket.

Finally, it was time to cut some grass. Suddenly, Ernie seemed to have acquired a great deal of knowledge. He walked slowly round the machine, examining various bits in some detail.

Finally, he stood up and said,

'How do you lower yon blade?'

Peter showed him how to set the cut lower, and alter the tilt of the blade.

'Tha cuts too high,' Ernie said.'Wastin' thy grass. Take it lower,'

Against his better judgement, Peter set the blade so that it was shaving the ground. Ernie examined it, and he seemed satisfied.

'Tha can cut ten swathes.' he announced.

'Ten?' Peter asked him, 'Why ten,'

'It'll take me a couple of days t' get yon into t' barn,' Ernie was serious.

Peter laughed.

'I'll bring the shaker over, and the rake. It'll be ready for taking in, in a couple of days, even if I cut the whole lot,'

The old man looked doubtful. He glanced over towards the western horizon.

'Well, I recon we'll get a couple of fair days,' he muttered.

Everything went according to plan, and a couple of days later, they were throwing the last of Ernie's hay up into the far corners of the barn.

The beams up there were thick with dust and ancient cobwebs that had collected over very many years.

Ernie knew that he had enough hay to get him over a long, hard winter.

He put his hand deep into his pocket and pulled out a handful of coins.

'Here Jim lad, put this in thy money box,'

He was well satisfied.

Nine

The big event finally arrived!

Susan had been trying to persuade herself that it wouldn't, but it was inevitable. The time has arrived for young Jim to begin his academic career. It was time for him to take his place among the other Dales children at Billingbeck County Primary School.

A letter had arrived at Nab's Head Farm, informing the parents of Mr James Barnard that the West Yorkshire Education Authority looked forward to the pleasure of James Barnard's attendance at the aforementioned school at the beginning of the autumn term.

The aforementioned James Barnard was in fact, looking forward to the event. He had talked of little else since the completion of haymaking.

There was a shop in Beddington that sold blue jumpers with 'Billingbeck County Primary School' emblazoned on the front, along with the school emblem, a ram's head. Jim was also fitted out with a couple of pairs of grey trousers and some gym shoes, two yellow shirts and a school bag.

He chose one with a big picture of a tractor on it.

The moment that they arrived home, Jim couldn't wait to try on his uniform. He stood there with a happy smile on his face,

Everything was rather too big for him and very new looking.

Peter noticed that Susan, although she was smiling, was also wiping a tear from her eye.

He put his arm round her shoulders.

'He's only going to the village school,' He said.

Perhaps men just didn't understand such things?

Finally Susan Picked Jim up.

'Oh, we are so proud of you, young man,' She put him down and whispered to Peter,

'Where has my baby gone?' Suddenly, Peter did understand.

Finally, the big day arrived.

Susan helped Jim to dress in his uniform; she noticed that he was careful not to drip any egg on his new jumper.

Because of the importance of the occasion, Peter had arranged to start work after Jim had been delivered to school. He didn't want to miss the occasion.

When they arrived at the school, they found twelve proud mothers and a couple of rather embarrassed looking fathers standing at the gates with their offsprings. The fathers, for the most part, wore the blue over-alls and cloth caps worn by farmers. Peter realised that he was wearing the same.

Just a grown up version of the kid's blue jumpers really.

He nodded to the other men.

'Good morning everyone,' boomed a voice from the direction of the school door.

It was Mrs Evans.

They had met Mrs Evans on several occasions.

She was the head teacher. Her 'school' voice didn't match her appearance at all. She was quite young and had very fair shoulder length hair worn loose, and she was wearing a long knitted pullover.

Susan had commented on her collection of long knitted pullovers, they had seen her standing in the school playground many times, and she always wore a long woollen pullover. They all seemed to be hand knitted. It seemed that Mrs Evans enjoyed knitting.

Mrs Evans smiled sweetly at the children.

'Would you like to follow me children? We'll go and meet Mrs Winstanley.'

The children surged forwards. Peter was reminded of the charge of the Light Brigade.

'Parents too.'

Mrs Evans beamed at the small assorted gathering of parents.

Susan smiled at Mrs Winstanley.

They knew her, of course, as Hillary, Geoff's wife.

She was of medium height, with fair hair. Very much a country girl. She was wearing a blue striped top and dark slacks.

She seemed very much at home among the children; Susan had the impression that Mrs Winstanley was well able to handle the wilder elements among Widdersdale's younger community.

She told the children to sit on the floor in a semicircle round her chair. There was a bit of pushing and nudging as the children jockeyed for the best places right in front of Mrs Winstanley.

'Quiet now please,' she clapped her hands. 'Now children, I am Mrs Winstanley and I'm going to be your teacher.'

'Aye, we know that,' muttered a red haired lad who had decided to sit on his own in a corner of the classroom.

Mrs Winstanley smiled at him.

'And, I know you Arthur. Now, please will you come and sit with the other children?'

Young Arthur was quite amenable to the request.

He strolled casually over to the middle of the arc of children and pushed his way in amongst them.

'Now, when I point to you, I want you to tell me your names.'

Mrs Winstanley pointed to the first girl.

It took a few moments because the child had been deep in a whispered conversation with the girl sitting next to her, but finally, the girl responded.

'Betty Arkwright,' shouted the child.

'Very good,'

Next she pointed young Arthur.

'Tha knows my name. We live next door to thee,'

'Yes, But perhaps the other children don't know your name,' pointed out Mrs Winstanley, with some patience.

'If they want t' know my name, they mon ask,' he muttered.

'Please,'

'Oh alright,'

He stood up for effect and brushed a bit of toast off his jumper.

'I'm Arthur Hebblethwaite from next door to Mrs Winstanley,'

He sat down again, muttering under his breath.

When Mrs Winstanley pointed to Jim, he shouted,

'James Barnard from Nab's Head,'

He stuck his thumb up to his parents.

Soon, all the children had been introduced.

'Thank you children,' Said Mrs Winstanley. Then, to the parents,

'I think we understand each other very well. There won't be any problems,' She smiled. 'Just remember to come back at half past three,'

All the adults, reluctantly and a bit self consciously waved to their offsprings and wandered outside.

Susan wanted to call at a couple of shops so, as the morning was fine, she decided to walk home, and the couple parted company.

Peter drove off to the mill, while Susan walked across the road in the direction of Mrs Eckersley's pie shop.

It seemed to be a very long day to Susan.

She was used to having Jim at home and the silence was very strange.

Susan was very aware that everything had changed. Jim was now a schoolboy.

Even Meg was quiet. She lay in the porch, constantly looking towards the Midge Hole, as though she expected Jim to appear at any moment.

Susan was outside the school gate well before half past three.

She joined the little group of parents who were waiting for their children.

'Good afternoon Mrs Barnard,'

Susan turned to face the woman who had spoken to her. She didn't recognise her.

'Tha doesn't know me. My lass is Betty Arkright, She started this morning, same as thy Jim. By gum, it's been a long day wi'out yon lass,'

'Yes indeed,' Susan smiled. 'It's been so quiet, hasn't it?'

'Oh no,' Mrs Arkwright pulled her face. 'It's been just t' opposite. Young Betty looks after t' other two. I've been doin' some washing, and t' other two have been crawlin' all o'er t' floor,'

Just as Susan was about to reply, a bell rang somewhere deep inside the school. Instantly, the door burst open and out shot the children.

All the new children were carrying a picture of a buttercup. All, that was, except Jim.

He looked fed up.

Susan knelt down and held her arms out.

'Where's your buttercup?' she asked him.

'Mrs Winstanley took it off me and pinned it on the wall,'

Jim wasn't happy.

Susan laughed,

'That's because it must be a very good picture,' she explained, but Jim seemed unconvinced.

At home, Jim enjoyed playing the role of 'hero of the day'. He sat, legs swinging, eating his tea.

'What did you have for lunch?' Susan asked him.

'Round meat and some potato and some peas,' He smiled, 'and orange juice and apple pie,'

Whenever Peter or Susan asked him what he had had for lunch, the answer was invariably, 'round meat'.

Tuesday was a perfect autumn day. Peter went off to the mill very early and Susan set off over the fields down to Billingbeck with Jim.

On the way down, they met a girl carrying a new looking school bag.

Susan recognised her. She lived in a cottage above the village.

'Morning Jim,' she called out.

The two children fell into conversation as they walked together down the lane. The girl walked along beside Susan, swinging her bag.

'How does t'a like livin' up at Nabsyead?' she said.

'Oh, we like it very much thank you,'

Susan found the girl quite amusing. She was skipping along, swinging her bag, and talking as if to herself.

'My dad thinks tha' must be crackers, livin' in that old place,' she said. 'We used to play in that old place up yon. It's got no windows,'

Susan assured her that they did have windows and that; Nab's Head was quite cosy.

The girl muttered something, but didn't look very convinced.

A few moments of silence, then the girl said,

'My mum was late for work this mornin' again,'

'What does your mother do?' asked Susan.

"She's a stripper,' The girl didn't look up.

Susan had met the girl's mother. She was a rather portly lady with a missing tooth. She didn't impress Susan as looking much like a stripper.

'Are you sure?' Susan said.

'Yes. A stripper. Tha' knows, in t' mill down at Oakendale. She strips wool of t' bobbins,'

They walked together down the road to where the school crossing lady was standing. Children were arriving from all directions, converging on the village school.

Suddenly, Jim lost interest in his mum and the girl.

He had spotted Arthur Hebblethwaite and a few of his new mates.

It was final proof that young Jim was quite happy to be at his seat of learning.

Peter didn't arrive home until about five thirty, most days.

Until then, Jim took over the role of farmer. He walked over the fields with his friend Meg and they chased off the odd sheep. Being a dog gave Meg an advantage. Then, when the job was done, they both had a good roll about in the grass and raced each other home.

Jim tried to cheat by shouting.

'Meg, sheep!' but Meg knew the game. She ignored him, and always got home ahead of Jim.

Gradually, almost unnoticed, the days began to shorten.

Autumn was a beautiful time of still, misty mornings and clear, bracing days.

But Peter and Susan noticed gradual changes. Leaves took on a dry, brittle look. Gradually, they changed colour to the reds and golds of autumn, while the fields took on the drab look of winter.

There was little sign now of the activity of summer, the spring lambs were almost fully grown and fewer cattle were to be seen in the fields.

There was an air of expectancy, everything seemed so still.

The hay was in the barns and already, the frenzied activity of haymaking was just a distant memory. The beck ran, cold and swift, its waters dark and mysterious as they rushed beneath leafless trees, down towards the distant river.

Elderflowers disappeared, to be replaced by lots of purple berries. There were a lot of blackberry bushes between Nab's Head and Willowburn Farm. Susan and Jim spent hours gathering the ripe, juicy fruit; Jim's couldn't resist popping the very best of the blackberries into his mouth.

Very soon, most of his face was purple. But, Midge Hole, lived up to its name. As the sun set, it was better to leave the area, or risk getting bitten by hordes of midges.

At this time of the year, the young cows didn't need telling that it was time to be wandering down towards the barn in the evenings.

When the evening was warm and the cows showed reluctance to abandon the fields, Susan soon discovered that a very efficient way to get them trotting down the hill, was to rattle a bucket with a handful of 'cattle nuts' in it. Of course, Meg was always on hand, waiting to move them on a bit.

Ernie seemed to enjoy passing on bits of information, and then there was always Old Ned, in the Black Bull.

'How's yon young 'uns getting along?' he would ask. 'Don't forget thy vitamin blocks an' plenty o' good clean water,'

Susan noticed that a lot of the good advice was given to her by other mothers, who knew little things that she may have missed, from a lifetime in the countryside.

Ned knew that Peter was working in the mill most days, and it was Susan who brought the cows in.

'Tha's doing a good job lass,' he said. 'What with gettin' young Jim off to school an' lookin after t' young 'uns,'

'No more that lots of other women on the farms,' Susan replied.

'Aye, but they were born to t' farms,' Ned pointed out. 'Thee, tha's not been up yon for a year yet. Tha' does very well,'

'What about me?' Peter said.

'Oh, thee, if tha's got any sense, tha does what tha t' told. It's wimmin that makes all t' big decisions,' He winked at Susan.

They soon noticed that Jim brought home his own bits of country lore. It wasn't only the children who lived on the farms; the ones that lived in the villages all seemed to know a great deal about rural matters. It was all part of growing up in the Dales.

Mrs Winstanley was, after all, married to a chap who knew most things about the Dale. If things were not going too well somewhere, Mrs Winstanley usually got to know. She appreciated the children's problems.

After all, they were part of the Dale, and one day, they would be the farmers and villagers.

Sometimes, she would talk with Susan about the future of the Dale.

'These children are going to have to adjust to changes,' she said. 'Nothing stands still, and the Dales won't escape progress,'

She smiled ruefully. 'I don't much like the idea of progress here. Is it progress, or is it just sometimes, just change for the sake of change?'

Susan had similar opinions,

'We can't fight this so called progress, but our children are going to lose out on a lot of things that have been a part of Dales life for hundreds of years. It worries me,'

Mrs Winstanley smiled,

Susan looked thoughtful.

'Perhaps the outlook isn't as gloomy as we think. After all, I don't see these children growing up to throw away all the things that matter so much. We are a stubborn lot. I mean us Yorkshire folk,' she laughed. 'Young Jim certainly knows where he is going,'

Susan often used to call at the village shop when she called to pick up Jim from school. She would sometimes buy an extra loaf for Ernie and a few extra groceries.

She didn't forget to purchase a red tin of Ernie's tobacco and a box of matches.

She knew that Ernie wasn't getting any younger and he didn't look after himself properly.

Ernie, on the other hand, seemed to have an endless supply of 'black treacle' toffee in little brown paper bags. He would produce a bag from his pocket when he called at Nab's Head.

'You shouldn't keep giving Jim black treacle toffee,' Susan scolded him. 'It's not good for young teeth,'

'Nay,' Ernie said. 'Its molasses. I were brought up on it. We always had a barrel of it in t' barn, for mixin' wi' t' cattle food. I used to spread it on a chunk o' bread.'

Susan could see that it was pointless trying to reason with Ernie.

'On Christmas day, we're having a little family get together,' she told Him. 'We would be honoured if you would come over to Nab's Head for Christmas dinner,'

Ernie nodded and thanked her, but, a few days later, he arrived at Nab's Head with a big brown paper wrapped parcel.

'I've brought a Christmas present for Young Jim,' he said.

Susan knew then, that Ernie would not be coming over for Christmas dinner.

Jim announced, a few weeks before Christmas, that they were rehearsing for the school Christmas play.

'Oh and where do you come into all this?' Susan asked him.

'I'm singing 'All Things Bright and Beautiful', and I'm a shepherd,'

He looked grim. 'Bill Raynard says I'll make a lousy shepherd because we don't have any sheep,'

Susan reassured him that he would be a very good shepherd.

'I have to have a towel on my head,' he grumbled. 'Can I borrow Meg as a sheepdog?' he asked. Hopefully.

'I don't think that Meg would be well behaved on stage,' his mother said.

'Why do we sing 'Forgive us our Christmases?' Jim asked.

'I don't know,' Susan was bewildered. 'I wonder why?'

'It's in the Lord's Prayer,' Jim said. 'Give us our daily bread and forgive us our Christmases as we forgive them that Christmas against us,'

Susan laughed and explained to Jim that, perhaps he had got it wrong.

After that one little mistake, actor Jim rehearsed happily and enthusiastically.

Slowly, but relentlessly, the autumn weather crept across the northern hills.

It was quite pleasant to see the mist hanging over the Dale.

Some days, it was like a huge lake below them. All that could be seen were the tips of tall trees that seemed to grow out of a smooth white cloud below.

The wet mist clung to clothes and eyebrows rather like a fine spider's web. Living in the high places was sometimes rather like living in a world that was separated from the rest of civilisation.

A week before Christmas, Peter Susan and Jim visited their parents in Guiseley. The first call was to Arthur and Ada.

Jim insisted on bringing his towel, so that he could do his shepherds bit and sing 'All Things Bright and Beautiful'. He put the towel on his head and said his lines very seriously,

'Is that Baby Jesus?' and 'Look at that bright star,'

He sat on his grandmothers knee and explained,

'Bill had that part, but he kept saying, 'Is yon babby Jesus in t' crib? So they made him into a wise man,'

Jim knew very well how to charm Arthur and Ada to maximum effect.

'I wanted to take Meg as a sheepdog,'

He usually got his own way with his grandparents, but not this time. They were visiting Billingbeck for the school concert and Peter had booked a meal at the Black Bull. A sort of get together for Arthur and Ada and Susan's parents Bill and June.

While Peter and Susan were visiting Guiseley, they also called at Bill and June's home.

Jim took the opportunity to do his acting bit all over again.

He made a final effort to get someone on his side about Meg becoming an actress.

'Not a good idea,' smiled June. 'Imagine what would happen if somebody whistled. Meg would go shooting off into the audience,'

Jim gave it some thought.

He giggled and said,

'All the children would love that,'

'Maybe, but I don't think that Mrs Evans or Mrs Winstanley would be very pleased,'

Jim realised that he was fighting a lost cause.

'Adults just don't understand,' he thought.

'This lad of yours has ideas about making a Hollywood epic out of the school concert,' Bill said seriously.

'Maybe he has a brilliant career waiting for him over there?'

Susan laughed at the thought of Jim taking the American film industry by storm.

'You've forgotten Meg. Where does she come into all this?' she said.

'Lassie did it, Why not Meg,' Peter was amused.'

'The two of them could easily take the world by storm. Maybe Mrs Evans could do the directing? And why not include Old Ernie? He has two dogs,'

Finally, the day of the concert arrived

There were to be two performances, one in the afternoon and one at half past six, because the school hall wasn't big enough to hold everyone that would be wanting to see this well established and much looked forward to production.

Jim arrived at school with his mum just after lunch.

Susan had volunteered to assist with the many tasks that needed to be done in order to be sure that everything would proceed smoothly.

'Or so it was hoped'. Already, harassed staff and helpers were making last minute adjustments to costumes, scenery, etc.

'Please miss, Henry's stolen my towel,'

One of the shepherds appealed for justice.

There was a thump and a howl! The irate shepherd got his towel back, but, in the process Mary's basket went flying across the room.

David recieved a left hook from Mary that sent him flying across the room.

'Yon baskets for putting Baby Jesus in,' Mary screamed.

'Children!'

Mrs Evans raised her authoritative voice, and all became silent… for about ten seconds.

'Give yon basket to me, or I'll gi' thee one in t' chops,' snarled Mary in a loud whisper.

She got her basket back and her voice became angelic again.

Mrs Evans beamed at her pupils.

'Now children. Do we all know what we are doing?'

'YES MISS!' It was unanimous.

'I know what I'm going to do. Give Sam 'ebblethwaite a thick ear,' muttered a ruffled David.

Slowly, the hall began to fill up.

Parents were eager to see their little darlings on stage.

Some children who had moved on to the Senior School at Ottershead had come along to watch the performance. A lot of these older children were the same kids who could be seen around the farms, dragging buckets of 'Lambing Nuts' around, or striding over the fields 'wi t' dog'.

Mrs Strickland wasn't one of the regular staff of Billingbeck School.

Her special talents lay in the field of music.

The school had a battered piano that stood in a corner of the hall, and Mrs Strickland could play it. Mrs Strickland was only too happy to oblige.

She lived in a pretty cottage close to the school, and was noted for her garden. She had the best vegetables and the most spectacular flowers in the Dale.

Mrs Strickland's one big problem was the fact that, over the years, her hearing had rather deteriorated.

As a result, her enthusiasm for pounding the piano keys was unstoppable. Mrs Strickland made the children shout.

Even when the piano subsided into silence, they continued to shout.

When it came to Jim's line about the bright star, he faced the audience and roared,

'Look at that bright star in the east,'

No doubt, sheep several fields away glanced at the school.

Mrs Evans was wearing one of her more spectacular hand knitted creations. Susan thought that the design may have been inspired by one of Mrs Strickland's floral displays.

To the intense relief of everyone concerned, the concert went more of less without a hitch. A few lines were forgotten, but Mrs Winstanley was at hand, hidden behind the curtain, to help out. Whenever a child forgot the script, loud whispering could be heard from behind the curtain.

Perhaps, if any of the audience had not been from Yorkshire, they would have had some difficulty understanding phrases like,

'As 'ta coom fro' Isrial?' or 'What's yon wise man's gawpin' at t'? Gold in t' sack,'

When it was all over, Mrs Evans stepped onto the stage and, surrounded by the children, thanked all the staff and members of the PTA for the work that they had done, plus the parents for the time that they had put in.

Special thanks went to the children. Finally, the lights went up and everyone started to talk at once.

Soon, children appeared wearing their outdoor clothes.

Henry gave David a thump for thumping him, and honour was satisfied.

Both Susan and Peter's parents had been invited to spend Christmas at Nab's Head. Susan spent most of Christmas Eve preparing food and making sure that the house would look at its best for their guests.

'You can get from under my feet,' she told Peter,

'I can get organised much better by being left alone. You do something useful like bringing logs from the barn,'

Peter had been trying to sneak a few mince pies out of the kitchen.

'Please can I have a couple of mince pies for Jim?' he pleaded.

'Ah, so that's your game. Mince pies for you and Jim,'

Susan put a couple of pies on a plate and poured a glass of milk.

'They are for Jim,'

She handed the plate and glass to Peter.

Peter stacked logs in the ingle nook and, assisted by Jim, dragged the big Christmas tree into a corner of the room.

The tree was spectacular. It had arrived courtesy of Geoff and his friends in the forestry. The room was decorated with holly and lots of balloons and the lamps were trimmed and filled with paraffin.

Jim's favourite bit was helping to lay the presents under the tree.

There were a considerable number with his name on them.

But, of course, most of his presents delivered personally by Father Christmas.

There they were, on Christmas morning, stacked up beside his bed.

He had placed a glass of milk and a mince pie on his bedside table for Father Christmas. The glass was empty and the pie had a huge bite missing.

If further proof were needed, the carrots that he had provided for the reindeer had gone.

'He's been,'

Jim came dashing down the stairs very early in the morning.

'Oh, come and look. I got some presents,'

Susan was putting the finishing touches to laying the table. Jim pulled at her skirt impatiently.

'Who's been,' she teased him.

'Father Christmas,'

Peter and Susan glanced at each other, making sure that Jim noticed.

'We'd better go and look what's going on,'

'Just look. All those presents. Can I open them?'

Jim was jumping up and down

'Let's wait a little while, Very soon, all your grandparents will be here.

I wouldn't be surprised if you don't get something else. Wouldn't it be fun to open everything at the same time?'

Reluctantly, Jim agreed.

He sat in the window from where he could keep his eye on the Midge Hole.

He didn't have to wait very long.

'They're here,' he suddenly shouted. 'The car's coming down the lane,'

They all went out into the yard and watched the green Ford chugging carefully along the track. As it drew into the yard, Jim ran across to it.

Bill wound down his window.

'Good morning young man. You seem to be pleased to see us,'

Both couples were loaded up with parcels. Susan hugged her mum, and Ada, who didn't often hug her son, picked Jim up.

'My, you seem to grow more each time we see you,' She planted a kiss on his face.

'Come on. Let's go into the house,' Susan said. 'Did you know that Father Christmas has been?'

Everyone looked surprised at the news.

As soon as everyone was sitting comfortably, it was time for Jim to open his presents. Of course, some of them were from Arthur and Ada, and others were from Bill and June, but they looked amazed when Jim opened the parcels.

'I wonder where the racing car came from,' Smiled Arthur.

It was he who had wrapped up the red racing car in its fancy paper.

'Father Christmas of course,'

Jim knew where everything had come from, but he read the little card that was attached to the wrapping paper.

'It says, 'To our little grandson Jim, from Ada and Arthur' on here,'

He looked up. 'I think that you gave this to Father Christmas?'

Dinner was late… something of an old family tradition.

But, Ada had taken charge, so everything went smoothly.

Peter and Susan had imagined that Jim's favourite toy would be the 'farmyard set'. But the red racing car was soon speeding round and round the rug.

The unfortunate Meg was lying right in the middle of the race track. She tried grumbling at Jim, but it had no effect.

You couldn't stop an important race, just because a dog had decided to lie down in the middle of the track. Meg got the message eventually, and moved to the other side of the rug, with much huffing and grumbling. She flopped down and glared at Jim, as much as to say, 'I ain't moving from here,'

The singsong was another old family tradition. Arthur gave an excellent rendering of 'Bless this house', and everybody joined in

'On Ilkley Moor baht hat'. With gusto. The unofficial anthem was, no doubt, being sung all over Yorkshire. There were a few party games and Jim was allowed to stay up later than usual.

Then, as Susan brought in the coffee and mince pies, and put the sherry on the table, plus a few bottles of Bill's favourite 'Newcastle Brown', the mood settled down, as they remembered Christmases gone by and old friends.

All too soon, it was all over.

Jim had nodded off on the settee, clutching his battered teddy bear, and surrounded by his new toys.

Inevitably, it was time to say goodbye. Nobody disturbed Jim.

He just got a few gentle kisses on his forehead.

There was frost on the windscreen of the old Ford.

Peter and Susan watched, arms round each others waists, as the car bounced along the track and disappeared among the trees. The last that they saw of it was the glow of the headlamps among the bare frosty branches.

'It's been a great Christmas,' Peter said, softly.

'Isn't it wonderful, being a family, all together,' Susan wiped her eye.

Now. There was nothing but darkness among the trees.

Peter carried Jim upstairs and Susan tucked him up cosily with his teddy bear.

Finally, the young couple sat by the fire, arms round each other.

The ticking of the clock seemed very loud as they silently watched the flickering fire. Susan couldn't help thinking about Ernie, sitting alone in his gloomy home... And, how many others?

'We are lucky people,' Susan whispered.

Ten

Now that the winter was upon them, Susan found herself considering the year ahead.

She always seemed to take stock of her life around the New Year.

Perhaps most people did, she thought. It was rather like being given the chance to sit down before a blank sheet of paper.

What an exciting prospect.

'I can't really believe that we have been here for so long,' she told Peter. 'The winter was only just over when we started working on Nab's Head. Now, here we are, on the edge of another winter. Remember how excited we were, settling down for our very first night up on the moors?'

'I certainly do,' Peter allowed his mind to drift back over the months. "In some ways, it seems as though we have been here for years, So much has happened. Jim's a schoolboy and we're farmers. Well, sort of farmers. But I agree with you, Perhaps it seems like a long time to me, because we have done so much,'

'I don't think we need to worry too much about the winter. We have the Land Rover and your working hours have changed. Above all, Jim's settled well at school, He's looking forward to the winter, all the snow. I must admit that I'm quite looking forward to the snow,'

Jim had been left out of the conversation, but he had no intentions of not having his say.

'I'm going to make a snowman,' he announced, 'And, I'm going to put some snow down Arthur Hebblethwaite's neck,'

'Maybe, he'll put snow down your neck,' His mum said.

'I'll hide behind Mrs Winstanley, she'll protect me,'

Jim seemed very confident.

The New Year celebrations at the Black Bull were only a couple of days away. It was one of Widdersdale's big social events of the year and people had been talking about it for weeks. Practically everyone would be there.

Peter and Susan had arranged for Jim to spend the New Year with Arthur and Ada.

Jim was quite excited at the prospect of going to Guiseley for a couple of days and, of course, getting a lot of his own way. He insisted on taking most of his new toys.So, on the morning of New Years Eve, he was delivered to the little terraced house on the outskirts of Guiseley.

Ada was busy polishing her already immaculate home. She saw the Land Rover pull up outside, as she was polishing the windows.

She opened the door and held her arms out to Jim.

'I hope you remembered to bring some toys,'

She picked him up and, as always. Planted a kiss on his cheek.

'Oh yes,' Peter told her. 'He remembered to bring some toys,'

There was hardly anywhere for him to sit.

The table had been laid in the parlour and all the brass ornaments were gleaming ready for the New Year, Tea was always quite a formal affair at the Barnards home. But, New Years Eve was special.

The parlour was for important occasions, and the gas fire had been lit early because Ada was conscious of a need to take away the slight chill and to give the room a more 'lived in' feel. She was aware that the home of Bill and June was rather different.

Perhaps, a little more in tune with the times?

Susan smiled, she couldn't help but notice that, at the end of the table where Jim would be sitting, there was a good supply of trifle and cakes within easy reach. Jim's expression showed that, he too had noticed.

Conversation over tea was mainly about events that had happened in and around Guiseley during the year that Peter and Susan had been away.

Ada seemed quite concerned about Jim's welfare over the coming winter, but Susan assured her that he would be very well looked after.

Arthur didn't have very much to say at all, he seemed content to listen to everyone else.

Finally, it was time to say goodbye to Ada and Arthur, and, of course, Jim.

'Be a good boy, won't you,' Susan said.

Ada put her arm round her grandson.

'Jim's always a good boy,'

Jim put on an angelic smile that didn't fool Peter and Susan.

It didn't take long to cover the few miles to Beddington.

As they turned into the narrow Dales road, they saw several cars on the road ahead.

'I think everyone is going to the Black Bull tonight,' Peter said.

'If they are, Ned'll be busy trying to save us a seat,' Susan laughed,

'Betty'll be with him and he'll have to wear his tie. Perhaps that's how we'll be one day,'

'If that ever happens, I'll put the tie round your neck and pull it tight,'

As they spoke, two of the cars ahead pulled into the square at Willowburn.

'Must be visiting relatives, or going to the Drovers Arms,' Susan said, 'Maybe we will be able to sit down,'

It was a dark night, the headlights of the Land Rover picked out the winding road ahead. As always, startled sheep ran up the slopes, away from the light and the engine noise. Peter wondered why they never got used to the lights of vehicles. They didn't seem to.

As they drove towards Billingbeck, they could see the coloured lights of the Black Bull. It looked like a small oasis in the middle of a vast desert of darkness. The car park was quite full, but Peter knew from experience just where he would be able to squeeze the Land Rover in.

Once inside, they found themselves in a different world.

.Everyone seemed to be talking at once and there was an atmosphere of expectancy that seems to always be in the air on New Years Eve.

The bar was very busy. People seemed to be crowded round, trying to order their drinks at the same time.

Bert was trying to work out who was next to be served, and, unusually, his wife Rita was also behind the bar. Peter noticed that there were also a couple of young ladies helping out. He looked more closely. Surely he was mistaken? He turned to Susan,

'Do you recognise the fair haired young lady behind the bar?'

Susan had been greeting a few friends that were standing by the door.

She looked towards the bar.

'Surely I'm mistaken. It can't be,'

'No. You aren't mistaken. It is who you think it is,'

The first time that they had seen the fair haired girl was at the chambers of Mssrs Ackroyd, Jones and Ackroyd, Solicitors and comissioners for oaths.

She was the young secretary of Mr James Ackroyd.

'Well! I wouldn't have believed it,' Susan laughed.

'It seems that there is more to that young lady than meets the eye,' Peter was amused.

While Peter joined the queue at the bar, Susan made her way into the back room. Music was provided by the same local group that had been playing the 'Beatles' music on the folk night when Peter and Susan first heard of the abandoned moorland farm that was for sale.

Ned had saved them a couple of seats. And, Just as Susan had expected, he was sitting upright, wearing his tie, knotted correctly under his chin. Unusually, his cap was not on his head. Instead, his rather unruly white hair was combed flat. Betty was wearing a dark dress with a cameo brooch at her neck. Her hair was, as usual, brushed back rather severely, but she had a smile on her face that rather belied her somewhat sombre appearance.

'Nice to see you Susan,' she said.

'And you too Betty, Peter is trying to get served at the bar. Crowded tonight, isn't it,'

'Yes indeed,' Betty looked round the room. 'I notice that the farmers are sitting down for a change. That's because they have their wives with them, I suppose,'

'Some of them often have their wives with them, but I suppose it's different. It's New Years Eve; they can't spend the evening talking about farming matter,' Susan said.

'I don't suppose they want to. New Year is all about family, isn't it,'

As they were talking, Peter arrived, balancing two pint glasses and two smaller ones very carefully, trying not to spill any of the contents.

Ned, who, up to now, had been sitting quietly, greeted Peter warmly.

'By gum Peter, we thought tha weren't coming,'

Peter explained that they had been over to Guiseley.

'We took Jim to Arthur and Ada's for the night,'

Soon, the band, who had been taking a break, were back onto the stage and, placing replenished pint glasses on the floor beside them, prepared to resume the evenings entertainment.

The room went quiet for a moment, as everyone waited to hear what the next number would be.

The red faced lad with the sleek, overlong hair and the dazzling smile picked up his microphone.

'And now, a song that you all know. 'I wanna hold your hand', which I am sure you all know,'

Peter and Susan smiled at each other; they remembered the last time they had listened to this song in the Black Bull. They had been sitting in the same spot all those months ago.

The mood was one of rather boisterous contentment; the room gradually became even noisier.

Ned took the liberty of loosening his tie. It didn't go unnoticed by Betty, but she just smiled to herself.

Only too soon, the fingers of the clock crept towards midnight.

Susan thought about Bill and June, and wondered what they would be doing. She knew that they were having a quiet evening by the fireside.

They had always preferred to be at home over the New Year.

Arthur and Ada would be having a quiet time too. Jim would have, long ago, been tucked up in bed. Then, her thoughts turned to Ernie.

What would he be doing? And the hundreds of other people who didn't have anyone. It must be a lonely time for them, full of memories.

'Cheer up Susan. You look as though you just lost a tenner,' Peter guessed Susan was thinking about.

They often commented about their uncanny ability to read each others thoughts.

Everyone had been checking the time every few minutes.

Suddenly, Bert and his wife Rita entered the room. As they walked across to the stage, the band stopped playing.

Bert raised his hands, indicating for silence.

'I make it two minutes to midnight,' he said, holding his pocket watch and looking at the dial.

Gradually, everyone stopped talking.

'One minute left,' he looked round the room.

'That's It. Happy New Year everybody,'

The room erupted into one big cheer.

Tables and chairs were moved and the band struck up with a not very tuneful version of 'Auld Lang Syne'.

Peter and Susan grabbed each other and, like most couples in the room, kissed and wished each other a happy new year.

Once again, Bert held up his hands. It took considerably longer this time, before he could speak.

'I want to just wish you all a very Happy New Year again, and to thank you for coming along this evening. And. I want to thank these lads behind me for providing us with a bit of good entertainment,'

There was a round of applause for the band. 'Aye, well, that's about it,'

Bert muttered. 'Oh yes. Just one other thing. If any of you have anything left in your glasses,'

He raised his own glass, 'A toast to the new Widdersdalians, Peter Susan and young Jim up at Nab's Head,'

There was a lot of laughter, and a few glasses raised in the direction of Peter and Susan.

Peter muttered,

'I'll have him for that,'

Susan laughed and raised her glass to everyone in the room.

'By gum, that a grand lot. Thanks for putting up with us,'

Ned had something to say. He wobbled uncertainly to his feet, despite Betty's efforts to restrain him.

He put his hands on the table for support,

'Tha's forgotten Jim's rabbit!'

He wasn't sure why he had said that, but it seemed to him that it needed to be said. He slid slowly back down into his seat.

Finally, the Bull's Head began to empty.

Betty helped Ned towards the door and stepped out into the darkness.

The cold night air was in sharp contrast to the cosy warmth of the pub.

To Peter and Susan, it had a clean, sweet quality that was exhilarating.

There was no moon, and the few lights of the village did little to detract from the strong feeling of remoteness that closed in across the Dale on such a night.

Tonight, it was perhaps, more noticeable.

The small group of revellers that gathered in the pool of light in front of the Black Bull were stepping into the very beginning of 1966.

The gathering seemed to be reluctant to go their separate ways.

There was much back slapping and laughter. It was as though the New Year had indeed wiped the slate, and presented everyone with a chance for a new beginning. Bert and Rita had joined their friends outside, and were busy shaking hands and wishing everyone a happy new year.

One of the farmers who Peter didn't know very well came walking rather unsteadily over to Peter and Susan. He was wearing a very long overcoat and his cap was rammed tightly on his head.

He put a friendly hand on Peter's shoulder and spoke, slowly and deliberately.

'Tha knows summat. When tha were thinkin' o' buyin' Nabsyead off Sam Turner, I thought tha were a bit daft. Comin' from t' town an' goin' livin' up yonder,'

He looked closely at Susan, as though he was having difficulty focusing his eyes,

'Thee too lass. But, tha's makin' a go of it! I wish thee all t' luck in t' world,'

Before they could reply, he staggered off and was lost in the crowd.

Ned laughed.

'That was Sid Rowlands. I never heard him admit that he were wrong before,' he laughed, 'Tha's got t' approval of Sid now. Tha must be doin' something right,'

Suddenly, he fell silent and looked up into the dark sky.

A hush fell across the little gathering.

Huge, soft snowflakes were drifting down into the light. It was the final magic, the perfect ending to a perfect night. Faster and faster, the great white flakes fell, seeming to gather speed as they drifted closer to the earth.

'Oh,' Susan gasped, 'If only Jim was here now,'

She was trying to catch one of the snowflakes. The whole gathering was silent. It was almost as though no-one wanted to be the first to break the magic of the moment.

By now, the snow was falling heavily. Peter looked round.

Gradually, everyone was turning white. Susan wasn't wearing a hat and her fair hair was taking on the appearance of a soft, white halo.

A few people were trying to gather up enough snow to make a snow-ball,

But, the evening couldn't go on forever. Slowly and reluctantly, more and more people gradually drifted away towards their homes, disappearing into the enveloping darkness.

Peter and Susan too, were reluctant to leave behind this dwindling gathering, but, Ned and Betty made the decision for them.

'Can't stand here all night,' Ned muttered.

Susan could not help smiling; his cap looked rather like a white sponge cake on his head.

'Goodnight then, we'll be off now. This snow isn't going to ease off,' Betty said.

As Peter and Susan walked to the Land Rover, Susan tugged at Peter's sleeve. Peter looked round.

Mr Ackroyd's secretary was just coming out of the Black Bull. She waved to Bert Eckersley.

'I'll be off now Uncle Bert. Glad I was able to help out,'

'Very much appreciated Edith. Thanks. Tell your mum that I'll be round when we close this afternoon,'

'Well, I never. So that's how she came to be behind the bar,' Susan laughed.

The Land Rover swung out of the car park, and into a world that was very rapidly disappearing under a white blanket.

The vehicle crunched the snow, compacting it beneath its tyres, and the headlights penetrated the blackness ahead. Thousands of snow-flakes drifted gently down, illuminated as they came into the arc of light in front of the Land Rover. They seemed to gather themselves together and make a final rush towards the windscreen, only to be swept aside by the wipers.

But, the snow was winning. Soon, Peter was peering through the only bits of the glass that were swept by the wipers. Everything Else was becoming covered in a coating of snow.

'It's absolute magic,'

Susan wiped a spot of condensation from the inside of the screen.

'It's like driving along through a tunnel isn't it,'

Peter was concentrating on his driving.

'Look out for the turning,' he muttered. 'If we miss that, we'll be heading for oblivion. We'll be driving halfway across Yorkshire,'

'There is nothing I would rather do,'

Susan was enjoying the journey.

Peter peered through the small clear arcs in the windscreen,

'Right now, there's nothing better than a good pot of tea and a warm bed,'

'O.K.' Susan laughed, 'Have it your own way,'

The following morning, it was still snowing.

Not quite as heavily, but there had been enough falling during the night to cause deep drifts to form in the hollows and behind the field walls.

The journey to Guiseley was unavoidable. Jim had to be brought home.

Arthur and Ada would, by now, have seen the snow, and would be wondering just how much deeper it would be in Widdersdale.

Ada particularly, would be feeling anxious. She would be worrying about the safety of Peter and Susan.

The roads were not bad enough to be beyond the capabilities of the Land Rover. It was rather fun, hitting the drifts and watching a wall of powdery snow, as it was thrown into the air.

Jim was on edge. He too had seen the snow.

Although very little had fallen in Guiseley, Jim rightly suspected that there would be much more of this wonderful, exciting stuff on and around Nab's Head.

'It'll be good to see Jim again,' Susan said, as they drove along the road that led to Guiseley, 'Isn't everything quiet without him around,'

'He's only been away for one night,' Peter laughed.

'I know. But I miss the young Tyke,'

Susan used the word 'Tyke' deliberately.

The real term Tyke was used to refer to a Yorkshire person, but, it was often used to describe children in an endearing way.

'Oh, don't worry. He'll have been living the life of a Lord. I'll bet he doesn't want to come home,' Peter said.

Jim was sorry to leave his grandparents, but the thought of the snow that was waiting at Nab's Head proved too much for him.

He had a few days of the holidays left. He spent most of the time outdoors, throwing snowballs at Susan and Meg. Meg seemed to think that they were balls, and kept trying to catch them. Only to snap at nothing, just a powdery ball of snow.

Each time, she did exactly the same thing.

Jim rolled over and over in the snow, laughing at her. But, Collies don't share the humour of humans. She failed to understand what Jim was laughing at.

Peter helped Jim to build a huge snowman. It had one of 'Big Teeth's' carrots as its nose and stones for eyes. He snapped a twig and made the snowman a pipe, and then he put one of his old caps on top to keep it warm.

Jim laughed.

'It looks just like Ernie,'

The next few days were bright and clear.

The skies were blue and the snow lay across the land, giving everything a soft and gentle appearance.

It was cold enough to not thaw the snow that had fallen among the bare branches of the trees; Susan looked over into the Midge Hole and saw a beautiful tracery of lace draped across the dark woodland.

There was just one other social event for Jim before he went back to school. It was the annual party laid on by the Widdersdale Young Farmers for the children of the Dale. Jim had been looking forward to it for weeks, and he wasn't disappointed.

Peter and Susan drove him over to Ottershead and pulled up outside the village hall. The moment that Peter stopped the engine, they could hear the noise of the party in full swing.

Jim was the first in.

He was wearing his favourite shirt. The only reason it was his favourite shirt was because Betty Edwards had told him that she liked it… and Jim liked Betty Edwards.

They were met at the door by two of the Jarvis brothers, looking rather embarrassed because they were wearing paper hats.

'Hello Peter, Hello Susan,' Jacob Jarvis greeted them, 'How's yon tractor?'

Peter remembered his mud bath.

'Oh, once it had dried out, it was fine,'

Jacob smiled at Susan.

'I bet you were glad when Peter had dried out,'

They didn't see much of Jim over the next couple of hours.

They knew that he was somewhere in the middle of the screaming mass of children.

Most of them lived in remote places and they hadn't seen each other since before Christmas. Jim had as much to say as any of the kids.

They each ate their share of sticky cakes and wobbly jelly.

Arthur Hebblethwaite and Betty Arkwright were sick, finally, they each were given a bag, containing even more sticky cakes.

Altogether, it had been a highly successful evening.

Gradually, the Dale returned to normal. The snow returned and made life very difficult in many ways.

It wasn't the heavy snow that had given the Dale its mantle of white over the New Year. It was fine stuff. Driven by the wind and piling up in great drifts against buildings and blocking the roads overnight.

There was little traffic in or out of Widdersdale.

The severe weather continued through January and most of February, then came the thaw.

Peter struggled to get down to the mill, sliding and slipping in the deep, half frozen ruts along the lane.

One morning in mid February, it was very misty and everything was hidden behind a cold curtain of wetness. Susan was up and about ahead of Peter. She looked out through the widow, across the mist shrouded yard and smiled.

'Do you know what day it is?'

Peter panicked. Had he forgotten an anniversary? Someone's birthday?

Finally, he had to admit that he didn't know what day it was.

'Thursday?' he said, hopefully.

'It's one year today since we first set eyes on Nab's Head. Remember the weather then?'

Towards the end of March, the very first signs of spring slowly began to appear. There were a few baby lambs about in the lower lying fields.

'Let's hope that the snow doesn't come back. Or worse still, the cold east wind. It never knows when to stop blowing,' Peter said.

Susan watched the lambs playing, jumping about, and watched by their mothers.

'The sheep farmers'll soon have them indoors, I suppose,'

Although it was only just after two o clock, Peter was home.

He had a quiet couple of days at the mill and he had been able to get away early. He glanced at his watch. He didn't want to be late getting down to the school to pick up young Jim. Susan had made some sandwiches and a pot of tea. She was sitting at the table with the 'Farmers Guardian', spread out in front of her.

'There's a farm sale coming up. Sally End Farm. Dispersal sale of livestock, machinery and land. The land to be sold in three lots of approximately fifty acres each. Lot three to include the house and buildings,'

'We knew about that,' Peter said, 'its Walter and Amy Holt.

They were talking about it in the Black Bull. They decided to move over to Bridlington. They don't have any children to carry on with the farm, and they want to have a few years to themselves. They've done more than their share of the hard work,'

Susan looked again at the advert.

'The sale is on the fifteenth of April. I wouldn't mind going to it. It's in the big barn at the farm,'

'Why not? But, you aren't thinking of expanding, are you?'

Susan laughed,

'I've noticed that your belly seems to be expanding these days,'

'Good living,' Peter held his stomach in.

The day of the sale finally arrived.

Peter and Susan arrived early, so that they could find somewhere to sit on one of the straw bales laid out in the big barn.

Most of the local lads were there. Some of them would be bidding for cattle or bits of machinery, but a few of them would, no doubt, see a chance to expand their land. Particularly the ones who were close to Sally End.

There were, as always, a few strangers too.

The sale started at ten thirty sharp.

The auctioneer was well known to most of the farmers.

Mr Andrew Hodge was a very popular character, noted for his sharp wit and even handed fairness. He had installed his desk from the auction house at Beddington. His secretary, Mrs Johnstone, was also well known to the farmers.

She sat, very upright and prim; her large glasses gave her the appearance of an owl, the impression heightened by her white, short hair and the practical brown smock that she was wearing.

Mr Hodge's gavel rapped sharply on his desk.

'Good morning,' he beamed at the assembled crowd. 'We'll make a start. We have a considerable number of lots this morning,'

The cattle were the first lots to be auctioned, followed by assorted machines, ranging from a Land Rover. Tractors and machines, to boxes of tools.

Then came the big one... The land.

Peter and Susan had discussed who would be most likely to be interested in the land.

Jacob Jarvis had land close by, as did Sam Turner. Because it was low land, both farmers would be almost sure to be bidding.

'Lot one hundred and thirty four. Forty six acres of prime pasture land comprising of five meadows with sound walls and a good water supply,' Andrew Hodge looked round.

'Will anyone start me at six thousand pounds?' There were no hands raised. 'Alright then, five, five hundred,'

Much to everyones surprise, a small chap who was standing by the barn door held up his catalogue.

'By the door, at five, five hundred,' Heads turned.

Who was this stranger?

The man standing by the door didn't look like a farmer.

He was wearing a dark, pin striped suit and a trilby hat. His swarthy face was totally devoid of expression.

No-one had expected the bidding to start at five thousand five hundred pounds.

There was only one other bid. Sam Turner went up to six thousand.

Immediately, the stranger raised his catalogue.

'Six thousand five hundred pounds, the gentleman by the door.

Any advance on six thousand five hundred pounds. Going. Going, for the last time… Any advance on six thousand five hundred,'

His gavel hit the desk top.

Mrs Johnstone recorded the stranger's number.

The same thing happened with lot one hundred and thirty five.

The final lot was the remaining forty four acres, plus the farmhouse and buildings.

There were two other strangers in the crowd, both of them glanced at the chap by the door, but his expression gave nothing away.

Peter was intrigued.

A few outsiders had recently started to buy small farms in the Dales.

But, this was different. There was something about the calm, almost indifferent attitude of the man who had just bought most of the land of Sally End Farm.

Susan leaned towards Peter,

'I think that our friend over by the door is going to be in on this one,' she whispered.

Peter nodded.

There was a hush in the big barn. Even the impassive Mrs Johnstone was showing interest.

The contest didn't last long, the two other strangers each put in a couple of bids, but each time, the man by the door raised his catalogue.

Mr Andrew Hodge seemed to pause rather longer than usual, but finally, his gavel tapped the top of the desk. Mrs Johnstone recorded the number of the new owner of Sally End Farm, and it was all over.

Instantly, the buzz of conversation began. Who was the stranger? Did anyone know him?

He didn't talk to anyone. As soon as the paperwork was completed, he just walked casually over to a white Jaguar and, throwing his briefcase onto the back seat, he drove off with little regard for the cars suspension.

'What an amazing auction,' Susan said.

One of the farmers overheard her.

'Dust tha know who yon chap is?' he asked her.

Susan assured him that she hadn't seen the new owner of Sally End before.

The farmer shook his head.

'Won't be long before we see more of yon chap,'

It was almost time to pick up young Jim from school.

Peter and Susan sat in the Land Rover, talking about the extraordinary events of the day.

'Sam won't be too happy. He really wanted a bit more land in the valley bottom,' Peter said.

'I got the impression that the stranger would have gone much higher with his bidding. No-one had a chance really. He obviously came to the auction with the intention of buying Sally End regardless of the cost,' Susan was looking at the school gates.

'We'll see some big changes, I think,'

Peter spotted Jim among the rush of children escaping from school.

'Here he comes. Ask him what he had for lunch,'

'Round meat,' Jim said, seriously.

Talk in the Black Bull was of little else but the auction, but no-one had any idea who the well dressed stranger was.

'Not short of a few bob,' Old Ned muttered.

'Nor art thou,' grinned one of the farmers.

'If I had the brass that this chap has, I'd be off t' Spain. A bit o' sunshine,'

But, for all the gossip. Everyone had to just wait and see.

Nothing happened for several weeks, and then, it all started to happen.

Workmen moved into Sally End Farm in droves. The house was transformed.

Large picture windows were fitted, the garden was landscaped with rockery and mature bushes, new fences and gates appeared, even where they were not needed. A large new building was erected, and a gravel drive was laid.

It was Geoff who found out who the stranger was.

He had been doing a spot of work at the mill, and decided to walk home across the old Quarry.

As he was passing the boundary of Sally End, one of the workmen who was busy digging out a post hole, spotted Geoff and, laying down his pick, he pushed his cap onto the back of his head and lit a cigarette.

'Evenin' mate,' he greeted Geoff. 'Nice day,' he glanced at his watch.

'Bit of overtime,'

Geoff detected no trace of Yorkshire accent.

This chap was from Birmingham.

'I haven't seen any of you guys in the Black Bull,' Geoff was indirectly leading the man on. He knew that he was about to get some interesting information.

'No, we go home when we finish work,' the man said. 'The lads who are doing the big jobs are contractors. They come from Leeds, but some of us come from Birmingham. That's where Mr Bradley is,'

Very soon, Geoff knew all about 'Mr Bradley'.

Naturally, it didn't take long for the customers of the Black Bull to find out about Mr Bradley.

Mr Bradley owned a large factory in Birmingham.

He did indeed have a bit of spare 'brass'! In fact, by Dales standards, he had quite a lot.

He wanted to become a farmer and he wanted to make a break from the midlands for reasons best known to him. He had a wife and two children, but the children were away at boarding school.

By mid May, Mr Bradley and his wife were living in the Dales.

They had obviously made huge sacrifices in order to struggle along in their new rural environment. The Jaguar had been replaced by a new Range Rover, and Mr and Mrs Bradley had bought green wellingtons.

One evening, the Range Rover pulled onto the car park of the Black Bull. Mr and Mrs Bradley were about to become part of the community.

But, it didn't happen. They chose to sit alone and merely answer the polite greetings of the villagers with what appeared to be mild indifference.

Then, one day, Mr Bradley visited the cattle auctions.

He very soon discovered that paying top price for Sally End Farm wasn't the end of it.

He seemed to have an interest in purchasing some Hereford cows.

A few had been delivered to Sally End in a large cattle truck that had come from the Midlands. Mr Bradley had bought wisely.

The cows were stocky and well formed; now, he was going to try his hand at bidding at the Beddington auctions.

Peter said a polite 'good morning' to Mr Bradley, but he got little response. Mr Bradley did nod to a few of the locals, and received a friendly nod or two in return. But, the moment he put in a bid, another bid was made. Up and up went the cost of Mr Bradley's cows.

It was customary to have lunch at the auctions cafe.

Peter was greeted by a few of the other farmers as he ordered his meal.

A space was made for him at the long, pine table.

'How's yon young lad, Jim?'

Peter found himself sitting opposite to Jacob Jarvis.

'Oh, he's fine thanks. Susan keeps us both under control,'

'Same as yon wife o' mine,' Jacob laughed. 'If tha does what tha t' told, tha'll be alright,'

Peter was intrigued about the high prices that Mr Bradley had paid for his three Herefords.

'Bidding went a bit high on those Herefords, didn't it,'

The answer came from Bert Dickinson, who was sitting at the end of the table.

'Peter, Tha't' a Yorkshire chap, and tha's been in t' dale now long enough to know what's going on. If someone comes into t' Dale thinking that they can spend brass to become farmers, us lads'll be happy to take a bit o' their brass,'

But, as it turned out, Mr Bradley was no fool.

That evening, Peter and Susan decided to visit the Black Bull.

Jim had dashed off to the games room and Peter had replenished Ned's glass, everything was quite normal.

The group of farmers were standing, listening to Sam,

He was telling them about Mary's sister. She had recently been on a visit to Willowburn Farm, and poor Sam had been pushed into the background by the constant talking of Mary's sister.

He wasn't getting much sympathy from his audience.

'It's about time someone put you in your place Sam,' Susan said.

Sam was just about to answer when Mr Bradley walked into the room.

It was quite obvious that Mr Bradley had something to say, and nothing was going to stop him. He walked across the room with a look of grim determination on his face. Right up to the farmers.

He held up his hand.

'I've got something to say to you chaps,' He looked unsure of himself. 'Those Herefords. They seem like good stock,'

'Oh aye,' Muttered one of the farmers 'Tha's getten good beasts,'

Mr Bradley smiled ruefully.

'Look lads. I know I made a bad start. I'm a pretty successful businessman. I honestly thought that I could run a farm without much thought.

After all, as I say, I've done alright. But, I can honestly say that I never came across such businessmen as you Dales farmers. I want to apologise.

I know I'm losing 'brass', and I know that I've so much to learn.

We want to fit in. You guys can teach me a thing or two. It's not easy for me to say this, but I met my match,'

There was a moment of silence, and then Sam said,

'Tha'll do for me lad," He held out his hand. "I'm Sam Turner from

Willowburn Farm. Tha trod on a few toes. But, it takes a man to say what you just said,'

Everyone was surprised when Old Ned spoke up.

'Tha made thy mistake when tha thowt that thy brass could get thee through. All t' local lads would do, is take thy brass off thee,'

Everyone laughed.

'Well, I guess that I can take my place among the real businessmen? My name is Ben Bradley. Wife's name is Maureen. Is there anything I forgot?'

'Yes,' a voice muttered from deep among the farmers, 'Tha forgot that we buy our rounds o' beer in turn. It's thy turn to get t' beer in,'

Eleven

Slowly, the final traces of winter were obliterated from the landscape.

Where there had been mile upon mile of greys and browns often hidden behind drifting mist, gradually the fresh greens and gentle colours of spring crept across the Dale, and on the high moors, the soft purple and white of the heather.

Gnarled old trees in the more protected and south facing slopes were the first to reluctantly take on the mist of gentle green, as the buds came back to life.

The beck still ran dark, deep and swiftly, its clear waters, cold and sparkling in the spring sunshine. The very stone of Nab's Head, just like all the other farms in the Dale, seemed to become alive.

Widdersdale had survived another winter.

Peter and Susan had been to the Cattle auction at Beddington.

After an early finish at the mill, Peter had picked Susan up in the village and, together, they had waited for Jim outside Billingbeck school. They put him in the middle seat of the Land Rover and informed him that he was going down to the auctions. Jim was delighted. He liked going to the auction because he had a lot of friends among the farmers who gathered there.

But on this occasion, they were only calling in to purchase a few bags of cattle feed. The cafe was still open, and so they decided to have a meal.

They soon found themselves in conversation with Ted Rowlands and a couple of Lancashire farmers. 'Or rather, Jim did'.

By the time they left the auctions, the sky was already darkening.

Although it wasn't much after half past six, the day was grey and miserable; the place to be was by the fireside. It was one of the spring days that the sheep farmers didn't want. It was quite cold, mainly because the wind was driving rain across the land in violent gusts.

Peter smiled to himself. The apparently un-repairable leaking door of the Land Rover was, as usual, allowing a steady drip of water to soak his right boot. As he drove along the flooded road through Willowburn, the place seemed to be deserted. But, suddenly, he spotted a lonely figure trudging along the roadside.

He knew immediately who it was. He recognised the long, black coat and the hat that looked so out of place in the awful weather.

It could only be Mrs Lord.

Local people knew very little about Mrs Lord, She seemed to only be around on Thursdays.

'Isn't that Mrs Lord?' Susan peered through the rain splattered windscreen and spotted the bedraggled looking figure trudging along in the rain.

'It certainly is,' Peter said. 'We can't allow this,'

They knew that Mrs Lord lived at the 'Sky House', a remote farm, high above Windy Edge. They also knew that Mrs Lord had just alighted from the last bus of the day from Leeds.

Each Thursday, Mrs Lord took the early bus out of the Dale bound for Leeds. She always carried the two carpet bags, and they always seemed to be full, both on her journey out of the Dale and later, when she returned.

She arrived back home on the six thirty bus, the last one out of Leeds.

She nodded politely to anyone that she happened to see, but she always chose to keep very much to herself.

It was Old Ned who first told Peter and Susan where Mrs Lord lived, he knew as much about her as anybody.

'She's been goin' t' Leeds on t' bus for fifteen years,' He told Peter and Susan. 'No-one knows why. She was married once. They went up to t' Sky House many years ago, an' they were raisin' sheep. Then, Mr Lord died. Everyone expected that Mrs Lord would move out of the remote moorland farm, but she stayed on,'

Ned shook his head sadly.

'That were fifteen years ago,'

'Oh, what a sad story,' Susan said, 'I wonder why she keeps to herself so much?'

'I don't know,' Muttered Ned.' She's educated, 'yon lass. Very quiet spoken. Only t' postman ever goes up yon. He were tellin' me that

Mr Lord's old car is still rotting in t' yard, an', Tha'll not believe this. His socks are still hangin' on t' washing line, rottin'!'

'Oh, the poor woman,' Susan was horrified. 'Has no-one tried to help her?'

'Oh aye lass,' Ned told her.' Many folk have tried, but she's one o' yon recluses. She won't let anyone near t' Sky House,'

Now, there she was, battered by the wind and rain, head down, heading for the lane that would take her up past Windy edge and along the steep, rocky track towards her remote home.

'Peter, we can't let her go up there alone on a night like this,' Susan was horrified. 'She must be soaking already,'

'Don't worry Susan, I don't intend to,' Peter stopped the Land Rover alongside Mrs Lord and jumped out.

'Mrs Lord isn't it?' he had to shout above the noise of the wind in the trees. 'I'm Peter Barnard from Nab's Head,'

'Oh, I know that young man. Good evening,' Mrs lord smiled politely.

It was as though she was standing in the middle of the village on a beautiful summers day.

'We can't let you walk all the way up to the Sky House in this awful weather. Jump in, and we'll take you up,'

Mrs Lord stood there, strands of white hair clinging to her fresh face in the driving rain.

'Oh, that's very kind of you young man, but it's no trouble. I'm quite used to walking,'

Susan put Jim in a comfortable place among the bags of cattle feed and got out of the Land Rover.

'We can't take no for an answer Mrs Lord,' She said. 'We insist that we take you home,'

Finally, after a considerable amount of persuasion, the reluctant Mrs Lord allowed Susan to help her into the cab of the Land Rover.

Her bags were placed carefully alongside the cattle feed bags, under the watchful eye of young Jim.

Peter put the Land Rover into gear and set off up the narrow, dark lane.

At first, it was a merely a matter of splashing along through the puddles, but as they passed the gaunt outline of Windy Edge, the track narrowed even more.

It became steeper and the surface that showed up in the lights of the Land Rover was black loose stone with water rushing down from some higher place. Tall rushes grew in great profusion along each side of the lane, and the cutting became so narrow that it was only about two feet wider than the Land Rover.

Higher and higher they climbed, the tyres slipping and trying to find grip on the wet rocks.

Suddenly, without warning, the land flattened out and they were driving across sparse, close cropped, sheep grazed grass.

There, just a few yards away, stood Sky House Farm.

It loomed suddenly out of the darkness, bleak and gaunt, silhouetted against the stormy grey sky. It was small and out of proportion. Not at all an attractive building. Quite high, with several lean to buildings that seemed to be propping the whole thing up.

Peter peered through the misty windscreen.

He could just make out the shape of a couple of small, deep set windows in the rough stone wall. Everything gleamed wetly in the lights of the Land Rover.

Mrs Lord had, up to this point, said nothing.

Neither had Peter or Susan. They were in awe at the sight of the grim looking farmhouse. Susan glanced back to where Jim was reclining among the sacks of cattle feed. He too was staring at the amazing place; his pale face looked a bit frightened, in the reflected light of the headlamps.

'This is where Mrs Lord lives Jim. She's home safely,'

Susan stroked Jim's hand.

He nodded, but he had nothing to say.

'Thank you very much, young man. I'll be alright now. You really shouldn't have put yourself to so much trouble,' Mrs Lord seemed apologetic.

'This will do very nicely, thank you,'

Susan jumped out and helped Mrs Lord to climb down.

Then, she recovered the heavy bags from the back of the Land Rover.

Mrs Lord took her bags, gripping them firmly. She seemed to be relieved to be holding them again.

'Thank you, young lady. You are so very kind. Thank you,'

With that, she was gone.

The last that Peter and Susan saw of the pathetic figure was as she disappeared round the side of the house, behind a mossy tumbledown wreck of a dry stone wall.

'Oh Peter, Isn't there something we can do to help the poor woman?'

Susan was very concerned. It didn't seem right to just abandon such a frail old lady out here on the wild moors.

'This is where she lives,' Peter said, 'There is nothing more we can do,'

As the Land Rover turned back towards the lane, there alongside the house, they saw an old Ford V8! A large grey car. It reminded Peter of the sort of car that would have been used by the mafia in America during the days of prohibition. It looked so out of place here, high on the moor above Willowburn.

It was obviously long since abandoned, its windows were covered in moss and its tyres were flat, resting, deep in the sheep grazed grass.

'Oh,' Susan gasped. 'It's Mr Lord's car,'

'It's a Ford V8. It was quite a car in its day,' Peter said. But it isn't going to go anywhere. I guess it's an old American army car from the war,'

There were no trees or bushes round the Sky House.

Nothing at all to soften the gaunt outline of the old house.

The windows had once been painted green, but now, the frames were rotting and cracked.

As they looked at the tiny downstairs window, a dim glow could be seen. It was Mrs Lord. They both saw her silvery white hair, silhouetted in the yellow light of the paraffin lamp that she was holding.

Then, it was all behind them. Once again, the steep wet track down towards the village. It was almost as though none of it really existed.

As though it had all been a dream.

Susan had picked up Jim and lifted him back into the front of the Land Rover. She cuddled him and he put his arms tightly round his mum.

'I feel sorry for Mrs Lord,' he whispered.

The rain was still heavy, lashing among the trees of the Midge Hole,

But it seemed to be a very friendly place, in absolute contrast to the

Sky House.

The following day was just as wet and miserable.

Susan lit the fire early, so that Jim could sit before it, eating his toast. Peter dropped him off at school, while Susan went over to the barn.

There were the cows to feed and water. She spent some time stroking their silky flanks and talking softly to them.

'You just stay where you are girls. It's not very nice out there,'

Daisy looked at her, as much as to say,

'We have no intentions of going anywhere,'

But, of course, Cows can't talk, Susan thought.

But then, perhaps they could in their own way? They had very gentle, expressive eyes.

Susan still had Mrs Lord on her mind. She looked at the well fed cows, chewing contentedly in the warm, dry barn.

Saturday morning was still miserable.

It may have been very slightly less windy, but the rain was there, and the heavy grey sky.

Peter dashed across the yard to feed the cows while Susan put the kettle on the stove. She wiped condensation from the window and peered out across the dismal soggy fields. She couldn't see very far because the mist was hanging low across the hills.

Suddenly, the porch door crashed open.

It was Peter returning from his expedition to the barn. His Waxed jacket was dark from the water that was clinging to it and his hair was flattened across his face. He was carrying an armful of logs.

'What an awful morning,'

He glanced at the stove. 'Good. You've put the kettle on. I wonder what happened to spring,'

'Did you feed Jim's rabbit?' Susan asked him, 'You may be sure that we won't see spring this morning,'

Peter laughed.

'Don't you worry about Big Teeth. He's munching away at his breakfast. Jim is better where he is this morning. In bed,'

By the time that Peter had got the fire lit, Susan had breakfast ready. They sat at the kitchen table, warming cold hands on the mugs of hot tea.

Peter had turned the radio on and they were listening to the morning news. Then the weather forecast. Apparently, the south of England was enjoying above average temperatures. Perhaps there may be an occasional shower.

But they were informed that the north may experience some rain, east of the Pennines.

'That's us,' Susan laughed, 'We should live in Lancashire. We are on the wrong side of the hills,'

Suddenly, she thought she heard a tap at the door.

The only people who could be out and about on such a morning were Geoff or Ernie, but neither of them would gently tap on the door.

'I thought I heard someone at the door,' Susan said.

Peter turned the radio down. Yes…

There it was again.

There was no mistaking it this time. Someone was tapping on the door.

Meg had noticed it and her eyes were fixed on the door, her ears erect.

Peter slid back the bolt and opened the door.

He saw a dripping figure wearing a long black coat and an old fashioned hat. Susan recognised her at once. It was Mrs Lord. She smiled and brushed a wisp of wet, silver hair from her eyes,

'Mrs Lord,' Susan was amazed. 'Come in,'

She stood aside and gestured that she was welcoming Mrs Lord into the warm kitchen, but Mrs Lord merely stepped into shelter of the porch.

'I can't stay young lady. But I would like to thank you very much for giving me a ride home in your motor car on Thursday,' said Mrs Lord.

She held out a damp, brown paper wrapped package.

'I'd like you to accept this little gift as a thank you,' she continued.

By then, Peter was at the door.

'Mrs Lord. You didn't walk all this way across the moor, did you?'

Mrs Lord looked rather like a child who was being told off.

'Oh, I'm very sorry,' she apologised, 'You were so kind. I just wanted to say thank you. That's all,'

A pool of water had formed round her shoes.

Behind her, the rain fell heavily, splashing in the puddles that had formed among the cobbles of the yard and dripping from the barn roof.

'I must go now,'

Mrs Lord looked as though she were about to burst into tears.

'Mrs Lord. You can't walk home in this awful weather. You must allow me to take you home in the Land Rover. You're already soaking,'

Peter found the whole situation amazing.

'No thank you,' She said firmly. 'I will walk over the moor,'

With that, she was gone. A lonely figure walking off up the field, towards the old Salt Track.

She was very quickly lost from sight in the mist.

'Oh, I can't let her walk over the top in this weather!'

Peter was exasperated.

'I'm afraid there is nothing that you can do,' Susan said.

Peter had reached for his damp jacket, but Susan laid her hand on his shoulder.

'Mrs Lord'll get far wetter, walking over the moor, than she would have done just walking up from Willowburn,'

Susan was still holding the package that Mrs Lord had given to her.

Carefully, she opened it. Inside, was a little red packet.

It was a packet of tea!

Mrs Lord would be plodding home across the wild, wet moor.

It didn't make any sense. But, perhaps it did to Mrs Lord.

The whole affair had saddened Susan.

'Oh, why can't we do something to help her?'

'I intend to,' Peter looked thoughtful. 'When the weather gets better, I'll go over to the Sky House. There are plenty of things that need doing.

If I only clear a couple of drains, it'll be something,'

The following day was wonderful. It was warm and spring like.

It was as just as though the bleak rainy spell had never happened.

All week, the good weather continued, and on the following Saturday morning, Peter decided to go over to the Sky House.

He had decided to use the tractor and go over the old Salt Track.

It was rough, even for the Land Rover. He put a pick and shovel into a box that he had fitted to the back of the tractor, and set off, chugging up the hill.

At first, there was nothing more than a poorly defined footpath over the tops. Peter, sitting high on the tractor, had the advantage of being able to ignore it in places, and cut across the moor.

He was enjoying himself.

He got the impression that nothing had been up here before except perhaps, someone on horseback, many years ago.

At last, he came to a collapsed, rotting gate, held together by the inevitable baling twine. So… someone had indeed been up here and mended the gate. Who would that be? Thought Peter.

There was no good reason.

The stone walls had collapsed long ago and sheep could just walk round the gate.

But, with the respect due to the unknown person who had mended the gate. Peter drove the tractor through, and carefully re-tied it behind him.

The old Track had been well constructed; after all, it had been a lifeline for the early hill people. Huge slabs of stone had been placed on the boggy ground, in two long tracks about four feet apart, to stop cart wheels from sinking in the soft peat. But now, the track was in bad condition. No doubt, some of the missing stones were now a part of someone's house or barn.

Slowly, the tractor lurched and swayed its way across the desolate moor.

Peter felt very isolated and cut off from the world.

He spotted a few sheep in the distance, and closer, a curlew suddenly rose from a clump of heather. Here and there, a large stone had been set on end, The reason was no doubt, to mark the line of the track when deep snow lay across everything, in winter.

Here and there, Peter saw the sculls and bones of sheep, bleached white by the sun.

Mrs Lord had trudged along this track alone only a week previously. Peter couldn't imagine what it had been like in the rain, leaning against the howling wind. What a hard world it was up here.

In spite of the spring sunshine. Peter shivered.

Suddenly, he arrived at a point from where he could see the Sky House. To his utter amazement, he saw Mrs Lord on the roof!

She was wearing a long army coat and a battered trilby hat, and she had a bucket balanced on top of the low chimney. She was obviously trying to put cement between the gaps in the stone.

Just as Peter saw her, she appeared to hear the sound of the tractor and glanced quickly to see where it was. Mrs Lord grabbed her bucket and climbed down her rickety ladder.

Peter was horrified.

He was reminded of what had happened to Sam Turner's dad.

Mrs Lord scuttled round the side of the gable end and disappeared out of sight. It took Peter some time to drive down to the farm. He pulled up alongside the abandoned car and stopped the tractor engine. Jumping off, he walked across the yard.

He could see much more in daylight.

He hadn't really believed all the village gossip about the Sky House, but, it was all true. Now, he could see for himself, the desolate, mossy yard and the fallen walls, the long abandoned car, the rusty bits of machinery and the washing line…

So, it was all true. Even the rotting washing line and the socks…

Peter half expected actors to appear. It was like a film set. But, there were no actors. There were no cameras, no mobile canteen, nothing.

This was real… There were no animals of any kind, no hens or ducks running about in the yard. Nothing but the wild bleating of sheep, adding to the feeling of utter desolation.

Peter knocked at the heavy door. Although in need of a coat of paint, it seemed to be in good condition. No-one answered his knock.

He tried again. After a long pause, a voice came from behind the door.

'What do you want, young man?'

'It's only me Mrs Lord, Peter Barnard from Nab's Head. Are you alright?'

'Yes thank you,' she replied.

It was so strange, having a polite conversation through a locked door, in the middle of such a wild and forgotten spot on the edge of the moor.

But, there was no conversation. It seemed to have come to an end. Peter was at a loss as to what to say next. He tried again.

'I would like to help you Mrs Lord if I may. It would be no problem for me to mend your roof. Perhaps I could mend a drain, or a few of the walls?

I could even paint your windows and door. It would give me pleasure to be able to help a bit. I wouldn't want any money. Perhaps Susan could visit you if you need anything…'

He was cut short.

'Thank you very much young man but I would prefer it if you were to go away,'

There was nothing more to be said. The door remained firmly shut.

Sadly, Peter climbed onto his red tractor. He could do no more.

He took a long final look at the lonely farm; it wasn't easy to just leave it.

He felt as though he were abandoning poor Mrs Lord. But it was her choice. She asked nothing of anybody.

She continued to travel to Leeds on Thursdays; otherwise, she chose to live alone with her memories.

Peter took the village road home. He was rather glad that he saw no-one. He wouldn't mention his attempt to help Mrs Lord.

It was strange, but he felt as though he had broken a trust.

When he arrived home, he told Susan all that had happened. She found it hard to believe.

'Surely, it would help if I were to go over. Perhaps she was nervous because you are a man,'

But, Peter knew that nothing would be achieved.

'If we see Mrs Lord plodding along in bad weather in the future, perhaps we should just look the other way,'

There was to be no more offering Mrs Lord a lift.

'I wonder how many more Mrs Lords there are out there in other remote corners of the Dales?' Susan said,

'It doesn't seem so bad with people like Ernie. He has a purpose.

He tends his animals and he enjoys coming over here for a natter and a mug of tea, and he will accept help,'

'I can't imagine that Mrs Lord enjoyed coming over here,' said Peter.

Everyone knew Billy Briggs.

He had a small farm over the top towards the next Dale, and he drove through the village very often. He would buy petrol at Bert Eckersley's pumps, and sometimes called at the post office or the shop.

He was a friendly soul, with a big grin on his face.

People always remembered Billy's grin. Probably because he only had one tooth, it was known as 'Billy's pickle stabber'. He never seemed to have a care in the world, to call him easy going would have been an understatement.

Billy was a scrap dealer and pig farmer. In fact, he was quite a good pig farmer. He owned an ancient Morris van that he used to take his pigs down to the auctions at Beddington. Billy's van was as well known as he was.

The drivers of the milk truck and the local bus dreaded getting stuck behind Billy's van. He always drove carefully at between twenty five and thirty miles an hour. Up hill and down dale, totally oblivious to the fact that there were several long, wide stretches between the villages.

He would think nothing of stopping his van right in the middle of Billingbeck or Willowburn to chat with some buxom lass that he recognised.

The trouble was that he had no regard whatsoever for any vehicle that was unfortunate enough to be stuck behind him. Even Policemen had been known to smile, as they stood discreetly in some doorway, listening to Billy's charming patter.

On the good side, he was a very generous and friendly chap who would go out of his way to help anybody, but, on the down side, he looked as oily as his scrap and always had a faint aroma of pigs. The strange thing was that the ladies seemed to like him.... from a distance.

Wednesdays was 'pig day' at Beddington auctions.

It was on the second Wednesday in April that Billy gained a totally different reputation for his driving. It happened just before lunchtime, the sun was shining, all was quiet and Widdersdale was at peace with itself.

Once each fortnight, the mobile library visited Billingbeck, and it was one of its allotted days. So, by Billingbeck standards, it was a very busy morning.

Susan was sitting on one of the benches in the village square, talking to Mary Turner from Willowburn Farm.

'How is Jim getting along at school?' Mary said.

'Oh, he seems to be doing very well, thank you. He gets along very well with the other kids,'

She looked across the road.

There was a small blue and white Police car parked outside Mrs Eckersley's Pie shop. She smiled to herself as two stalwart members of the West Yorkshire Constabulary came out of Mrs Eckersley's shop, each carrying a paper bag which obviously contained their lunch.

They got into the blue and white car and, placing their pies carefully on the back seat, the driver set off round the side of the church and up the lane leading towards Folly Edge.

Susan knew that there was a pleasant little spot in the shade of the trees that was just hidden from sight. A nice place indeed to relax for a few moments with one of Mrs Eckersley's pies, followed perhaps by the luxury of a fag.

It was very fortunate for Billy Briggs that the two constables had decided to go 'off duty' for a few minutes.

Mary Turner was the first one to notice it.

'Listen,' she raised a finger, 'Can you hear that?'

Susan Listened.

'It sounds like an aeroplane,' she said. 'It seems to be very low,'

They could both hear it.

A high pitched whining sound that was rapidly becoming louder. People looked up in alarm as they grouped together in doorways staring in the direction that the sound was coming from.

It sounded as though the 'Round Britain Rally', was approaching.

It was Billy Brigg's van.

It came hurtling out of the hills, doing all of seventy miles an hour.

Right down the middle of the high street it came, swaying and rocking over the cobbles of the square, past the Black Bull.

It so happened that the milk truck was coming up from the direction of Beddington. The driver saw Billy's blue van coming towards him at what appeared to be a hundred miles an hour. He got a glimpse of Billy, gripping the steering wheel with white knuckles, a look of grim determination on his face. The only place for the milk truck to go was up the grassy bank beside the road. Spectators could not help but admire the skill of the milk truck driver, as he avoided Billy's van by inches.

With no reduction of speed, Billy was gone. Hurtling round the bend and on towards Willowburn, leaving behind, a faint trail of pale blue smoke.

'Well, I never!' Mary spoke at last, 'That was Billy Briggs, wasn't it?'
Susan was glad that the children were safely in school.
'It was. Whatever was wrong? He is usually such a careful driver.'
Billy shot straight through Willowburn at top speed, and carried on; lurching round the sharp bends leading down to Beddington.

The ancient blue van swung violently into the auctions car park, and shuddered to a halt in a cloud of steam and loose granite chippings, only inches from the main building.

The only witness was the chap who wheeled the trolleys full of cattle feed out to waiting vehicles. He had been sweeping the yard.

He leaned on his sweeping brush and pushed his cap onto the back of his head.

'By gum Billy lad, tha were shiftin' a bit. But, tha's getten damn good brakes,'

As if from nowhere, Billy suddenly found he had quite an audience, attracted by the sound of his dramatic pit stop. He just sat there, pale faced and shaking with emotion. They had to prise him out of his seat and lead him into the canteen.

Billy Briggs was in shock.

It was some time before he was able to speak. He gripped his mug of tea tightly in trembling hands and closed his eyes. Finally, he was able to tell the crowd who had gathered round him, what had happened.

His cargo was a load of weaners, 'little pigs'. And little pigs can get quite excited. One of them had wriggled between Billy's legs and had sat down on the accelerator pedal. It also blocked access to the brakes, so, in effect; the pig was driving the van. It had, of course, allowed Billy to steer.

There were dozens of little weaners in the van, so the culprit could not be identified.

Billy never again drove at more than twenty five miles an hour.

He even got a certain amount of begrudging respect from the milk lorry driver and the bus drivers. And the ladies too! But, he had learned his lesson.

Very soon, Billy changed his vehicle.

Young Jim was one of the first to know. Unknown to anyone. Billy came up with a clever idea to separate himself from his pigs, while on the road.

His plan was to buy a four wheel drive vehicle and a pig trailer.

But, being Billy, it wasn't just a mere Land Rover that he bought.

He had found out where he could get good value for money, so, he went over to Preston. There was a place just on the outskirts of Preston that specialised in selling Ex Military vehicles. He soon found what he was looking for. He bought a Willis Jeep.

It had only had one careful previous owner… The American army.

But, the American army hadn't been very careful with Billy's Jeep.

It looked as though it had been involved in most of the major battles of World War Two.

Billy was never slow to exploit any situation to his maximum advantage. He just couldn't lose. Soon, he took to chewing gum and, when he was talking to the ladies, he developed a very strange accent.

Somewhere between Yorkshire and New York.

It was as he was deep in conversation with one of the local ladies that young Jim spotted him.

He had parked his Jeep near the village school and he was sitting, talking to the lass with one leg draped casually over the side of the Jeep.

Just as he had seen the G.Is do it at the Picture Palace in Oakenhead.

A few of the older ladies remembered the 'Yanks', and their seemingly endless supply of nylon stockings.

Jim stood, open mouthed, staring at Billy in his Jeep.

The big white star on the battered bonnet was catching the dappled light of the sun filtering through the trees. It gave the effect of camouflage. Jim could imagine a German tank rumbling round the corner.

'Sure, honey,' drawled Billy, 'I guess tha's getten nowt t' worry about,'

Jim didn't know why the lady should be worried, and he didn't care. He just wanted to tell his mum the news. Susan saw Jim's excited expression as soon as he came running out of school.

'BillyBriggshasajeep,' he gasped.

'Hey,' Susan laughed, 'Now, slow down. What did you say. Billy Briggs has some sheep?'

'No. Billy Briggs has a Jeep,'

Young Jim was jumping up and down.

'Please can we get a Jeep,' he pleaded. 'I think it has a gun in the back,'

'No Jim. We can't get a Jeep,'

Susan was amused at the thought of Billy Briggs cruising round in a Jeep with a machine gun in the back.

It wasn't very long before Gossip in the black Bull turned to what was happening up at Billy Brigg's farm. Something strange had been noticed.

Billy didn't much like anything to be 'noticed', up at Dingle Bottom Farm. Just as long as he was making a 'bit o' brass' he would rather be left alone.

But, this was something that wasn't at all normal.

Billy had a washing line strung up between his house and one of the many dilapidated sheds.

And, the washing line had several shirts and long undergarments on it, flapping gently in the summer breeze.

Billy's yard was an absolute goldmine to anyone seeking some obsolete and otherwise unobtainable bit of agricultural engineering. And, if Billy hadn't got it, he knew where to get it.

To anyone else, Billy's yard was just a nightmare of old junk.

But, to see a washing line! It was very soon the talk of the village.

'Perhaps he's started going to Church,' Old Ned said.

'Nay, he's not religious,' Sam laughed, 'I recon that he's tryin' to live like yon Yanks do. It'll take more than a clean shirt,'

'I know,' someone said. 'Perhaps he's getten a washing machine that actually works,'

'Nay. If he had, he'd sell it,' said Ned.

'If tha' sold a washing machine, tha' could buy thyself some beer,'

No-one knew who said that, but it raised a laugh at Ned's expense.

One of the lads drove past Dingle Bottom Farm most mornings, and he kept a close eye on the place. One bright morning, he glanced over towards Dingle Bottom as always, and quickly looked again.

He saw a young lady hanging out some washing.

She had a wicker basket at her side, and she was pegging out some of Billy's shirts.

He didn't recognise her. He was sure that she wasn't a local lass.

Very soon, the whole village got to know more about the mysterious lady.

A few days after getting the news about Billy's young lady, Peter and Susan happened to be in the village, doing a spot of shopping.

It was well into May, and Peter had decided that he was going to need a couple of 'farmer's friends'.

Billingbeck High Street was at peace with itself.

There was a pleasant haze in the air. A lazy sun and not a breath of a breeze.

The only movement was an old, unaccompanied Collie dog.

It seemed to know where it was going, and it seemed to know that it wasn't allowed to go there. It kept glancing over its shoulder with a guilty expression.

There was only one vehicle in the street. Billy's Jeep,

It was standing outside the Post Office.

From the direction of the Black Bull, a couple of farmers appeared, heading towards the ironmongers. Several women came round the corner, making their way towards the pie shop. Billy's Jeep attracted no attention, until his much discussed, but never seen, lady friend walked out of the Post Office.

Peter and Susan watched, as she went over to the Jeep.

She was quite attractive in a rugged sort of way.

She was wearing a tartan shirt and a pair of jeans. Maybe she was slightly overweight for such a fashion, but she had a pretty face and her fair hair was tied back. She had a little beret on her head.

Casually, she smiled and nodded towards Peter and Susan.

'Nice day,' she said.

'It is indeed,' Susan tried to place the strange accent.

'Got to dash. The pigs need feeding,'

She tossed her shopping bag into the back of the Jeep and jumped nimbly over the sill of the vehicle, wartime Jeeps having no doors.

There was a healthy roar and a puff of blue smoke. The Jeep had been facing downhill, but it swung in a tight circle and accelerated away as though it was being pursued by the whole German army.

Since his unfortunate experience with the pigs, Billy had become a very steady driver. Not so this young lady.

The Jeep sped swiftly away, leaving behind a group of astonished villagers. Just above Billingbeck a few ramblers were happily wandering up the road. The Jeep had lots of room, but the ramblers stood to the side of the road, watching the approaching vehicle.

One of the ramblers, a middle aged gentleman wearing rather over-sized shorts, looked over the top of his glasses.

'By gum Ralph. It's one of them American things!'

Ralph, a small, rather overweight chap, adjusted his rucksack and smiled.

'Perhaps, t' driver doesn't know that t' wars over,'

They were suddenly lost from view as the Jeep roared past them, a thick cloud of dust trailing along behind it.

Twelve

Jim was playing with his rabbit in the pen that Peter had built in a corner of the yard. It was Sunday. A 'no school day'. He didn't feel like going anyway.

He had big plans.

He was going to help his dad to dig out a broken field drain.

He was really looking forward to it. It promised to be a nice, messy job.

'Lots of mud,' Jim said to the young rabbit. He was at peace with the world.

He sat Big Teeth on his knee and gently stroked his soft fur.

Meg, who wasn't allowed in the pen, was lying stretched out in the warm grass, thinking, no doubt, about the injustice of life. To add to all her trials and tribulations, she had a fly buzzing round her ear.

Suddenly, she stood up. She had heard something.

She was staring towards the trees in the Midge Hole. Jim looked up, but he could see nothing.

Meg however, stood, ears erect, causing Jim to put down the rabbit and listen.

Yes. Now he could hear it too. There was a vehicle driving through the Midge Hole. As it came into view, he recognised the familiar green Ford.

Excitedly, he ran to the house

'Mummy, Daddy, Grandma and Granddad are here,'

Susan came to the door. Her hands and even parts of her face were coated with flour. She looked towards the trees. Sure enough, her Mum and Dad's car was driving down the lane. Hurriedly, she grabbed a towel, in an attempt to rub some of the flour from her hands and face. She ran out into the yard to greet her Mum and Dad.

'What a surprise. It's really nice to see you,' June laughed,

'You've got flour all over your face,'

'I'm making a few buns,' she told her Mum.

'Great,' Bill said. 'We just arrived in time,'

'Well, young man. You didn't expect to see us today, did you,'

June put her arms out and Jim ran eagerly across the floor. She picked him up and kissed him.

'I hadn't started making dinner,' Susan said.

'That's why we came a bit early,' Said Bill. 'Don't bother. We felt like having lunch at the Black Bull. All you have to do is scrape some of that flour off your face,'

'Where's Peter?' June asked.

'Oh, he'll have heard the car. He's somewhere out there,' She waved a hand. 'Mending a field drain or something.'

'Are we really going to the Black Bull Grandma?'

Jim hoped that it was true.

'We certainly are young man. On a day like this, you can be sure that some of your friends will be there,'

As they were talking, Peter came striding down the field with a shovel over his shoulder. He looked very hot and dishevelled.

He kicked off his muddy boots in the porch.

'Hello, I thought I heard the car,' He shook hands with Bill and hugged June, as he always did.

'When do we get fed?' he asked Susan, 'I'm starving,'

'Just as soon as you are clean and tidy,' She replied. 'We are invited out for lunch,'

'Wonderful. We don't go out for lunch very often these days,' Peter said.

'Well, better make the most of it,' Bill said, 'It's on me. So it may be years before it happens again,'

Susan made a pot of tea, while Peter, who couldn't hang on 'till lunchtime, sneaked himself a chunk of bread, liberally covered in butter and topped with a great slice of cheese.

Eventually, it was time to drive down to the Black Bull.

They all managed to fit into the Land Rover. Peter driving and the two ladies in the front, Bill and Jim sat in the back. Considering the good weather, the car park wasn't too full.

Peter parked the Land Rover and followed everyone else into the pub.

As always, the small group of farmers were standing to the side of the room. Ned was there with Betty, and Sam Turner was sitting at a table with Mary. There were a few strangers, no doubt, motoring families, but most of the children had disappeared in the direction of the games room.

It didn't take Jim long to join them. He had spotted Mr and Mrs Hebblethwaite, and guessed correctly, that Arthur would be in the games room.

Much to the surprise of Peter and Susan, Ben Bradley and his wife Maureen from Sally End were sitting at a corner table, looking very much at home. They were accompanied by another couple who looked as though they were friends of Ben and Maureen. 'Perhaps from Birmingham'. Susan thought.

Everyone was busy gossiping and not taking much notice of who was arriving, but suddenly, the level of noise decreased.

A few people were looking towards the door.

Peter had been talking to Susan, but he looked up to see why everyone had gone silent.

Billy Briggs had just walked in, accompanied by his young lady.

Perhaps it was the group of farmers who were most surprised?

This was a Billy Briggs that they hardly recognised.

He had abandoned his usual oily overalls and he was dressed in a very respectable jumper and trousers, and his shoes were nicely polished.

His usually unruly hair was brushed flat.

But without any doubt, the star of the show was his companion.

She was wearing a very attractive, pale grey tweed two piece and just the right amount of makeup. Her fair hair was well brushed and tied back.

She was very aware of the interest in the room, but she chose to ignore it. But her laughing eyes showing her amusement at the situation.

Billy could hardly expect his young lady to stand with the group of farmers, and so, with a show of chivalry that surprised Susan, he led his partner to a vacant table right beside Peter and Susan.

With impeccable manners, he moved a chair for her to sit down, and stood there looking rather self conscious. Finally. He realised that he was the only one standing, and sat down himself.

Ned was grinning. He couldn't resist making his comment,

'By gum Billy, I didn't know that tha' owned a tie,'

Billy turned a bit red, but chose to say nothing.

There was little doubt that, if they had been alone, he would have had plenty to say.

Susan smiled and addressed Billy's partner.

'I must say, you do seem to be a good influence on Billy,'

Billy's lady friend smiled back in a friendly way.

'I hope so,' she held out her hand. 'We met in the village didn't we. I think I know who you are. You're from Nab's Head,'

Susan was surprised.

'Yes, you're right. My name is Susan,'

She introduced everyone,

'This is my husband Peter, and my mum and dad, Bill and June,'

The young lady shook hands and introduced herself,

'My name is Andrea.' She explained, 'Billy's friend,'

Susan smiled,

'It's a pleasure to meet you Andrea. Where do you come from? I can't quite place your accent,'

'Perhaps its better that you don't,' Andrea laughed.

'Why do you say that?' Susan was intrigued.

Andrea glanced over to where the farmers were pretending to be involved in the serious business of drinking their beer, but they were unusually quiet.

Andrea said quietly,

'Just watch those lads' faces,'

She spoke in a louder voice,

'I'm from Nelson in Lancashire,'

The farmers couldn't help knowing that it had been said so that they would hear.

A small red faced chap wearing a large cap raised his glass in a friendly way.

'By heck. I'll tell thee what lass. If there are any more like thee in Lancashire, they can come to t' Black Bull anytime,'

Everyone laughed and a few of the farmers raised their glasses towards Andrea. Poor Billy turned bright red, but he was secretly quite relieved because has Lancashire girl friend had been accepted.

It wasn't long before Susan and Andrea were deep in conversation.

They quickly discovered that they had a great deal in common, in spite of very different backgrounds and upbringing.

Suddenly, everything else took second place as young Jim casually wandered in. He didn't say anything; he sat beside June and listened to what Susan and Andrea were talking about.

But, Andrea had seen him.

'Now, who is this young man?' she asked. 'Let me guess. He's certainly a Barnard. There's no mistaking that. Perhaps a bit more handsome than his dad. Am I right?'

Susan laughed.

'You are right Andrea. Meet Jim, our son. But, let me warn you. He's very good at turning on the charm,'

Andrea was immediately captivated by the little boy with the tousled hair and the big open smile.

'Oh, he doesn't need charm. He can count me as one of his fans already,'

But Jim was staring at Billy Briggs. He remembered seeing him in his Jeep.

Jim knew all about Jeeps. He had a picture of one in a book, and like most little boys, he had a fascination for such things.

'Come round here young man and tell me all about yourself,' Andrea said, 'do you go to the village school?'

'Yes, but I'm only in year one. I sit next to Arthur Hebblethwaite, but he keeps on talking, so he gets moved,'

Peter had been listening to the conversation.

Up to now, he hadn't said anything much, but he was curious to know just where Andrea was from.

'You mentioned Nelson. I know a chap from Nelson. He drives a lorry and comes to the mill sometimes,'

Andrea explained that she was brought up on a smallholding near Nelson. There were two girls, Andrea and an older sister.

Their mother had died when they were quite young, and they had been brought up by their father. They had a small milk round in those days, delivering milk door to door in the area. They never had more than twenty or so cows, but it gave them a living along with selling a few eggs, plus the money that their father managed to bring in by a bit of expert 'wheeling and dealing', as she put it. Meaning of course, buying and selling all sorts of things.

Then suddenly, tragedy had struck again. They lost their father.

A tractor had slipped and overturned while he was spreading lime, and their father was trapped. He had been rushed to hospital, but he died the following day.

The two girls, who by then were in their late twenties, had carried on running the farm, but it was obvious even in those days, that small dairy farmers were struggling to make a decent living. Andrea and her sister had opened a market stall selling various dairy products and other groceries, and managed to get along quite well.

Then, one day, out of the blue, Billy Briggs arrived at the farm.

He had been interested in a quantity of scrap that was lying abandoned in a corner of the yard. As always, he had put on his charm, but it had little effect on Andrea.

A few days later, he came back to load some scrap iron on his trailer and mentioned his pigs.

Andrea had always wanted to keep pigs, so they found that they had a common interest.

All of this had been over two years ago.

Andrea had visited Billy and gradually a friendship developed.

The outcome was that Andrea decided that a partnership would work out well, and there came a time when she left her sister to run the farm in Nelson, and moved to Widdersdale. It had been, without doubt, Widdersdale's best kept secret.

But eventually it all came out into the open. Billy's much improved appearance couldn't be kept secret, then, one day, Andrea arrived in the village, driving the Jeep.

'Well, that's the story of my life,' Andrea said. 'You know the rest,'

Finally, Billy spoke.

'There's a bit more to it than that,' he said. 'Andrea has really changed things at Dingle Bottom Farm. She came up with a few ideas that make things run along much better,'

'All I did was move things round a bit. It didn't make much sense to have the feed in shed miles away from the pigs for instance,'

Susan was intrigued by all of it.

'You weren't at Dingle Bottom when Billy had his unfortunate encounter with the weaner that wanted to learn to drive, where you?'

Andrea glanced over the group of farmers.

'Yes, I was. I told you that some things go unnoticed in the Dale. Maybe those guys are not quite as smart as they think they are.'

Susan noticed the quick little smiles that passed between Billy and Andrea. It was obviously a very good, mutually advantageous relationship, but. Susan knew, with the instinct that women have, that there was more to it than that. There was a genuine affection between this couple.

Bill and June were very interested in the conversation.

Andrea had worked so hard, and that the two sisters had done well to overcome the tragedy in their lives.

The meal was excellent.

Jim was happy because he got his sausage and chips. But, he seemed to be deep in thought.

Finally, he could contain himself no longer.

'I have a picture of a Jeep in one of my books,' he told Billy.

Billy smiled.

'The Jeep's outside, young man. When we go out, you can sit in it.'

So, when, eventually it was time to leave the Black Bull, Jim was the first one out, He was in the car park in a flash. Everyone smiled.

He was standing beside the battered Jeep with a look of someone who was very privileged. He was gazing at the dent in the wing and imagining that it had been caused in battle. In his mind no doubt, he could see this vehicle dashing across the shattered landscape of wartime France,

Peter looked at Jim and he saw himself as he had been at that age.

He could still vaguely remember the vivid imagination of a child's world.

Andrea picked Jim up and lowered him into the driver's seat.

He looked very small, sitting behind the large steering wheel, but, in his day dreams, he was no doubt much bigger and wearing khaki green clothes and one of those round American helmets.

Bill and June looked thoughtful; they were old enough to remember the grim reality of war.

'It was really nice meeting up with you tonight,' Andréa said. 'We only decided to come down here for a meal on the last minute, but we found much more. We have enjoyed the company of friends. And I discovered young Jim,'

'It was nice to meet you and hear something about you. You're a bit of a mystery in the Dale you know,' Andrea nodded,

'I realise that, but it surprises me. Remember that I come from a rural community too, and I know how news gets round,'

'I know only too well Andrea. We've only been in the Dale for just over a year you know. But I can honestly say that almost all the people that we have met here have turned out to be really nice folk,'

Susan looked thoughtful for a moment,

'Tell you what. Why don't you come up to Nab's Head some time? We don't get too many visitors, we would be glad to see you,'

'We'd be only too pleased to,' Andrea said.

She turned to Billy,

'How does that sound?'

Billy scratched his head and glanced at Peter,

'I'll tell thee what Peter,' he muttered, 'It doesn't half change thy life. havin' a woman organisin' it!'

'Oh, you get used to it in a few years,' Peter said,

June listened to the interchange of comments with some amusement,

'I see a big difference in Peter since Susan took him on,' she said,

'He's changed beyond recognition,'

'Thanks mum," Susan laughed, "It hasn't been easy,'

'It's not been easy for me either,' muttered Peter.

The following week was one of great activity. Once again, haymaking time was fast approaching, and the machinery had to be checked over.

Peter wasn't particularly looking forward the using the so called 'farmers friend', to sharpen the blades of the mowing machine.

He took the precaution of making sure that the box that contained their first aid stuff had a bottle of TCP and a few packets of assorted plasters in it.

Towards the end of the week, Jim was playing with Meg out in the field beside the house. Meg was rushing around like an idiot while Jim pretended that she was herding sheep. Jim stood in the middle of the field with a stick in his hand, trying to whistle.

Meg got the message. But she probably thought that Jim had gone mad, she loved running about just for fun. From where they were playing, it was possible to see part of the lane running through the Midge Hole.

Suddenly, both Jim and Meg rushed into the house. Susan was sitting in the big comfortable chair, reading a book. Peter was doing the crossword puzzle in the 'Farmers Guardian'.

'The Jeep,' Jim gasped, 'it's coming through the Midge Hole,'

Jim dashed outside again because he wanted to see the Jeep arrive in the yard.

Susan looked at Peter,

They went outside and saw the Jeep coming along the lane.

Andrea was driving, with Billy in the passenger seat.

Or, maybe it wasn't Billy.

'What on earth is that?' Susan said.

'It looks as though someone's sitting on Billy's knee,' Peter was intrigued.

Whatever it was, it had pointed ears and a beard and it was wrapped in a blanket. As the Jeep drew nearer, it was easier to make out what it was.

A goat...

The Jeep swung into the yard and came to a halt in front of the porch.

'Hello,' Andrea called, as she jumped out, 'We've brought you a present,'

The goat had a collar on, and it was on the end of a length of baling twine.

It quickly wriggled free of its blanket and jumped out of the Jeep, followed by Billy,

Jim was delighted.

'A goat,' Susan exclaimed, 'Oh isn't he lovely,'

'Do you mean the goat?' Andrea said, without smiling.

Billy handed the 'lead' to Susan, but, being a goat; it took its opportunity and instantly escaped.

To Jim's delight, it ran into the house!

'Come in,' said Susan, 'It looks as if the goat didn't need to be invited,' In the kitchen, they were greeted by the sight of Meg being chased round and round. She had met her match. Ears down and tail between her legs, she was looking over her shoulder.

It was easy to catch the goat. Meg slid outside and the goat lost interest in her. It had its front feet on the table and was busily munching away at half a loaf of bread. It was allowed to keep the bread and to stay in the kitchen for the time being, but it was firmly tied to the door handle.

Billy Briggs hadn't been up to Nab's Head before.

He looked round with interest,

'You've certainly brought this place back to life,' he said, 'after all those years of standing empty,'

'Yes, we're beginning to see a light at the end of the tunnel,' Susan said, 'it's been hard work, but we got a lot of help from friends,'

She put the kettle on the stove and said,

'Sit down. There'll be a pot of tea in a few minutes,'

Everyone sat round the table. Everyone that was, except Jim.

He had made friends with the goat! It was allowing him to stroke it, while gently nibbling his hair.

'Look at that,' Andrea said, 'Best of friends already. We got the goat as part of a deal we did with John Seymour over at Oakendale. I thought of young Jim right away.'

'Keeping busy on the farm, gives us little time to get out and meet people,' Andrea explained to Susan, 'We seem to get along with you very well, so we thought we'd pay you a visit, and bring Jim his goat at the same time.'

For her part, Susan didn't know too many people of her own age around the Dale. Most were farmer's wives and they were kept pretty busy helping around the farms and raising their families.

'I'll show you round if you want,' Peter said to Billy, 'When you've finished your tea.'

He had noticed that the girls seemed to have plenty to talk about, and Jim was playing with the goat to the utter disgust of Meg, who had crept back in.

By now, the goat had decided to lie on Meg's rug.

Jim wasn't too happy. His friend Meg was under threat, but, Peter very soon put things right. He lifted the goat from the rug and beckoned to Meg.

Meg dashed over and lay on the rug. She was wagging her bushy tail wildly and very obviously grovelling. It was her way of saying 'Thank you'.

Andrea was interested in all things that were going on round the Dale.

She had been quite worried about what impression she would make at the Black Bull.

'I don't think you need to worry about that Andrea. There were a few chaps that would change places with Billy anytime.'

Before they left, Jim was given a ride round the fields in the Jeep.

He was allowed to sit in the front, beside Billy, while Susan and

Andrea sat in the back.

'Jim'll be telling his mates about all this on Monday morning,' Susan said. 'A ride in a real American wartime Jeep,'

'Why don't you come over to our place next weekend?' Andrea said, 'It would be nice to have visitors. We don't see many people,'

'We would love to. We don't often get out in the Dale. Everyone seems to go down to the Black Bull, so we do see a lot of our friends there, but we rarely visit anyone. Even when we do, it's usually to do with farming. As you know, we've only been here for a sort while our- selves, so, we learn a lot. But, I must say that everyone has gone out of their way to make us welcome,'

It was arranged that they would go over to Dingle Bottom Farm on the following Saturday.

As they approached the farm, it became obvious that things had changed very considerably. There was a new gate that swung easily on its oiled hinges and there was not a trace of baling twine. There was a notice on the gate. It announced that 'New laid eggs', were for sale. Also, there was another, less permanent notice. It read 'Jeep for sale'!

The junk that was lying around the yard looked less like junk and more like useful agricultural spares.

The house too had undergone a transformation.

The visible bit was the new curtains and polished windows, but, although Peter and Susan had never been inside, they both knew that Billy would never have lived in such a tidy way.

Andrea came to the door and greeted the three visitors with obvious pleasure.

The hall light had a new looking shade and a colourful bowl of flow- ers had been placed on a table just inside the door.

'Billy will be back in a moment. He's just gone over to our neighbour with a dozen eggs,' she stood aside. 'Come in,'

The room was not at all what they had expected.

It had modern wallpaper and an oak fire surround with an oval mirror above it. The furniture had obviously been recently polished and the cushions washed. On the wall, hung a picture of Billy, looking very self conscious.

He was wearing a white smock and was standing beside a pen of pigs. It had obviously been taken at an agricultural show. Billy was holding a large rosette.

Andrea noticed Susan looking at the picture.

'I found the picture hiding in the attic. It's Billy at the Royal Lancashire Show,'

She was fussing round like a proud mother hen. She picked up Jim and planted a kiss on his cheek.

'And, how's my little friend. How are you getting along with the goat?'

'We called it Beatty and it ate all the flowers in the garden,'

Andrea laughed. Her eyes sparkled.

Peter and Susan, knowing something about her tragic life, had the impression that she hadn't laughed very much in the past.

At that moment, the Jeep turned into the yard.

Billy had seen the Land Rover and he had a big grin on his face as he came into the room.

'By heck, it's good to see you. I'm right glad tha' could come,'

He turned to Andrea, 'I got a regular order for eggs from Mrs Eckersley,'

Peter didn't think that Mrs Eckersley would sell many of Billy's eggs.

Most people who lived in and around Billingbeck kept a few hens or bought their eggs from nearby farmers. But he wished Billy well. He was trying.

'I hope you brought your appetite with you?' Andrea said.

She had laid the table in the dining room with the best china.

Nothing had been overlooked; it was obvious that she was really enjoying her new role as hostess.

Peter couldn't help noticing that Billy looked a bit self conscious as he took his place at the head of the table. He looked like a typical red faced country lad. A bit out of his depth perhaps, in his unaccustomed position as host. But, he was obviously so proud to be sitting there.

Billy's whole life had been transformed.

A family man and now, guests... Although He had first met Andrea two years ago, it had taken them both so long to get the courage to actually invite guests to Dingle Bottom Farm. Billy looked at Andrea with pride as she carried in a dish of roast potatoes. For pudding, it was Jam sponge and custard.

Peter and Jim glanced at each other. Susan smiled at Jim. It was their favourite.

'Well Andrea, I can honestly say that you produced a perfect dinner.

You're cooking is superb and what made it all so much more enjoyable, was being in the company of such nice people,' Susan spoke with sincerity.

'I notice that there is a lot of curiosity about my living at Dingle Bottom. That really amuses me because no-one actually asks me outright about my relationship with Billy, or how we met and why I came to Widdersdale, but I have let bits of information out, and I notice that it gets round the village pretty fast,' Andrea said.

Susan told her about the time that they had called in at the Black Bull, only minutes after completing the signing of the documents for the purchase of Nab's Head,

'Bert Eckersley knew almost before we did, and within half an hour, Old Ned came in and told us that he knew all about it!'

Andrea laughed.

'I suppose it's the same in all country areas. It certainly was where I used to live,'

Getting round to hay time again,' Billy suddenly changed to subject.

'We don't have a baling machine,' Susan said. 'But we only cut about ten acres. We were discussing hay time only yesterday,' Andrea told them that her father had never owned a baler.

'It's much more fun getting loose hay in,' she said. 'I would love to come over and help. It would remind me of my childhood, when we were all together as a family,'

Just for one brief moment, her face showed sadness, then, she was the usual smiling Andrea once again, but her moment of sadness hadn't gone un- noticed by Peter and Susan... Or by Billy.

'What a great idea,' Susan said, 'We'd love to have you over at hay time. Its hard work, but I love it. It really does take you back to your childhood doesn't it? Maybe it's the everlasting summers that we re- member so clearly,'

'I wonder why it never seemed to rain during our school holidays,' laughed Andrea.

'I see you're selling the Jeep,' Peter said to Billy.

'Aye, t' winter isn't too far away. I know that it's only July, but we re- ally need something wi' doors,'

Jim was listening to the conversation. His expression showed that he couldn't understand how anyone could sell a Jeep.

'Why don't you go down to Willowburn? Have a word with Wishbone at Kestrel garage. He usually knows where there's a bargain,' suggested Susan. Andrea laughed,

'Billy's a true Yorkshire man. He won't spend any more brass than he needs to,'

She addressed herself to Billy, 'You have to spend a bit sometimes, to get more in. 'Hay in t' barn's money in t' bank' as they say,'

Peter was surprised to hear Andrea say that. It was one of Old Ernie's favourite sayings.

⁓

The pressing urgency now was hay time. It seemed to Susan, to be only a few months since they had been so nervous about their first haymaking, but she realised that a year had gone by. So much had happened.

As for Andrea, Susan was happy to have her as a close friend.

A couple of days after the Barnard's visit to Dingle Bottom, Andrea spotted Susan down in Billingbeck. It was a lovely morning.

They decided to spoil themselves and buy a couple of Mrs Eckersley's sticky cream buns with icing on the top. They went over to the churchyard and found a bench in a shady corner under the great yew tree.

'I noticed that a few of the farmers have already started haymaking down at the bottom of the Dale,' Andrea said.

Susan laughed because Andrea had a huge smear of cream on the end of her nose.

Andrea looked a bit embarrassed and wiped it off.

'We begin a few days after them, being much higher,' Susan said,

'Old Ernie will be over, no doubt, telling us that the weather will be settled,'

Susan thought that it was a pity that the school holidays weren't a few weeks sooner. Jim had really enjoyed helping with the hay last year.

But, now he was a schoolboy, he would miss some of the fun.

'Don't forget that I want to come over and help,' Andrea said.

'We need all the help we can get,' Susan said. She remembered the race to beat the rain last year,

'Are you and Billy going to the Widdersdale Summer Fair?'

Susan changed the subject.

'Billy hasn't mentioned it. We certainly didn't go last year, but I don't want to miss it again,' Andrea said.

'No, we didn't go last year either. We were too busy getting Nab's Head ready for the winter,'

Susan had mentioned the Fair to Peter, and they had decided that they were certainly not going to miss it this year.

'It's sometime in early August, just after the children break up for their summer holiday,'

By now, the fields across the Dale were taking on the familiar patchwork of greens and soft yellows as hay time progressed, and the air was heavy with the sweet smell of the 'cooking' hay, it was most noticeable as the days cooled and the long summer evenings crept over the dales.

Once again, the snarl of tractors could be heard late into the night, as bales were moved into the barns. Headlights shone across the gloomy meadows, showing where the late work was in progress.

The following weekend saw Peter with four clear days to get started. Not only did he have the Saturday and Sunday, but Ralph had made sure that he wouldn't be needed at the mill over the following few days.

Peter and Susan decided to make their move.

As soon as Peter arrived home on the Friday, he was out with the mowing machine. Susan and Jim stood watching, as swathe after swathe of tall sweet grass fell cleanly under the swishing blades.

By dusk, there were five acres of cut grass lying over the first of the two meadows.

Ernie had, of course, been working for several weeks with his scythe. He was cutting places where the tractor couldn't reach.

Peter had been watching him. He noticed that, over the year, Ernie had slowed down a bit. He was a very methodical and steady worker, but there was more of a pause now as he straightened his back after a few hours of swinging his scythe.

No-one was really sure of Ernie's age, but Peter was sure that he was well into his seventies. Ernie used to give Peter advice on how to keep going into old age.

'Sithee now, young man. Tha takes a spoonful of cod liver oil every morning,' He pointed with his pipe, 'If tha does that, thy joints'll go on forever,'

Peter and Susan had gradually come to regard Ernie almost as family.

As far as they knew, he didn't have any family of his own. He very rarely mentioned his childhood in Cumbria.

On Saturday morning, Andrea was up and about early.

By seven o'clock, the hot sun was burning the last of the dew off the grass, and a bright haze across the Dale promised a perfect day.

Billy planned to spend the day in his workshop, making a couple of gates for one of their neighbours, so, Andrea knew that he wouldn't be using the Jeep.

'I think I'll pop over to see what Peter and Susan are doing,' she told him, 'On a day like this, I'm sure that they will be starting on the haymaking,'

'Aye, I was thinking that. Thee go over. I'm sure you'll find them out in t' meadow,'

Billy reached for the teapot.

'I've got lots o' things to do in t' shed,'

It was well before eight o clock when Andrea arrived at Nab's Head, but Peter had already been out in the meadow for an hour.

As she drove into the yard and cut the engine, she could hear the tractor in the meadow, but, Susan was still in the house.

She glanced through the window,

'Your friend Andrea's here in the Jeep Jim,' Susan turned to Jim.

But, he was already heading for the door because he had heard the Jeep.

'I think Andrea's come to help us with the hay Mum,'

In his hurry to get outside, he collided with Andrea in the doorway.

'And what are you rushing about for, young man?' She tousled his hair and propelled him back into the house.

'I think you've made a hit with young Jim,' Susan laughed.

'No Susan. It's the other way round,' Andrea looked at the little boy,

'With charm like he has, he's going to have to fight off the girls. Is Peter out in the meadow? I could hear the tractor when I arrived,'

'Oh yes. He's already cut the first field. We were at it last night too,' Susan handed Andrea a cup of tea.

When they walked over to the second meadow, much of it was already lying in swathes. Peter saw them coming and stopped the tractor.

He greeted Andrea with a wave,

'Good morning Andrea,' He looked at his watch; it was just half past eight.

'It was a nice morning,' he joked,

Then, more seriously,

'We can't do much more here for a few hours. I shook the other meadow this morning, and I don't want to cut the last half of this one.

How about going over to see how Ernie's getting along,'

'Great idea,' said Susan. 'He'll certainly be hard at work,'

Susan and Andrea went on ahead with Jim running round and round as children everywhere do.

Ernie was in his cowshed.

As they walked down the hill, they could hear the clatter of buckets, and a wheelbarrow stood beside the open door.

'Good morning Ernie,' Susan called out.

The old farmer appeared in the doorway. He shaded his eyes as he looked into the bright morning sunlight and smiled as he recognised Susan.

'Good morning young lady,' he said.

He puffed on his inevitable pipe and was lost for a moment in a cloud of smoke.

'Mornin' young Jim,' he said, 'And, who's this young lady?'

'Andrea, Billy Brigg's young lady,' Susan introduced Andrea.

As they were talking, the tractor came chugging down the hill, towing the mowing machine. Ernie looked at it in surprise.

He hadn't expected Peter to come over so soon. But, he recovered instantly and took over his favourite role of 'boss'.

He walked over to Peter and pointed over to the meadow behind his house.

'Tha can cut a bit o' yon field for me,' he shouted above the sound of the tractor engine. "Make sure tha lowers yon blade, young man. I don't want t' leave a lot o' grass on t' field,'

Peter drove into the small meadow and jumped off the tractor.

In a moment, he had lowered the cutting arm to what he considered was the point where it was going to shave the grass to the roots.

Ernie re-lit his pipe and inspected the machine with no expression on his face.

'Aye, well, I suppose tha can't go down a bit,' he grumbled.

Andrea looked on in silence. She was totally captivated by the old man.

'If this weather holds, all the hay'll be got in safely,' Andrea was addressing Susan, but Ernie overheard her.

'And what dust thou know about t' weather,' he said. 'Tha comes from t' other side o' t' Pennines. Weather's different o'er yon,'

Andrea was amused,

'And how do you know where I come from?' she asked him.

'Thou ar't Billy Briggs young lady. I know tha comes from Nelson i' Lancashire,'

'And, I know that you come from Cumbria,' Andrea had him.

Ernie muttered something unintelligible and turned to Peter.

'Right now young man. You can cut us a few swathes,'

He turned to Susan and Andrea.

They were laughing and discussing Ernie's cantankerous attitude, but he didn't know what they were talking about.

'It's a wonder thou ever gets owt done. You lasses never stop talking,'

Andrea laughed.

'I'll tell you something Ernie. If I'd met you before I met Billy Briggs, I recon I'd have been after thee,'

'By gum,' Ernie's face broke into a big friendly smile, 'Tha could have done much worse. But, yon Billy Briggs needs a lass like thee,'

'So do you Ernie,' laughed Andrea.

'Well, there's nowt much wrong wi thee and young Susan. Tha's getten thy men on t' right track,'

He thought for a moment.

'Hasn't thy got a sister in Lancashire?'

'Oh yes, but she's worse than me. I'll tell her about you,'

As far as Jim was concerned, all this was grown up talk. He had no interest in any of it.

He was playing with Ernies dogs.

It didn't take very long to cut Ernie's five acres.

He inspected it all carefully, almost inch by inch. Finally, he seemed to be satisfied.

'Go and turn thy hay lad. T' weather'll hold for t' rest o' t' week,'

The following morning, Andrea was back.

She brought Billy along because he had nothing much to do at Dingle Bottom, and he wanted to spend a bit of time over at Nab's Head with their new friends. By the middle of the day, the hay had been raked into rows, where it would finally dry out ready for getting in.

Ernies hay was turned too. Ernie tried out his humour on Billy, but he got back as good as he gave.

'I hope tha's not getten any more weaners for t' auctions,' he grinned.

Billy knew what Ernie was referring to, and his answer was instantaneous,

'Time means brass Ernie. I got to Beddington in ten minutes,'

They both laughed.

Billy had something to tell Peter.

'How would tha like another tractor?' he asked him. "I've getten one, if tha wants it. Thirty pounds,'

'I didn't know you had a tractor,' Peter was surprised.

'Nay. I bought it from a chap in Oakendale. He didn't use it and I'd done him a few favours in the past. He wouldn't let it go for less than thirty, but, I thought you could use it. A spare tractor's useful,'

'What sort is it?' Peter asked.

'It's a Little Grey Fergie,'

Peter was delighted.

The grey Ferguson tractor was fast becoming a part of folk legend among the farming community. It was first produced in the late nineteen thirties and had been used right through the war on thousands of farms.

By the nineteen sixties it was a bit underpowered and newer and bigger tractors were in common use, but the 'Little Grey Fergie' as it was affectionately known, had found its place in the hearts of the British farmers.

It was more than Peter could resist. Soon, the 'Fergie', was at Nab's Head.

Andrea drove Billy over to Oakendale, and he had the tractor running in minutes. A drop of oil in the engine and some air in the tyres, and it was running like a sewing machine.

Jim wanted to paint it right away, but Peter told him that it needed a bit of rust scraping off and a spot of priming paint first.

He promised Jim that he could help with the restoration job.

Finally, everyone in the Dale finished haymaking, and the farmers found time to call in at the Black Bull for a pint. Life settled down into its usual late summer routine and Widdersdale braced itself for the school holidays.

Finally, the day of the great escape arrived.

Mrs Evans and Mrs Winstanley stood at the school gate, saying goodbye to the children, but few of them responded. They were free.

Each child carried a blue folder containing artwork that they had done over the term.

Jim got a pat on the head as he rushed out.

'Have a good holiday Jim,' called Mrs Winstanley.

Jim looked up at her and said,

'Thank you Mrs Winstanley. I'm going to help my dad to paint the new tractor,'

Mrs Winstanley stuck her thumb in the air and winked at Jim.

Up went Jim's thumb and a big smile spread across his face.

Mrs Winstanley smiled and shook her head. She looked rather sad.

Susan, who had seen all of it, waved to Mrs Winstanley.

As soon as Jim arrived home, he pulled his blue school jumper over his head. It was his way of saying 'No school for a few weeks,'

But, he rather wished that he could see a few of his friends a bit more.

The problem was, being such a spread out community, some of the children lived a considerable distance from Billingbeck. Others lived on remote farms and seldom came into contact with neighbours. A lot of children went to the auctions with their fathers. There they would greet other kids like adults, with just a casual nod and a comment about the stock on their farm.

But, the big act didn't last long.

After all, they were not 'real' adults. And so, very soon they were dashing about playing, as children all over the world do.

Thirteen

Without any doubt, the big social event of the year was the Widdersdale Summer Fair.

It was the time when all the Dales folk had the chance to meet together and enjoy themselves for a day. For as long as anyone could remember, it had been held in one of Sam Turner's lower meadows. For days before the event, the lads of the Dale were busy erecting huge marquees and marking out the main arena and running tracks.

Peter and Susan went down to Sam Turner's meadow and helped where they could, but there was not much to do because the Young Farmers Club had more or less taken over. During the week before the show, Sam's meadow was transformed. The main arena was fenced and several huge marquees were erected. Part of the main arena was set aside for the equestrian events.

Bert Eckersley personally supervised the erection of the 'beer tent', while other people were busy putting the final touches to their various stalls.

There was a lot of enthusiasm among everyone who was involved in getting ready for the big event so, there wasn't really much that Peter and Susan could do.

Equestrian events were organised by the Pony Club, and the Young Farmers were planning a sheepdog trial. Jim wanted Meg to take part, but Peter explained to him that, perhaps Meg would be likely to roll on her back and wag her tail at the judges.

'I can teach Meg how to do trials as soon as I learn to whistle properly,'

Jim was supremely confident that his friend Meg could easily beat the opposition.

'Perhaps next year you'll be a good whistler,' Peter said.

'Meg is the best,' Jim muttered.

Jim did however, have a painting in the junior art competition. It was entitled simply, 'Meg'.

Finally, the big day arrived.

The morning broke, bright and warm, with the promise of a perfect day. Peter Susan and Jim were on the field early. They walked round the various exhibits. The Women's Institute had a huge array of home made cheeses and jams as well as cakes and bread. Most of the ladies were involved in running various events,

That left a lot of the men free to wander over to the beer tent.

Situated right next to the beer tent was the spot where the Ottershead Brass Band was playing. It was very hot work, playing in the Ottershead Brass Band. Most people agreed that the band played much better after a couple of visits to the beer tent.

Suddenly, there was a cry from somewhere in the crowd,

'Susan, Peter,' It was Billy Briggs and Andrea. 'We knew that you were here. We saw the Land Rover in the car park,'

Andrea bent down and beckoned Jim over to her side,

'Good morning Jim. How's my best boyfriend?' she said.

'I have a picture in the art tent,' Jim said.

'Well then, it's sure to be a winner. What's it about?'

'Meg,' Jim said.

The showground was becoming crowded; it looked as though everyone was there.

Ned and Betty were helping out on the 'stick makers' stand.

'Morning,' he called out, as he spotted Peter and Susan. 'By gum, t' weather couldn't be better. Does tha want t' buy a new stick?'

Peter looked over the array of carved walking sticks and shepherds crooks that were on display.

'Some fine carving Ned,' he said. 'But I think that I will keep with my old stick. I only use it to wave at stray sheep,'

Ned tried again.

'Tha could hang a good stick o'er thy fireplace,'

'I'll hang thee over our fireplace, if you keep on trying to sell me a new stick,' Peter tried to look stern.

'Aye. So tha doesn't want a stick,'

Ned abandoned the idea of selling a stick.

'We'll go and watch the Morris dancers while you two get some beer from the beer tent.' Susan knew that Peter and Billy would want a beer by now. 'We'll be sitting on those straw bales,' she said. 'What do you want Andrea?'

'Half a bitter please,' Andrea said.

'Me too. And a glass of orange juice for Jim,'

Susan smiled as the two men walked off in the direction of the beer tent.

'Quite well trained, those two,'

Andrea looked at the two men disappearing into the gloom of the tent.

'Oh, I must admit, they usually do what they are told,'

Jim was getting restless,

'Let's go and watch the sheepdogs,' He said. 'I bet Meg would have been the best,'

'The sheepdog trials haven't started yet,' Susan said. 'We're going to watch the Morris dancers,'

'It's daft,' Jim said. 'Grown men dancing about wi'flowers on their hats,'

'Wouldn't you like to be a Morris dancer?' Andrea teased him.

Jim didn't even bother to answer her. He had seen John Thompson's big sister, Jean. She was in class two. Most of the boys had a crush on Jean Thompson,

Jim was no exception.

Jacob Jarvis and his sons were in the beer tent, so was Geoff Winstanley and the young vet from Dobson's veterinary surgery.

He was wearing a bowler hat, because he was the vet for the show.

Peter saw Mr Ackroyd's secretary who was also Bert Eckersley's niece, serving behind the bar.

'Good Morning Mr Barnard,' she managed to make herself heard above the noise of a lot of thirsty farmers. 'What would you like?'

'Two pints and two halves of bitter and a bottle of orange juice,'

Peter managed to shout his order to her.

The two girls were sitting in the sunshine enjoying the colourful spectacle of the Ottershead Morris dancers jumping about, waving their blue and green handkerchiefs in the air.

'Why don't you join the Ottershead Morris dancers?' Andrea asked Billy, innocently. He almost choked on his beer.

'They look like a lot of girls, wi' flowers on their hats,' He muttered. 'Tha't joking,'

Meanwhile, Jim had disappeared! Actually, he was only a few feet away, deep in conversation with Jean Thompson. Most of Jeans face was hidden behind sticky candy floss, but Jim was totally besotted. He was gazing into her eyes.

When he saw the bottle of orange juice however, his thirst overcame his love for Jean Thompson.

'My dad's back. See you after the holidays,' He abandoned Jean Thompson.

A lot of young girls were wandering about, trying to look sophisticated in their black riding hats and tweed jackets. Most of the lads on the other hand, tried to look like their dads in their overalls and caps.

The big event as far as Jim was concerned, was the sheepdog trials. They were held on the sloping field behind the main showground, where the land rose gently towards the higher part of Willowburn Farm and towards Lower Brigg.

The Barnards and Billy Briggs and Andrea had no choice in the matter. Jim was adamant.

'Come on,' he said, 'Time for the sheepdog trials,'

Bales of straw had been placed on the edge of the slope, so that spectators could see the whole course, while sitting in comfort.

The judges were not local men.

They were experts who knew every trick and method used by these devoted sheep men. Most of the competitors, on the other hand, were from Widdersdale and the surrounding countryside. Jim didn't sit on the bales with his parents. He was fidgeting and looking carefully at the dogs.

As soon as the first dog was sent up the slope to bring the little group of sheep together, Jim was totally engrossed in what was happening.

He seemed to anticipate the sharp whistles of the shepherds and their dog's reactions.

The first dog ran rapidly round the nervous sheep and sent them off

Towards the first turning point. It was running, ears erect, belly to the ground, eyes fixed on the sheep.

'Yon's Lassie, daughter o' Gess, from Ilkley,' Jim told his parents.

They were amazed. Firstly, by Jim's sudden local accent and secondly by his knowledge of sheepdog trials.

'How do you know all that?' Susan asked him.

'Oh, Jack Riley told me, at school. His dad's on next.

He has a good chance. Their dog is called Timothy. It's three years old.

He'll beat Lassie, I think,'

'Wow!' Peter muttered. 'It seems that our lad is something of an expert. Perhaps, if we had allowed him to enter with Meg, they would have won the junior Widdersdale cup,'

'No, I would need to train Meg. She's too young yet,' Jim was quite serious.

'You have a future champion there,' Billy said. 'Maybe you should buy him one of Ned's shepherd's crooks,'

Timothy did indeed beat Lassie, but he didn't win the cup.

The big event of the day was, without doubt, the tug o' war!

Willowburn had won it for the last three years and the Billingbeck lads were out for revenge. The opposing teams lined up and spat on their hands.

They were burly farmers sons for the most part. Weight and muscle was what mattered. They rubbed their hands together and gripped the rope with grim determination. They were well aware that a lot of the lasses from both villages were standing in the front row of spectators.

Old Ned appeared from nowhere, with Betty. He was holding a pint of beer in his gnarled hand.

'Come on lads,' he shouted. 'Tha's not goin' t' let the Willowburn lot win again,'

A few of the Willowburn lasses giggled. It was their way of mocking the Billingbeck team. In reality, it served to make the Billingbeck team even more determined to win.

Suddenly, the whistle blew. Both the teams dug their boots into the turf and took the strain. Muscles rippled and faces turned bright red.

Very slowly, the ribbon on the rope inched towards the Willowburn end.

Then back again.

Several times… The Willowburn girls screamed. Victory was in sight again.

Perhaps it was Ned's comment that did it. Suddenly, the ribbon shot over towards the Billingbeck end and it was all over.

The exhausted lads sat on the ground, sweaty and muddy, but they all had big grins on their faces.

One of the Willowburn lads shouted out,

'I slipped on a cow pat. Just thee wait 'till next year,'

Peter laughed and commented.

'I'll bet Bert Eckersley put that cow pat there. There'll be a lot of celebrating in the Black Bull tonight,'

There was a lot of laughter. There was still plenty to see and do.

Small girls on small ponies jumped desperately, each clear round earning a cheer from doting parents. A very small boy holding grimly onto a St Bernard dog won the cuddliest dog award, and still the band played on.

But eventually, all good things must come to an end.

Rosettes were pinned on assorted hot small girls, standing in rows holding hot small ponies. In the Arts and Crafts tent, a card had been pinned below Jim's picture of Meg. He had been awarded second prize.

'I didn't think I would beat Betty Edwards,' Jim was satisfied with second place. 'She's good at art,'

Susan suspected that there was a bit of chivalry involved.

Best dogs were rewarded, and their owners, for the most part, consumed vast amounts of beer.

The queues outside the toilet tents lengthened, the band finally played the unofficial Yorkshire anthem, 'On Ilkley moor baht 'at.' and by so doing, drew a line under the days events. Then, abandoning their instruments, they made a dash for the beer tent, conspicuous in their blue and gold uniforms.

The Women's Institute sold off most of the home made jam and cakes at bargain prices and the farmers loaded trailers with assorted animals and made their way slowly towards the field gate. Small groups of people started to drift homewards as the perfect sun sank down towards the western rim of the Dale.

As soon as Jim was put in the Land Rover, he fell asleep. As far as he was concerned, it was all over for another year.

⏎

The following morning brought an early autumn mist.

Widdersdale was back to normal.

Over at Appleburn Farm, Annie Dickinson looked into the cowshed. She had seen Bert backing his trailer up to the door and wondered what he had in it. She knew that it was auctions day and guessed that Bert had called in, as he often did, to see what was on offer.

To her surprise, she saw three young Hereford calves.

'What on earth have you bought calves for?' she asked him.

'It's getten nowt to do wi' thee,' Bert winked at her. 'It's time that young Peter and Susan next door got a couple more beasts. They've got lots of winter feed an' I got yon calves at t' right price,'

'Well, tha'll be able to tell them,' Annie said. 'Their Land Rover is just coming through t' Midge Hole,'

Bert looked up the lane. Sure enough, Peter's Land Rover was just coming into view under the trees.

Bert stepped into the lane and raised a hand.

'Mornin' Peter, Mornin' Susan. I saw that young Jim got second prize at the show. Good picture,' Jim grinned.

'Betty Edwards got first prize. She painted the village square and the Black Bull,'

'Well, I've not stopped thee for nowt,' Bert said. 'I've getten summat t' show thee,'

'I thought perhaps you wanted something from Billingbeck. We're just going down there,' Susan said.

'Nay lass. Come and look what I've got in t' barn,'

Peter stopped the Land Rover engine, and they followed Bert to his barn.

He opened the top of the door and pushed his cap onto the back of his head.

'Just tell me what tha thinks about those young ladies,' he said. 'Tha'll not get any better,'

Peter and Susan looked at the three red and white calves standing in the straw. They knew that they were looking at very good youngsters.

The calves stood, stocky and solid, gazing towards the open door.

'I thought maybe tha' would want 'em,' Bert said. 'Tha's getten lots o' good hay, an' I can give thee a bag o' Gold Top milk for feedin' 'em,'

Susan turned to Peter,

'Well Peter. It looks as though our minds are made up for us,'

She explained to Bert that they had been discussing buying a couple of calves.

'Tha'll not get any better. And, they haven't been in t' auctions. I bought 'em out of Jim Holt's trailer,' He looked at Peter,' If tha' wants 'em, Fifteen pounds each,' he smiled, "Tha'll get no scourin', they haven't been in t' ring,'

Peter understood what he was talking about. Calves that went through the auctions could pick up 'scouring', from other calves. Scouring, was a stomach bug that caused loose bowels, and could easily cause the calf to die, or at best, to retard its growth considerably.

'We'll buy them,'

Susan made up Peter's mind for him.

To make sure that he couldn't refuse, she lifted Jim up, so that he could see the little calves.

'Are we buying them Dad?' Jim said.

It was a devious move on Susan's part.

'Come on inside. We don't see very much of you these days. I'll put the kettle on,' said Annie. 'I've got some home made ginger beer for Jim,'

Peter was worried that the calves might injure themselves in the back of the Land Rover, but Bert soon put him at ease.

'I'll show thee how to keep 'em safe in t' back o' thy Land Rover,' he said.

He went into one of his sheds and came out carrying three sacks and three small wooden wedges that looked like pencils.

Expertly, he lowered one of the calves into a sack, back end first, with Peter's help. Then he gathered the neck of the sack together and put a peg into it, so that the calf was safe inside a sort of sleeping bag, with only its head sticking out.

'It's safe now. It can't jump about and injure itself,'

Really it was so simple and obvious. But, simple ideas are often the best.

Jim got his luck money from Bert. He said,

'Thank you very much,' as Bert handed him a pound.

Feeding the calves was the next thing to get right. Susan knew that they must mix the milk powder with warm water and they had seen Ernie feeding calves from a milk bottle, using the finger of a rubber glove as a teat.

It worked very well.

Later, it was time to teach the babies how to suck the milk from a bucket. Ernie had shown them how it was done.

He had put his finger into the warm milk, and they watched, as the calf sucked at his finger. Patiently, Susan lowered his finger into the milk until the calf was sucking at the contents of the bucket, without realising it.

Ernie was over at Nab's Head the morning after they acquired the three calves.

'How are yon calves doing?' he asked,

'How do you know about them?' Susan was genuinely baffled.

As far as she knew, Bert Dickinson had just moved them to Appleburn Farm, and not mentioned it to anyone. But, Ernie knew.

Ernie pulled his pipe from his mouth and tapped the side of his nose, grinning.

'Tha can't keep secrets in t' Dale,' he said.

His next comment didn't surprise either Peter or Susan.

'If tha gets some scourin', I've getten something in a bottle. Don't you go telephoning yon vetinary chap,'

'Oh,' Peter said. 'We wouldn't dream of it. But the calves haven't been in the auctions,'

Ernie just grunted in acknowledgement. He sat beside the fire and gratefully accepted a mug of tea.

'Well,' he said, 'All t' hays in and t' fairs over wi' for another year,'

He was silent for a moment.

'Lot of walkers about Ernie,' Peter said.

'Who would have thought that folk would come walking in t' Dale just for t' fun of it. Never saw anyone in t' old days. T' Black Bull had oil lamps in those days. Even t' church. Beer were in barrels behind t' bar, an' there were sand on t' floor,'

He hadn't mentioned the old days before.

'Petrol pumps! No petrol pumps in t' yard. Bert Eckersley weren't born then. I remember t' first motor car in t' Dale. It belonged to Doctor Threlfall. He's been dead for many a year,'

'How old were you when you came to Widdersdale?' Susan asked him. But he had said all he was going to say.

'Oh, I were just a lad,' He puffed on his pipe and withdrew into his memories.

Peter couldn't imagine the changes that had happened over the years.

He knew that Billingbeck had been different. There had been a butchers shop and a shop selling clothing and shoes. There had been an apothecary too. There had been a lot of woollen mills in Yorkshire in those days.

Milk, eggs and cheese were all provided by the farms, as well as butter, and ham from the 'home pig'. But gradually, rural folk were attracted to the big towns. In Leeds, it was possible to rent a house with a tap.

Peter had been daydreaming. He shook his head and came suddenly back into the world of nineteen sixty six.

Ernie laughed.

'Tha were far away then Peter,' he said.

'I was trying to imagine how things were sixty years ago,' Peter smiled.

'Best forgotten,' Ernie said. 'They were hard times,'

Jim was almost ready to go back to school.

The holidays had passed so quickly.

Arthur and Ada came to stay with them for a week, and Jim was treated like the Lord of Widdersdale. They saw Jim quite often, because Peter and Susan visited Guiseley every few weeks. But it was different, having his grandparents at Nab's Head for a whole week; he made the most of his celebrity status, as children do. But finally, it was all over.

Jim was going back to school as one of the old hands now.

No longer the timid little boy aged five, so out of his depth.

Now, he was in class two. He walked confidently down the lane with Susan, and greeted Mrs Winstanley with a wave. His school jumper had faded a bit. He looked at the new children, clutching their mother's hands nervously, and smiled. He was growing up fast.

He made good use of the Library van that came to Billingbeck once a fortnight. He usually chose adventure books with lots of pictures.

He was full of questions about everything he read. He would lie on the rug alongside Meg, elbows propping his head with a book open before him.

Susan would look at him, lying there, and smile.

Meg showed no interest in reading, but she loved the closeness of her friend Jim.

The calves were doing well. There had been no 'scouring', and they were sturdy and strong. It was obvious that the cattle at Nab's Head were going to winter well.

By now, it was well into November. Peter and Susan found time to relax in the evenings, and just enjoy the sheer pleasure of where they lived.

They both knew that they would never take it all for granted.

Peter's new toy, the Little Grey Fergie, was often to be seen working around Nab's Head Farm. It amused Susan to see Peter wiping a spot of mud off the bonnet, or going round it with an oil can.

Ernie found it very amusing. He pointed out that Peter had forgotten to paint inside the tool box, so he made sure that it was indeed painted grey.

As nightime fell, light rain drifted into the valley.

It crept silently across the Dale in the darkness like an invisible hand gently stroking the cheek of a sleeping child.

Peter and Susan were surprised, because, earlier in the evening, they had walked to the top of the higher meadow and gazed across the moors.

The sun had been setting across the broad expanse of gently waving cotton grass. The sky was lit up with every shade of red and gold and the colours were reflected in the contours of the moor. Deep shadows were beginning to form in the hollows, but there was a clear sharpness in the evening sky. Nothing moved. The land was at peace.

Jim looked towards the horizon in awe.

It was one of the magic moments that remain clearly in the memory of a child for ever.

But, it was something that would be gone in a short time.

Nothing more than the coming together of nature's miracles few moments.

A mere Will o' the whisp. A proof, if proof be needed, of the creator of all things.

'Where is there a Cathedral anywhere in the word, with such magic?' Susan whispered.

Peter glanced at his family.

They were standing, gazing across the gradually darkening land.

Their faces glowed in the light of the setting sun and their eyes shone brightly. How often had this magic scene gone unseen by human eyes up here on the wild moors? The little group, standing on the edge of the wild countryside, were indeed privileged.

By the time they had walked down the gently sloping field, the moment had passed. As they walked round the side of the barn, they heard a deep 'moo', from inside. One of the young cows had, no doubt, heard them.

It was as if they were being welcomed home. Jim was almost asleep on his feet. Susan lit the lamp as he drank his milky cocoa, and he didn't need to be told that it was bedtime.

He muttered 'goodnight and God bless', and gave Peter his goodnight kiss, and then, knowing that his mum would be right behind him, he started to climb the stairs towards his tiny bedroom. In a few moments, he was being tucked up in his bed, while Peter laid a few sticks in the empty fireplace.

Very soon, the room was glowing in the flickering light of the fire. Susan came down the stairs, smiling.

'We won't hear much from Jim, He was asleep even before I tucked him in,'

Peter handed Susan a mug of cocoa,

'Jim didn't have much to say did he? But he certainly appreciated the magic of it all. Did you notice his expression as he looked across the moor and watched the changing colours of the sunset,'

Susan sat on the battered settee and smiled.

'It's been a perfect day, hasn't it?'

'Indeed it has,' Peter put his arm round Susan's shoulder and stretched his legs towards the fire.

'Where does time go? With the school holidays behind us and the shortening days. It isn't far off our second Christmas at Nab's Head.

Out there, on the moor, I couldn't help thinking about all the generations in the past who must have stood and gazed in awe at a sunset just like that. They all had lives and families, and they all had our fears and uncertainties too,'

Susan rested her head on Peter's shoulder.

Peter gazed into the flickering fire,

'Really, when you think of it like that, I suppose that none of it belongs to us. One day, Jim'll be standing with his family, seeing it all. He'll remember tonight and reflect about the passing of time,'

Gradually, the fire died down to nothing more than glowing embers and the room dimmed, the only light coming from the oil lamp.

Still, the silence was broken by the gentle, slow ticking of the Grandfather clock. Somewhere, far away on one of the distant farms, a dog barked, perhaps disturbed by a marauding fox.

From that time on, the shortening days became more noticeable, and the nights became cooler. The woodpile was topped up ready for the winter and the buildings were given a fresh coat of lime wash.

Preparations for the school Christmas play were going ahead under the Supervision of Mrs Evans and Mrs Winstanley.

It was the turn of the new children to wear the towels this year.

Jim had a new role as a sailor in a comedy sketch. He was well pleased with his sailor's hat. He was even more suited by the fact that the girls sang 'All the nice girls love a sailor', and he had Betty Edwards on his arm, but he didn't want to admit it.

The new class one children seemed to be rather more sedate than the rebels of the previous year had been, but perhaps it only appeared so.

Perhaps it was that year two had finally discovered that it was impossible to beat the system?

An older and wiser young Master Hebblethwaite played his part to perfection.

⌒

The Christmas party at Nab's Head was a foregone conclusion.

In fact, it was to become something of a tradition over the years.

Peter and Susan planned a family party once again.

They planned to invite Billy and Andrea along.

Both Peter and Susan's families would be staying overnight, and Ernie was going to be there, even if it meant Peter taking the Land

Rover to Folly Edge, and collecting him.

Geoff and Hillary Winstanley were invited.

They were delighted and accepted the invitation,

It was going to be quite a gathering.

Andrea planned to go over to Nab's Head on the day before the party, to help Susan with the preparations.

Peter was ordered to stay well out of the way, but, Jim was allowed to take on the role of head of the kitchen. His job consisted of testing the cakes and trifles. The party was set for Christmas day.

Christmas dinner at Nab's Head.

The party at the Black Bull was on the following weekend.

Christmas Eve morning was spent over in Guiseley, visiting friends and picking up Arthur and Ada.

'Have you noticed how different it all seems now?' Susan said, as Peter was driving towards Guiseley.

'Have I noticed what?' Peter asked her.

'Well, everything really, I suppose that nothing much has changed here, but, we have. After so long, living in Widdersdale, Guiseley seems so different. It's still Yorkshire, and it still has its charm, but maybe I see it differently now. Everything seems to be organised somehow.

In the Dale, it's rather like living in a different time. That's how I would describe it. Perhaps it's because we live with nature more,'

'Yes, I agree,' Peter said, 'two worlds in harmony with each other,'

'Perhaps because its Christmas, we are both thinking about the past,' Susan said. 'A time to reflect,'

'Maybe?' Peter thought about it, 'Yes, maybe you're right,'

They were home early in the afternoon, because Susan and Andrea had so much to do. Peter took his Dad over to Appleburn Farm, to visit Bert and Annie Dickinson, but, Ada wanted to help the girls in the kitchen.

That was O.K. by Jim, just as long as everyone knew who the boss was.

There was the 'now familiar', enjoyable task of putting a lot of Jim's presents beside his bed after he had gone to sleep. When it was done, Susan made a late supper for all of them.

'It seems no time since we were putting Peter's toys beside his bed,' Ada smiled at Susan.

'You'd have a problem trying to fit a 'Little Grey Fergie' beside his bed,' said Susan. She had to explain what Peters toy, the Little Grey Fergie was.

'I remember dragging a bike up the stairs,' Arthur said. 'It only just fit round t' banister rail'

Christmas morning was bright and sunny. Billy and Andrea arrived at Nab's Head early. Ernie had been told that dinner would be about two o clock, and he was instructed by Susan to be on time. Susan introduced Billy to Arthur and Ada. They had of course, met Andrea the previous day.

They shook hands rather formally, but soon, they were nattering away like old friends. Arthur was intrigued by Billy. He hadn't really ever met anyone like him, and he was full of questions.

Billy quite enjoyed the attention and soon, he was telling Arthur all about life as a pig farmer in the Dales.

Ada was much more relaxed with Andrea and she was quite at home in the company of the two girls. Susan saw a side of her that she hadn't seen before. She had a humour than Susan had never suspected.

Jim, of course, was in his element with three women fussing round

There was a knock at the porch door and Jim rushed to open it.

He knew that Mrs Winstanley was coming, but, suddenly coming face to face with her away from the environment of the village school rather took the wind out of his sails.

'Good morning Miss,' he said, as though he had just arrived at class.

Mrs Winstanley found it difficult not to smile.

'Good morning Jim,' she answered.

Jim stood aside to allow Mr and Mrs Winstanley to enter.

Geoff soon put Jim at his ease. He bent down and whispered in Jim's ear.

'Mrs Winstanley is really called Hillary, but I'll tell you a secret. I call her 'Cork'. I'll tell you why. We have some hens and they strut about shouting 'Kaaawwk'. Sometimes, Hillary talks back to them. She loves animals. Just wait 'till she sees Meg,'

Jim found it impossible to believe that Mrs Winstanley actually talked to hens. Perhaps teachers were just like everybody else?

His Mum would talk to hens. There couldn't be much wrong with people who loved animals.

The next guests to arrive were Susan's parents, Bill and June.

Jim heard the car pulling into the yard and he ran outside to greet them.

'Merry Christmas Jim,'

June was loaded with presents, but, Bill swept Jim off his feet.

Susan gave her parents a hug and Peter rushed to assist June with her brightly wrapped parcels.

Just as everyone was being introduced, there was another knock on the door. Peter was nearest, so he went over the porch and opened the door.

There was only one guest still to arrive and Peter hadn't been too sure that he ever would, but it was indeed, Ernie. It wasn't the Ernie that he knew so well who was standing there. This Ernie was wearing a collar and a tie and he had shaved very carefully. The transformation was remarkable. Ernie looked every inch a country gentleman. His appearance emphasised the character that had been etched on his honest, open face. His intelligent eyes were bright and belied his age, but he was obviously slightly ill at ease as he looked round the room,

Susan understood the mixed feelings of the old farmer. After all, it wasn't every day that he was invited into someone's home, let alone to share Christmas with a family.

'Ernie. We are really glad that you could make it. I saved your favourite chair for you. First thing'll be a cup of tea,'

Ernie knew Billy and Andrea of course, and Geoff.

He had seen Hillary in the village; he knew that she was Geoff's wife and a teacher at Billingbeck School.

He looked at Arthur and Ada.

'Ernie, I'd like you to meet my parents, Arthur and Ada,'

'So, Young Peter's thy lad,' he had his old twinkle in his eye, 'He isn't a bad 'un, I'll make a farmer out o' him yet,'

Arthur laughed,

'We've been told a lot about you Ernie. It's good to meet you. Merry Christmas,'

'And to thee,' Ernie said.

He sat in the corner, on his favourite chair.

'Where's young Jim?' Ernie asked. 'I've getten something for him,'

Jim was sitting beside Hillary, playing with Meg.

Ernie beckoned him over. He gave Jim the parcel that he was holding and bent close to his ear.

'Merry Christmas, little un. This is for thee,'

Jim thanked him and looked a bit uncertainly at his mum.

'Go on then. Open it,' she said, 'Ernie brought it for you,'

Everyone watched Jim as he tugged at the wrapping paper.

As he finally caught sight of the contents, his eyes opened wide.

It was a model of a 'Little Grey Fergie'.

'Oh, Thank you so much,' he muttered. 'Look dad, a Ferguson,'

Susan knew that it was Jim's very best present.

She had waited until this moment to give Ernie his present.

She picked it up from its resting place under the Christmas tree, and handed it to Jim.

'There you are. Father Christmas didn't forget Ernie,'

Jim handed the gaily wrapped present to Ernie.

'Can I open it now?' he asked.

'Oh yes. I opened all mine,'

Jim was curious.

What had Father Christmas brought for Ernie?

Ernie unwrapped his present with a touch of drama.

Father Christmas had given Ernie a new pipe and three red tins of his favourite tobacco.

Erne smiled at Peter and Susan,

'Thank you Father Christmas,' he said.

Susan winked at him.

She had noticed that Ernie had brought something else with him.

He had an old sack tied with string. Whatever it was, he was keeping it tucked carefully away in the corner beside his chair.

The great table had been laid earlier and finally, Susan and Andrea were finished with the final preparations for Dinner.

'Dinners ready,' Susan announced. 'If everyone can sit round the table, we can get started. You'll find a little card with your name on it,'

It was no accident that Ernie was seated between Arthur and Bill. They would find plenty to talk about.

Dinner was traditional. The soup was creamy vegetable and it was followed by a huge turkey, carved by Peter, and a large dish of Andrea's roast

Potatoes and a choice of vegetables. Gravy and sage and onion completed the meal. Christmas pudding and white sauce was followed by a choice of Port or Sherry. Peter stood up and looked round the table,

'I would like to wish everyone a Merry Christmas and a Happy new Year,' he raised his glass, 'To all of you, Family and dear friends, and to our Dale. May we all find peace and happiness in the coming year,'

Everyone raised their glasses.

Jim was in big demand, but he really wanted to play with his new tractor.

Hillary told Susan that Jim was a very different child to the rather shy little chap who had arrived at the village school just over a year ago.

He had gained a lot of confidence. He very was quick to come to the defence of the quieter children if there was any sign of bullying. He was listened to. His opinion was even asked for on occasions. Susan told her how upset he had been because he didn't bring his buttercup out of school.

Hillary laughed.

'You explained to him that it went on the wall because it was the best picture,'

Susan nodded.

After dinner, everyone settled down with a glass of sherry or a mug of beer and a large plate of mince pies was placed on the table

Jim was ignoring the jelly! A sure sign that he had eaten too much, but he made sure that Meg came in for a few treats and Susan saw him wandering outside with a bag of goodies. Quietly, she followed him.

He went into Beatty's shed. There was nothing that wasn't on Beatty's menu.

Peter and Susan looked round the room,

How things changed. Last year, they had been new to the Dale, they knew a lot of people, but not really well. They had been a family unit then, but in a different way. Not only had so much changed, but without realising it, they had changed too. They had been eager to fit in, but they realised now that 'fitting in', was something that just happened.

Ernie seemed to be content to just sit in his corner, in his comfortable chair, listening to what everyone had to say. Andrea was impressed by him.

She got through his natural reserve simply by using her honest, friendly charm. It wasn't long before the two of them were chatting like old pals.

Andrea was laughing, but sometimes looking quite sad. Ernie was telling her tales of the old days. She had a glass in her hand. And much to the surprise of Peter and Susan, so did Ernie.

Andrea had insisted that he have a Christmas drink with her, but he wasn't a drinking man. In fact, he never called in at the Black Bull, and there was never a bottle of anything on his shopping list. But, he was contented.

He had a twinkle in his eye and his face glowed.

Peter went over and spoke to him,

'By gum Ernie, how do you manage to charm the ladies? I never suspected that you had such hidden talents,'

Ernie grinned at him.'There's a lot of things tha' doesn't know,'

He tapped the side of his nose.

Andrea smiled,

'I thought I was talking to another Yorkshireman, but Ernie is a Cumbrian. I'll tell you something Peter, this one has seen good and bad times,'

Ernie looked round.

'Where did I put yon sack?' he asked.

His sack was where he had put it, safely tucked beside his chair.

He began to untie the string that held the neck closed.

Then, to everyone's amazement, he lifted out a violin case.

He laid it on the table and opened it. He lifted out a very fine looking violin and a bow.

'Haven't played this in a good many years. We used to play in t' barns after harvest time at t' big houses. I was a lad then, T' other farmers as could play'll be long gone,'

He pulled on a couple of the strings with his rough, work worn fingers. Carefully, he adjusted a couple of pegs. Finally satisfied, he put the violin under his chin and began to play it, eyes closed.

The music that filled the room was so sweet.

Old Ernie, the farmer who lived alone over at Folly Edge, was a fine and accomplished musician.

'What talent,' Susan whispered to Peter.

He nodded.

Ernie broke off his playing.

'Well,' he said, 'Move yon chairs an' I'll play a couple o' jigs,'

With a big happy smile on his face, he brought the old violin to life.

It was impossible to just stand there listening. His sweet, lively music demanded that feet came alive.

The first one was Jim. In no time, the scene was one of merriment and movement. It was a step back in time to the long ago, days of the harvest home jigs of the nineteenth century.

Ernie had a far away look in his eyes as he became at one with his old violin. The years drifted away from him. He was a young man again, in his old life so far away in some Cumbrian valley where he had spent his childhood.

As Susan watched him. She had a tear in her eye.

It was as though he had his family round him and a lot of long gone faces, some of them lost in two World Wars, some of them gone long before their time, killed by overwork and hard living, Long hours spent on the land in all weathers, damp old sacks over their shoulders as protection against the rain.

Such was the magic of Ernie's music.

Susan watched the old man, battered and hardened by a lifetime spent farming on the northern hills. His white hair framing his honest face, his bright blue eyes shining with happiness as he was taken back to his youth.

How many Christmases had he sat alone in his remote little hill farm, just Ernie and his dogs? What sadness had gripped his heart?

Susan had a picture in her mind of a lonely old man, sitting by his flickering fire in the twilight, with his dogs for company and a pot of tea at his elbow, thinking about times long gone.

At that moment, the remoteness and wildness of the distant reaches of the Dales was brought home to her. She looked round at her little family.

Peter was jigging up and down the room with young Jim. Both of them were laughing.

Susan wiped the tear from her eye. What would Mrs Lord be doing at that moment? Sitting alone with her memories, no doubt.

Fourteen

'Goodnight girls,'

Peter glanced round for a final time, to be sure that the cows were settled down, picked up his lantern and made his way into the yard.

He was greeted by a scene that could have been from a Victorian Christmas card.

In the short time that he had been attending to the animals, the world had been transformed; great snowflakes were floating down out of the night sky. The ground was already covered with a thick coat of powdery snow.

It only took him a moment to grab an armful of logs and carry them over to the porch, but, in that short time, he was himself covered in snow.

Most of January had been quite mild. There had been a few sharp frosts, but for the most part, skies had been deep blue and the views across the Dale had been bright and clear. But towards the end of the month, the wind had turned towards the North West and, with a cold, moist blast, came grey skies and a warning that snow was not far away.

Jim looked up as his dad walked in looking like a snowman.

'It's snowing. Mummy, it's snowing,'

He was sitting by the fire, reading an old 'Rupert' annual that had been handed down to him by his granddad Jackson. But nothing would keep him indoors now that he knew about the snow. He pulled on his wellingtons and rushed outside, closely followed by Meg. He was so excited that he forgot that he was wearing his pyjamas. Susan reached for his coat, but Jim was too fast for her. Bedtime was forgotten… His journey upstairs would have to wait.

Susan didn't realise that Jim had managed to gather up a snowball until it landed on the back of her head. Peter laughed and bent down to grab some of the snow, but he was too late. Susan beat him to it and hers landed on his shoulder and sprayed cold powdery snow all over his face.

The biggest snow enthusiast was once again, Meg.

She dashed round, rolling and tumbling in the sparkling snow, trying to grab great mouthfuls until she had a little white mound on top of her nose.

Back indoors, Jim had to be fitted out with dry pyjamas and have his hair dried. But he wasn't very interested in going to bed.

By morning, the sky was once again, bright blue. The Dale below looked sparkling and fresh in the early sunshine.

February and March brought more heavy snowfalls.

Soon, drifts built up against the walls and in the gullies. Sometimes, sheep had to be dug out of the drifting snow and farmers were kept busy carrying bales of hay out into the fields. They took out buckets of 'sheep nuts', and vitamin supplement blocks.

Thankfully, by the end of March, there was a thaw.

Early grass had begun to appear behind the sheltered south facing edges of the field walls. The clear waters of the beck ran dark and deep, sparkling brightly in the spring sun, as they dashed over the mossy rocks, down ever down, towards the valley far below.

Jim was the first to spot one of the early spring lambs.

He was running on, ahead of Susan, as they made their way across the fields on their way to school. Suddenly, he stopped and looked carefully towards a corner of one of the fields. There stood a wobbly, uncertain lamb, beside its mother. The rather bewildered looking mother was busy cleaning another one. Twins!

Jim was over the moon. But, he was a bit concerned.

He thought that they should be indoors. Susan reassured him that everything would be fine. The morning was dry and beginning to warm up in the early sunshine. It promised to be yet another wonderful spring day.

Reluctantly, Jim wandered off down the slope and towards school.

He couldn't wait to tell 'Miss', about the baby lambs. Very soon, the fields were full of lambs, jumping and cavorting about rather like children in a playground. Each day it was possible to see them growing stronger.

Perhaps the danger was over? The weather seemed to have settled down and there was little sign of any problems among the spring lambs.

The morning was overcast. It was cool, a grey sort of morning with a slight drizzle of rain. Peter was in the hayloft, whistling, as he nailed a new piece of wood across a hole in the floor. He was feeling quite happy about life. After all, it was spring and there was still hay in the loft.

The young cows were out, wandering over the fields, contentedly pulling at some early grass and lazily swishing their tails.

Peter noticed that they always seemed to be bigger when they were in the cowshed, but they had wintered well.

Suddenly, his thoughts were interrupted by the arrival of Ernie's dogs.

Meg had been lying in the hay down below, waving her feet in the air, but she jumped up as the other dogs burst into the barn. After greeting each other, they lay on the floor, tongues hanging out and tails wagging.

Peter came down from the loft and fussed the dogs.

Any moment… Yes, he could hear the clatter of hobnail boots on the cobbles outside.

'Art thou in t' barn?' Ernie called out.

'Aye,' shouted Peter.

Old Ernie clattered into the barn.

His cap was pulled well down against the grey morning, and he had a sack tied round his shoulders. He nodded to Peter, his weather-beaten face, unshaven as usual.

'How are you this morning, young feller?'

'Just mending a hole in the loft floor,' Peter replied.

'Well, tha'shouldn't be. Tha' had some sheep in t' top meadow,'

'Come in the house Ernie. Let's have a pot of tea,'

Ernie followed Peter into the house. The dogs decided to lie in the porch.

'Good morning Ernie,' Susan said. 'I just got back from school and I was about to put the kettle on,'

Ernie nodded his thanks and sat by the fire.

He had gone suddenly quiet and merely sat gazing into the flames.

It was very obvious to both Peter and Susan that he had something on his mind.

Gratefully, he accepted his mug of tea and held it in his hands.

Susan wondered what he was thinking about.

He usually had something witty to say, some little comment about what Peter and Susan were doing. Susan knew that, often, when Ernie sounded serious, it was to put her off her guard. Only the twinkle in his eyes giving away the fact that he was pulling her leg.

But there was no lively twinkle in his eyes this morning, no light hearted conversation.

As Susan looked at the old man, sitting by the fire, she saw an Ernie that she hadn't seen before. She saw a vulnerable old man.

He suddenly seemed to be smaller and older. She wanted to go over and put her arm round shoulder in a protective gesture.

Some time later, mugs replenished, Ernie pulled his battered old red tin from his pocket and stuffed some tobacco into his pipe.

He didn't have a match, so he bent towards the fire and lit his pipe with a scrap of blazing newspaper. A cloud of blue smoke hid his face for a moment.

Finally he spoke.

'I want thee to come over t' Folly Edge when tha's got time Peter,'

He puffed at his pipe.

'It's nowt urgent. But, make sure tha comes late. I don't want thee stoppin' me from working, taking up my time when I could be doin' something useful,'

Conversation after that became more relaxed.

'Best thing that ever happened to Billy Briggs was gettin' yon lass from Lancashire, Andrea. By gum, it's been t' making of him,'

Peter smiled.

'Thee too young feller. If tha hadn't got thy lass behind thee, tha wouldn't be half t' chap thou art. Tha's got a good lass,'

'Thank you,' Susan was amused. 'That's just what I keep on telling him,'

'Oh, make no mistake young lady, it's not all thee,' Ernie was his old self. 'Tha's getten a good chap,'

Finally, the old man stood up and straightened his back.

Susan noticed a slight pause. Then he put his cap well down over his face and pulled the old sack across his shoulders. His dogs jumped to their feet and stood eagerly behind the door.

'Don't thee forget t' come over. Anytime in t' next few days,'

Then, he was gone.

'Well, I wonder what all that was about?' Susan said.

'We'll soon find out, I'll go over to Folly Edge tomorrow night when I get home from the mill. I expect that he'll be thinking about muck-spreading.

And, he'll be wanting to pass on some more of his experience,' He grinned ruefully, 'We sure do need that,'

As the day drew on, it developed into the real 'Dales' version of rain.

It drifted in great clouds across the high ground and hid everything above about eight hundred feet from view. It dripped from the stumpy trees and ran down the gulleys between the rocks in ever increasing amounts.

Peter was at the mill, and therefore sheltered from it all.

He usually worked until about five thirty. Coming from the mill, he glanced up at the grey sky and grimaced as he dashed over to the Land Rover.

One thing that owners of older Land Rovers will agree on is the fact that, sitting in one, is no guarantee that the driver or passengers will remain dry in rainy weather.

As Peter drove away from the mill, a familiar drip of water entered his right boot. He had tried many times to find the source of the leak, but without success. Most people who live in country districts will have noticed farmers rattling along in ancient Land Rovers, wearing a cap and waxed jacket.

There is a good reason for that. Also, the Widdersdale rain often travelled horizontally over the ground, pushed along by the strong wind.

Peter drove the Land Rover into the yard and grabbed the hand-brake. Then, he made a quick dash over to the porch.

He was reminded of a painting he had once seen in one of his school books.

It had been entitled, 'Shelter from the raging storm'.

Susan had seen the Land Rover winding its way along the lane, and by the time Peter had finished taking off his boots in the porch, there was a homemade steak pie on the table.

It usually started to go dark about eight o clock at this time of the year, but tonight, darkness came earlier because it had been gloomy all day.

Susan had lots of work to do about the house and Jim seemed to be quite happy, bashing his toy Land Rover across the furniture.

Peter did the few jobs that needed to be done around the farm.

It didn't amount to much really. Cleaning out and feeding the few cows and carrying water in, feeding the goat and checking on the rabbit.

He didn't need to do anything there because Jim always made sure that 'Big Teeth', was cleaned out and overfed, whatever the weather

All the jobs finished, he decided to go over to Folly Edge Farm.

'Well, I'll be going over to see Ernie now. I hope it's nothing serious,'

Peter filled the storm lantern with paraffin and trimmed the wick.

'Can I come with you?' said Jim, hopefully.

'It's your bedtime, young man,' Susan said, firmly. 'And it's dark and very wet. Anyway, Daddy wants to talk with Ernie. You'd be bored,'

Jim knew that he wouldn't be allowed to go out so late, but there had been no harm in trying.

Meanwhile, Peter had pulled on his already damp coat and rammed his cap tightly on his head.

He gave Jim a goodnight kiss and smiled at him.

'It's tough, growing up, isn't it,'

He hugged Susan, more as a joke really because his coat was cold and damp.

'I shouldn't be too long dear. I'm sure that Ernie is just feeling a bit down. He needs someone to talk to I expect,'

'One thing that men are good at,' Susan pushed the damp Peter away. 'Discussing the injustice of life with each other. But, I think you are right.

Ernie isn't himself at all. He needs to discuss something. I hope we can help,'

Peter lit the lantern and picked up his stick. Then, with Meg at his side, he set off across the dark field.

He made his way carefully down the hillside towards Ernie's farm; he could see a dim light glowing in the farmhouse window. As he drew closer he made out the feeble yellow glow of another light in the grimy window of the cowshed.

As usual, Ernie was looking after his animals.

Peter's boots slid on the wet cobbles as he crossed the yard and pushed open the low door. Ernie was sweeping the cowshed floor with what had, at one time, been a yard brush. He looked up with a smile.

'I'll tell thee what, young 'un. I never thought I'd see thee on a night like this. Tha should be in thy house, by t' fire wi' a cup o' tea,'

It was what Peter had expected. No welcome. No thought that it was he, Ernie, who had asked Peter to come over.

Peter was carrying a small bag full of groceries that Susan had put together for Ernie. He held it out without speaking. Ernie took it from him and peered inside it.

'I bet young Susan thought about this. She's getten more sense than thou'll ever have,'

Ernie's face lit up as he extracted a red tobacco tin from the bag.

'By gum. I were a bit short o' tobacco,'

Suddenly, he disappeared into one of the darkest recesses of the cowshed.

He was back in a moment.

'Half a dozen eggs,' He held up a brown paper bag, and then put it on a shelf just inside the door. 'For Jim. Don't forget yon, when tha goes,'

He put what remained of the ancient brush into its corner and reached for the lamp that was hanging on a rusty hook that had been hammered into one of the beams.

He held the lamp in front of him and made his way towards the door. Carefully, he closed the door and fastened it by putting a bit of bent wire in the hasp, and then he crossed the wet cobbles of the yard, clogs rattling.

He glanced over his shoulder to be sure that Peter was following him.

Then he opened the porch door and disappeared inside.

Peter hesitated, not sure what to do.

A voice from inside made his mind up for him.

'Come on, young 'un. Kettle's on t' hob. Hang thy coat on t' nail in t' porch. Fetch that dog o' thyne in by t' fire.'

It was as though people often dropped in to visit him. But as far as Peter knew, no-one had ever set foot inside Ernie's home.

Stooping under the low door frame, Peter looked round the porch.

It had at one time been whitewashed, but few traces of white remained.

Only scraps of lime hung from the flaky walls, perhaps held there by cobwebs.

The floor was of stone flags, cracked and broken and there were several stone shelves set into the walls. That was it.

On the shelves there was a jumble of articles. A rusty scythe, a couple of buckets full of junk, some ancient spanners, a few old fashioned milk bottles and some mouldy bits of horse harness. There were several sacks containing, who knew what.

Peter ducked through another low door and he was inside Ernie's home. He looked round slowly.

The room was quite large. There were smoke blackened beams and an equally black ceiling. Curtains hung at the small windows.

They had, at one time, been covered in some sort of floral pattern.

Now they hung, limp and cobwebby. There were a few faded sepia pictures on the walls, but Peter found it impossible to see what they were, partly because of the dim light and partly because the glass was yellowed and grimy.

One was without doubt, a picture of a young man wearing the uniform of a soldier of the First World War, and another was a faded picture of several young men in shirtsleeves, some of them little more than children. They were standing in a field and holding scythes.

The room was dominated by a huge iron fireplace with a tarnished brass fender. A heavy iron kettle hung from a chain over the fire, its lid bouncing as the water inside boiled, sending clouds of steam up towards the ceiling. There was a large old table in the centre of the room. Covered in all sorts of seemingly useless objects. Peter could see an axe and an old hammer, a box of very rusty nails, bits of antique farming implements, several broken 'Farmers friends', yellowed copies of the *Farmers Guardian*, several dog eared stock record books and, in the middle of it all, a sleeping hen.

'Sit thee down an' I'll bring t' teapot,'

Ernie bent down and brushed yet another sleeping hen from a chair by the fire

Peter sat in the battered armchair, on a cushion made out of an old army greatcoat covered in hen's feathers.

It was surprisingly comfortable.

Ernie disappeared through a low doorway into what must have been the kitchen. He took the lamp with him. Peter had left his lantern in the porch. So the only light in the main room was the flickering fire.

Peter was amused to see another disgruntled hen, followed by a cat appear from the gloomy kitchen.

Peter had forgotten about Meg. He looked round the room and saw that she had quietly curled up in a corner with Ernie's dogs. After all, this was where she had begun her life.

Ernie returned, carefully balancing a teapot and a bottle of milk in one hand and the lamp in the other. He used his elbow to clear a corner of the table, and then he set down the lamp and laid a copy of the *Farmers Guardian* as though it were the finest Irish linen.

He carefully placed two large mugs on the newspaper and, with much ceremony, used his scarf to hold the steaming kettle He filled the teapot with smoky smelling, boiling water.

His weather beaten face glowed in the firelight as he beamed at Peter,

'Just give it a moment to brew,'

Ernie sat on the other chair and pulled his pipe from his pocket.

He opened his red tin and stuffed his pipe with tobacco.

He picked a small piece of blazing wood from the fire and lit the pipe with obvious pleasure. A long practiced ritual. For a moment. Ernie just sat puffing away at his pipe, and then he poured the tea into the two mugs.

He handed one to Peter,

'Drink thy tea before it goes cold,' he said.

Peter cautiously sipped the hot liquid. Surprisingly, it didn't taste at all bad.

'I don't invite many folk to Folly Edge,'

Ernie picked up a blazing bit of newspaper and re-lit his pipe.

Peter was very aware of how the old country folk saw no reason to rush anything.

Ernie took a deep draught of his tea, apparently unaffected by the scalding liquid.

'I've been keeping an eye on thee, young man. And that lass o' thine. One day, tha'll make farmers,'

Coming from Ernie, that statement meant about as much to Peter as being awarded an M.B.E.

The two men sat in silence for a while, each deep in his own thoughts.

A sleek looking cat jumped on the Ernie's knee and the old man began to stroke its silky fur. Peter was fascinated, just soaking up the atmosphere of the Ernie's home. It felt rather like being transported back in time a hundred years or so. There was total silence, except for the ticking of a clock and the soft moaning of the wind outside.

Ernie was in a reflective mood as he gazed into the fire.

'It's a lot different for you youngsters nowadays,'

His mind was far away. He almost seemed to be talking to himself.

He told Peter how he had been born in a village deep in the hills of Cumbria. He was the eldest of a family of eight children.

His parents ran a smallholding owned by the 'Master', at the big house.

At the age of eleven, he had been taken by his father to the 'Hiring fair', at Keswick. He had stood in a line of children, all hoping to be hired out as farm lads. Eventually, he was noticed by a farmer who was looking for a 'cow lad'.

The farmer walked all round young Ernie, and then felt his muscles.

'Not that I had any in those days,' Ernie was smiling.

He seemed to just accept that he should have been there in that line of children.

Eventually, after answering questions about cows and general farming, he had been offered a years work. The farmer was willing to pay him six pounds for the year, plus his food and keep. Accommodation on offer was in the hayloft over the cow shed, but he ate his meals with the family.

Breakfast was usually cattle bran with milk poured over it.

The family fared little better.

On Sundays, he was allowed to go to Chapel and say ' thank you' to his God for his good fortune, then, after Chapel, he could walk the eight miles, whatever the weather, to spend a few hours with his family.

He told Peter how, after several years of 'hiring', he met a young lady from his own village who worked in the 'big house' as a kitchen maid.

She had to get permission from the lady of the house and the butler to walk out with Ernie.

Eventually, they married.

She was a pretty girl and a hard worker. Ernie brought his young bride to Widdersdale. Folly Edge farm was up for rent and so they started farming there. But, within two years, his young bride was dead. A victim of consumption. They had no children.

Ernie looked so small and alone sitting by the fire, as he told Peter about the tragedy.

'I never re-married. I loved yon lass with all my heart.

Eventually. I bought t' farm and ever since, I've been here wi't' cows and t' dogs. It were all a long time ago. I took my bride back to t' village i' Cumbria. She's buried there, among t' hills, wi' her family,'

Peter wasn't able to say anything. His throat was choked with sympathy for this lonely old man.

There was silence once again. Just the ticking clock and the wind on the moor.

'Tha'll do alright, young'un. Tha's getten t' right lass wi' thee,'

Ernie broke the spell, but Peter was to remember that moment for the rest of his life.

'What I wanted to see thee about, young man is… Well, I'm not gettin' any younger I've been thinkin' Mebbe I don't want yon top meadow o' mine, and t' top field up by thy place. Its getten good water and t' walls are sound.

Dus't tha want t' make me an offer? Sam Turner's been showing' an interest, but he'll not want thee to miss t' chance. He'd rather thee have it, an' so would I,'

Peter was astounded.

'Of course, we'd be more than interested. But, you'll be alright.

We can always spread your muck and get the hay in for you,'

Ernie smiled.

'I've given it plenty o' thought Peter lad. If tha wants it, make me an offer,'

Ernie was not an easy man to do a deal with, but, eventually, a fair price was agreed. Ernie held out his gnarled hand to shake on the deal and Peter did the same.

'I'll go down to see Mister James Ackroyd at t' lawyers, and get t' papers sorted out. Tha doesn't need to worry about payin' yet. Tha can do some work for me, wi' yon machines o' thine. And, tha'll have too much hay.

Tha can gi' me some o' that too. But, tha does all t' work, carryin' it,'

Although it was late, Ernie didn't seem to want to be alone with his thoughts.

Peter understood.

Ernie had opened his heart in a way that he hadn't done for many years.

'What about your family in Cumbria Ernie? Do you ever see any of them?'

'No lad. It's been many long years. I don't belong there now.

My sisters are married an' two o' my brothers still have the farm.

It's bigger now. There's about three hundred acres, an' they own it.

My young sister Maggie writes every Christmas, but there's only four still living. They wouldn't want old Ernie back in their lives,' he laughed and glanced round the room,

'They live a bit different,'

Ernie was telling Peter things that he would never mention to anyone.

He knew that none of it would go any further.

'Anyway, I've getten good neighbours now. Tha does some o' my work, and t' lass makes sure I don't starve. An' young Jim. Tha's got a bright star there Peter. Yon lad'll grow up t' do thee proud,'

He paused for a moment.

'I've getten summat I want Jim to have,'

He stood up, holding the edge of the table, and walked over to a cupboard beside the window. He opened the door and lifted out an old sack.

Peter knew what it contained, because he had seen it before.

'Oh no Ernie. You can't do that,'

'Tha can't stop me,' Ernie grinned. 'I see something in young Jim. He'll be carrying something on for a lot more years after I'm gone,'

He lifted his violin from the sack.

'There's a block o' rosin for t' strings on t' bow,'

He held up a small piece of resin. 'I'll put t' violin in a plastic fertiliser bag, t' keep it dry. Tell Jim, I'll come over an' teach him how t' play it,'

'Ernie. Are you sure?'

Ernie was giving away a part of his life.

Ernie said nothing. He put the violin carefully back into its case and lowered it into the sack, then, he went into the kitchen and brought a large plastic fertilizer bag.

'That'll keep it dry,' he said. 'Well young man. I've kept thee too long.

I were glad o' thy company, and t' deal wi't' land's fine. Tha'll be doin' a bit o' work for me,'

He re-lit his long forgotten pipe.

'Tha'd better keep yon sheep off. Now, go back to thy wife. She'll be wondering if tha't safe, wanderin' all oer't' moor in t' middle o' t' night,'

Peter went to the porch door and put on his jacket and cap.

Meg was instantly eager to be off, but Ernie's dogs didn't move.

Ernie handed him the violin and reminded him to pick up the duck eggs.

'Take care, young 'un. And thee take care o' thy lass and young Jim,'

For a moment, he looked sad.

'Tha't just startin' off Peter. I wish thee well lad,'

It was with a heavy heart that Peter picked up his lantern and headed out across the yard.

He reached into the cowshed and put the bag of eggs in his pocket, then, with a wave, he headed off along the edge of the field wall, leading to Nab's Head. The stormy weather hadn't eased off.

The rain was lashing across the moor and the sky was totally black.

Peter was a lonely figure as he trudged along, up the field, swinging his lantern. Nothing but a little pool of light out on the desolate hillside,

Meg trotting along close beside him. But, Peter's thoughts were not on the weather. He hardly noticed the raging wind or the lashing rain.

His thoughts were with Ernie.

There was no doubt that the old man was thinking about the future. Peter could imagine him sitting alone by his fire, reflecting on his life and thinking how different things would have been if only his young wife had lived, and if there had been children.

Suddenly, Peter realised that he was walking across the top field.

Now, it was a part of Nab's Head! But he had little enthusiasm.

He would have given up a lot, if he could have helped Ernie.

But, perhaps they could. Wasn't that what good neighbours did.

He remembered what Old Ned had told him, sitting in the Black Bull, well over a year ago now.

'Tha can't do without thy neighbours Peter. One day, tha'll depend on them. But they'll not let thee down. Not in't' Dale,' he had said.

Sam Turner hadn't made an offer to Ernie, because the bit of top land would be good for Peter and Susan.

Peter thought about the many times when things had just happened.

A tractor at the right price, a couple of good calves, help with hay time...

It was a long list.

Peter suddenly realised that it hadn't all happened by chance.

Now, they were in a position to be able to give a bit back.

There had been a lot of wisdom in what Ned had told him.

Susan was worried. What if something had happened.

She had expected Peter back a couple of hours ago.

Jim was tucked up in bed and she was sitting by the fire, listening to the storm and trying to read, but, she couldn't concentrate on the book. Then, suddenly she heard the porch door open, and the clatter of Peter's boots.

'Oh Peter. Thank Heaven that you are safe. I was worried,'

Peter stood there with water dripping from his wet coat.

He pulled off his cap and laid the stick in its corner.

'I'm really sorry,' he said. 'But I didn't realise what time it was,'

He pulled off the wet coat and blew out the storm lamp. A very wet Meg lay on her rug beside the fire.

'I have so much to tell you,'

Susan didn't see him put the fertilizer bag carefully down in the corner.

They sat beside the fire and Peter put his arm round Susan's shoulder. Gently, he laid his head against her cheek. He could feel the warmth of her body and he allowed himself to close his eyes for a moment.

He was thanking God for his little family and for the chance that had been given to them.

Finally, he spoke.

'Ernie was telling me something of his life Susan He is a wonderful old man, and he's seen some real tragedy.'

He told her about the bewildered child who left his family and his village at the age of eleven, to work out in all weathers on a strangers farm.

He told her about a frightened little boy, sleeping in the hay over a cowshed, alone and so far from home.

He told her about the young man who, so full of hope and love for his new bride, had left his home county and set out for a new life in Widdersdale, and how, after a few short years, everything collapsed in awful tragedy.

He told her of Ernie's love for his bride, and how he had never really come to terms with his loss, even over the years.

He told her how Ernie faced his new life alone, devoting himself to his small herd of cows, the only life he knew.

He told her of a disaster that had happened in the hills of Widdersdale, so long ago.

Peter didn't find it easy to tell Susan the entire story.

When he looked at her, there was a tear on her cheek.

'Oh, poor Ernie. How could life be so cruel. The poor man. What can we do Peter?'

'There is something we can do. We can't put right whats gone.

No-one can ever do that. But we better that anyone can do something.

Do you remember when Ned told us about the Dales folk? We were sitting in the Black Bull, and we had just moved into Nab's Head,"

Susan nodded, wiping her eye.

'Something else that Ernie told me tonight.

He thinks that we are O.K. We are good neighbours and we've got something that he saw in his life, all those years ago. Really, it's a different time and everything is so much easier. But, we are at the beginning of the journey. He believes in us Susan,'

Peter told her about the extra land, and how it was a chance to take some of the pressure off Ernie.

'We'll not need all that hay for years,' Peter explained. 'So, we stick it in Ernie's barn. There are lots of things we can do. Right now, it's a bit of shopping and being able to make his life a bit easier, But, There is so much more we can do. He isn't getting any younger Susan. All we've got really is a family member over the hill. Ernie hasn't had a family for all those years,'

Susan was quiet for a moment.

'Well, he has now,' she whispered.

'Look what he sent for Jim. I tried to refuse, but he had made his mind up,'

He opened the plastic bag and lifted out the violin.

'Ernie's had this most of his life. Think of all the happy times.

Think of the jigs at the end of harvest time. Think of Ernies good memories, working in the fields with his dad and his brothers. He had a mother then and sisters too. Think of the summers as a child in his native Cumbria, He would have gone to the village school, no doubt. His happiness was cut short... As you say, an awful tragedy. But, he wants Jim to have this. He told me that it's a chance for him to do something for Jim. He wants to be remembered,'

'Oh Peter. I was so worried because you were late home. How fortunate we are. We have each other. Little else matters. Think of all the people who live in Widdersdale. People like Sam and Mary. People like Geoff and Hillary. Old Ned and Betty. All of them. Billy Briggs and his

Lancashire lass,' she smiled.
   'We are part of all of it,'
   She put her arms round Peter.
   'Oh, I love you so much,'
   'And me you,' Peter said quietly. 'And, now we have another family
member,'

⤸

   In the gloomy little valley over the top of the hill, a dim light glowed in
the window of a lonely moorland farm. But, there was no-one to see it.
   Nothing but the wild wind and the sweeping rain.
   Inside, a white haired old man, asleep in his chair beside a dying fire.

THE END

About the author

Anthony Gilroyd is the pseudonym of Arnold Long.

He lives by the shore of Lynn Padarn, deep within the mountains of Snowdonia with his wife and son, their scruffy old Collie dog and two hens.

He comes from a line of Longs who lived, and still do, in the village of Horsforth Yorkshire, for more than four hundred years.

Now retired, he spent some years living and working among some of the amazing and loveable people described in his novel. He was compelled to write 'Barnard's Hill' by his strong desire to share such characters before they became lost in the mists of time.

Many times, he became discouraged because he was seeking perfection, and over the years, his work sometimes gathered dust for long periods. But, driven by his need to tell his tale, he returned to his writing and finally, with the help of good friends who are established writers and the patient help of an understanding editor, 'Barnard's Hill' slowly emerged.

He has written several short stories and is at the moment, editing his tale of the adventures of 'Young Arnold aged eight', which he put onto the B.B.C. Peoples War site.

It was given a 'recommended story' rating by their editorial staff.

ISBN 142514480-2